The No-Hopers Christmas Club

And Other Festive Stories

Geraldine Ryan

First published in 2022 by Wrate's Publishing

ISBN 978-1-7396165-7-1

Copyright © 2022 by Geraldine Ryan

Edited and typeset by Wrate's Editing Services

www.wrateseditingservices.co.uk

Cover illustration and design: Rachel Middleton

All rights reserved. No part of this publication may be reproduced, stored in a retrieval system, or transmitted, in any form or by any means (electronic, mechanical, photocopying, recording or otherwise), without the prior written permission of the publisher.

This book is a work of fiction. Names, characters, places and incidents are either a product of the author's imagination or are used fictitiously. Any resemblance to actual people living or dead, events or locales is entirely coincidental.

A CIP catalogue record for this book is available from the British Library.

Geraldine Ryan

To my reader,
Pour yourself a drop of what you fancy, help yourself to a mince pie, put your feet up and take some time for yourself this festive season.

Contents

The No-Hopers Christmas Club	1
Secret Santa's Pickle	14
A Soft Touch	38
A Bit of a Situation	48
The Prodigal Father	71
Being Gerald's Wife	110
A Rocking Horse Christmas	119
Gemma's Night Out	130
The Love and the Laughter	156
She's Leaving Home	161
When Sally Met Holly	188
My Stupid Lies	196
Bearing Gifts	213
Forbidden Feelings	218
Just How Far	242
Gabriel's Story	254
After Christmas	272
Nicole's New Year	286
Acknowledgments	309
About the Author	311

The No-Hopers Christmas Club

It had taken Joy a great deal of courage to tell Neill that she was really sorry, but she had no choice. Somebody was going to have to keep popping over to the dog sanctuary throughout the Christmas period to check on any dogs they hadn't managed to find homes for. And since they didn't have small children or family coming to stay, she'd volunteered her time, so the other helpers wouldn't have to.

His response was just as she'd predicted. 'So, what am I expected to do while you go gallivanting off there?' he demanded.

'You could come with me,' she replied.

His look of contempt said everything. As long as they'd been married, she'd always encouraged Neill to pursue the things *he* was enthusiastic about, but when it came to her own enthusiasms he'd never really reciprocated.

But she wouldn't give up looking after the poor abandoned dogs. They were like children to her. And Christmas was a busy time. The dogs were flying out of the kennels to new homes right now and she had to be there to groom them and make sure they looked their very best for when their new owners arrived to take them away.

Neill made her late because of his tantrum. On her arrival at the sanctuary, Sandra, one of the volunteers, greeted her with some exciting news. Someone had brought in a stray pregnant bitch, and only a couple of hours previously, she'd produced three lovely puppies. She squealed as she grabbed an equally excited Joy by the arm and dragged her along to have a peep at them.

'At least we won't have to worry about finding *them* homes,' Sandra said, as the two women watched, captivated, by the half-blind pups as they stumbled their way to their mother's teats and began to suck greedily. 'Talk about super cute.'

Joy nodded in agreement, her heart heavy. She knew exactly what Sandra was getting at, and it troubled her as much as it troubled the other woman. Yes, everyone loved puppies, and everyone loved dogs with shiny coats, wet noses and sunny dispositions.

But what about the others, the no-hopers, the remaining four dogs who'd been here at the sanctuary longest and who still hadn't been found homes and at this rate never would be?

There was Butch, the Staffordshire Bull Terrier cross, for instance, who spent most of his days cowering in the corner of his kennel, whimpering, so fearful was he of humans. Then there was Fugly, the Pug, who thought he was a Jack Russell. His distraught owner had brought him in more than three months ago, because he'd snapped at her youngest child. No one wanted a dog that didn't get on with children. Especially at Christmas.

Added to this couple of reprobates was the Lurcher, whose owner had brought him in claiming the dog had seriously let him down. He'd thought he was buying a guard dog but this one, it appeared, was stone deaf. Last of all there was the three-legged Labradoodle with one and a half ears. No matter what she said about his lovely nature, none of the visitors to the kennels in search of a pet seemed able to get past his physical appearance.

'At least the no-hopers will have some company over the holiday,' Joy said to Sandra. 'The puppies will have to stay with their mum, and I'll be popping in when I can to give them a bit of exercise and a cuddle.'

'You are good, Joy, giving up your Christmas so willingly,' Sandra said, getting up from her knees. 'Now, before I forget, I'm going to ring up those people on my list we promised any new puppies to and fix a time for them to come and have a little peep at them.'

Joy mulled over Sandra's words, once she was on her own with just the puppies and their fat, contented mum for company. Neill's face, irritable and cross, loomed before her. Sometimes this place wasn't just a refuge for dogs, she thought.

There was a woman in his office he'd started mentioning – Jean or Janet or Jeanette, one of those names. She should have felt jealous, but, oddly, she felt nothing. Except, perhaps, if she looked inside herself long and hard enough, maybe a tiny bit of relief.

Sandra came and found her half an hour later as she was trying to coax Butch out from his kennel.

'You don't give up, do you?' she said.

Joy smiled.

'Right. I've lined up three hopefuls for the pups,' Sandra said. 'I've told them they'll be ready to be picked up in the new year. Though what will happen to the poor old mum is anyone's guess.'

'Another candidate to join the no-hopers,' Joy said, gloomily.

'You'd think, at Christmas, there could be a happy ending, wouldn't you?' Sandra said.

Neither of them wanted to think about the inevitable – that the four remaining dogs would be put down if no one wanted them after a certain time had elapsed. So, they went about their work. Thankfully, there was plenty to do.

It was a relief to get back to the sanctuary the next

morning, after another frosty evening spent with Neill. The day was quieter than usual, since one by one all the strays, bar the usual suspects, the newborn puppies and their mother, began to leave for their new homes.

The highlight of the day had been meeting the prospective owners of the new pups, all of whom at various times had come to visit and pick out the one they wanted, a difficult choice since they were all just too gorgeous for words.

First to arrive had been the excited mother of a little girl who had no idea what she was getting for Christmas.

'Finally, we've moved from our poky flat to a house with a garden and a lovely park nearby,' the woman said, choosing the one with a brown patch over its eye and a cheeky face. 'I was brought up with dogs,' she said, 'and I miss not having one terribly. But I always said we could never even consider getting another unless we could look after it properly.'

This woman knew dogs, that much was easy to see. Joy was reassured. Equally reassuring was the rather gruff older lady, an ex-headmistress, she said, who claimed the snowy white one. Since her retirement she didn't get the exercise she was used to, she added, and a dog would be just the thing.

Joy was pretty sure that it wasn't just exercise the woman craved. Sometimes dogs were better company than humans. Neill hadn't been in when she'd arrived home the previous night. When he did rock up there was alcohol on his breath and someone's sweet perfume on his jacket.

The last to call in, on his lunch break, he explained, was a man in his early forties, pleasant-voiced and with smiley eyes. She liked him immediately when he said that he'd take whichever pup was left.

'Only right the little girl's mum should have first pick,' he said, when she explained the other two had beaten him to it. 'And to be fair, they're all equally brilliant.'

Since it was so quiet, Joy decided she might as well lock up for the day and go home. She made her final round and said goodbye to the dogs who were staying behind, each in turn.

She was startled out of her task by the appearance in the yard of a woman bundled up in a big coat against the winter chill. She was holding tight the hand of a small, equally bundled up, girl. It was hard to tell which of them looked the most distraught.

'How can I help you?' she said. 'Have you come to take home a dog?'

It flashed through her mind that here was an opportunity to offload one of the four remaining dogs, but her hopes were quickly dashed.

'It's Lily Allen.' The little girl lifted her face so that Joy could see the pools of tears in her huge dark eyes.

'Our dog. We think she might be here. You're our last hope. We've tried everywhere, haven't we, Mummy?'

The woman nodded. 'She's expecting and she went wandering off," she said. "We haven't seen her in two days, but the police said to try here.'

'Well, we do have a bitch who has just given birth, yes,' Joy said. 'But I don't know if it's your dog. Perhaps you'd better come and have a look.'

Half an hour later, she waved the two off. It had ended happily enough for the little girl and her mother, reunited with Lily Allen and gleeful at the sight of her pups, all of whom they wanted to take home in the New Year as soon as it was safe to move them.

But what on earth was she supposed to tell the three people she'd promised the pups to? She sat and worried about it all evening. She had plenty of time to do so since it was the middle of the night before Neill turned up. She could have asked him where he'd been, but she kind of thought she already knew. The lipstick on his collar told her everything. Once more she was taken by surprise by how little she cared. Was it really over between them after ten years of marriage?

Next day was Christmas Eve. Neill was still in bed when she left for the shelter. As soon as she arrived, she phoned all three people who'd imagined they were getting new puppies with the news that their hopes were dashed.

Each, in their own way, was disappointed. Mrs Simpkins, the woman who'd always had a doggy companion as a child said she was gutted; the ex-headteacher wondered what she was going to do with the dog basket and all the toys she'd bought and the man with the smile in his eyes said it was just his luck.

To each she said the exact same thing. 'We've got fully grown dogs here all desperate for homes. You could come and take a look.' She didn't add, "if you're desperate", but that was what she meant. Two of them agreed to come, arriving within minutes of each other.

The man, however, Mark Ashworth, refused point blank. He'd thought he was getting a puppy, he said. He wasn't in the market for an animal nobody else wanted. She didn't blame him, but she couldn't help wondering how she could have misjudged him so easily. He'd seemed so lovely the first time they'd met. But then, so had Neill. She'd been wrong about him too.

'The thing is,' said Mrs Simpkins, who was the first to arrive, 'I've got it into my head that we really *must* have a dog now. For my little girl's sake as much as mine. She needs to have something to love and care for, just like I did as a child.'

Joy took her round to see each of the dogs in turn. Mrs Simpkins didn't think they could take a dog that didn't like children, and she wasn't sure about caring for a disabled hound either. That meant Butch was the only dog left. Joy's heart sank.

'This dog's been so badly treated,' she said, opening Butch's kennel door. 'I'm not sure anymore if he can be socialised. Believe me, we've all tried.'

But Mrs Simpkins ignored her protests. She moved towards the little dog, speaking to him gently and holding out her hand. And instead of shivering with fear as he usually did whenever he was approached too closely, Butch raised his head, stood up and cautiously began to move towards them.

'I don't believe it,' Joy said.

'I did tell you I have this thing with dogs,' Mrs Simpkins replied. 'They know it, too.'

'So, you're going to take him?' Joy said, hardly able to believe her luck.

'You bet,' Mrs Simpkins said. 'Where do I sign?'

It was just as easy with the next dog. Miss Potter, the ex-headteacher, didn't mind that Fugly wasn't good round children, since she didn't know any these days. He'd keep her on her toes and be a bit of company, and if she could take him off Joy's hands then she'd be doing her a good turn. That much was true, Joy mused, cheerfully waving the two of them goodbye.

She felt bad though that there were still two dogs left.

'I'm sorry, guys,' she told them. Was it her imagination or did they know they'd been rejected yet again? 'But I'll be in tomorrow. And now the other two have left you'll get their Christmas presents as well as your own.'

Someone had let themselves into the yard and was walking towards her. She was surprised to see Mark Ashworth.

'I know what I said.' He held up his hands in a gesture of peace and apology. 'It was stupid. And selfish. Those puppies belong with their mother and the family of the mother. So, if you still think I can be trusted with one of the four dogs you said you had left, well, here I am.'

Maybe she wasn't such a bad judge of character after all, Joy mused, as she led Mark over to meet the two remaining dogs, apologising for the lack of choice.

'So, it's a deaf Lurcher or a three-legged Labradoodle, is it?' he said, with a grin.

Joy's phone pinged. That would be Neill, asking her where the hell she was. She decided to ignore it for now. It was far more interesting watching Mark and the Lurcher interact. They were getting along like a house on fire.

'Looks like he's made his choice,' she grinned.

'He's cool,' Mark said. 'And there's one advantage to having a deaf dog. I can play my music as loud as I like.'

'Well, if you're sure and you're not just doing this out of some sense of guilt.'

'No, no, no. I was a prat.' He was adamant. 'Does he have a name?'

'Well, we just call him Lurch,' Joy said, slightly embarrassed.

'Lurch it is, then.' He held out his hand.

She shook it awkwardly. 'It's a deal, then,' she said.

His hand was warm, just like his smile and his eyes. She felt suddenly very lonely.

'So, there's just you and me left, Hopalong,' she said, stroking the labradoodle's one remaining complete ear tenderly as the man and his new dog disappeared from sight.

He looked up at her trustingly. If only she could take him home. But there was Neill and his annoying aversion to dogs. Remembering she'd had a message, she groped for her phone.

It was from Neill, all right. Short and sweet. 'I've left you. Taken all my stuff. Moving in with Jeannie. My solicitor will be in touch in the new year.'

'Not even a Happy Christmas, Hopalong,' she said to the dog. 'What do you think of that?'

It was a cold, crisp day. Just the weather for walking your dog on the heath.

'Right, Hopalong.' Joy knelt to unfasten her new dog's lead.

In a flash he was off. For a dog with a missing leg, he could certainly move. Standing there, the wind blowing around her, she felt just as exhilarated as her pet clearly did. This morning, she'd had a letter from Neill's solicitor, just as he'd promised. He was out of her life, and she had a much better companion now.

She couldn't possibly have left Hopalong on his own at the kennels on Christmas Eve, so she'd brought him home where they'd spent a very companionable Christmas together. She hadn't missed Neill one bit.

It wasn't long before an excited Hopalong reappeared, this time with another dog in tow. A dog who seemed very familiar. *Lurch?* Could it be? She felt suddenly flustered. If Lurch was here that meant his new owner couldn't be far behind. And now here he was, striding towards her, his eyes bright from the cold and his smile as welcoming as ever. *Mark.*

'Two old friends,' he said, glancing at the dogs who were sniffing round each other as only dogs do. 'They remember each other, don't they!' He shifted his gaze to her. 'And what about you? Did you have a good Christmas?'

'I did as a matter of fact,' she said. 'Just me and the dog. It was perfect.'

'Same here,' he said.

So, he was single then. Just like she was.

'I know it's a cliché,' he said. 'But do you come here often?'

She laughed. 'First time. We've been taking things slowly.'

'Always the best way,' Mark replied.

They smiled at each other and continued their walk, the dogs running around playfully at their feet.

'But now I know this is where Lurch hangs out, we might make it a regular habit,' she added, shyly.

'Good,' Mark said, equally shyly. 'It would be a shame, now they've found each other again, for them to lose contact.'

'Exactly,' she said. 'Just what I was thinking.'

First published 2014, *Woman's Weekly*

Secret Santa's Pickle

The memo from the new supervisor was the sole topic of conversation during the coffee break that morning.

'It's Jane Markham's way of getting us to bond,' Margaret Parker sniffed. 'I don't know why she can't just get on with the job she's paid for and leave the social work to those who are qualified.'

It was common knowledge that Margaret Parker had been turned down for the supervisor's job.

Emma Hope, just 18 and the youngest employee in the general office at Futura Fashions, was reading the label on the back of her cellophane-wrapped flapjack. Should she eat it now, she wondered. If she did, she wouldn't be allowed a jam tart at tea break that afternoon. It was a debate she entered into daily – and invariably lost.

'What's going on then?' she asked, giving in and

ripping off the cellophane. She never read memos if she could help it. Usually, her friend Fay read them and relayed the contents to her at coffee break, but Fay was off sick today. Not that Emma believed for a moment that Fay was actually ill – not unless you could call having a massive hangover being ill, that is.

Fay and Emma went everywhere together, and Emma was feeling her friend's temporary absence badly. She hoped she would be back tomorrow so she wouldn't have to drink her coffee with this ancient bunch of crones again.

Iris Smith swallowed her last drop of coffee. She had been at Futura Fashions for 40 years. All her working life, in fact. She'd been there from the beginning, when the company had been a family firm, Raymond's Raiments, run by old Mr Raymond. He was long retired now, and five years previously the firm had been taken over by Futura Fashions, who ran it as a subsidiary, making upmarket lingerie.

Just one more year and Iris would retire. Everyone imagined she was counting the days. She was, but not in the way most people imagined. The fact was, she was dreading it. If her Edward were still alive to share it, then things would be different. They'd had such plans for their retirement. They both loved travelling, and although they couldn't afford to stay in the best hotels, having their own caravan had made it possible for them to visit places that other couples could only dream of.

Since Edward's death almost a year before, Iris hadn't even been able to set foot inside their mobile home. She knew it would still be spotless inside – if a bit dusty and damp – because Edward had spent the fortnight leading up to his death getting it shipshape for the summer. Almost as if he knew he'd never use it again, she often thought.

The outside, though, was beginning to show signs of neglect – a spot of rust here, a patch of flaking paint there. When Iris looked out of her bedroom window first thing in the morning, it blocked her view of the garden, its bulk staring accusingly at her.

She supposed she'd have to sell it once spring came around again. People never thought about rubbing shoulders with wide open spaces in December, when the days were short and the wind and rain slogged it out between themselves in the garden, but in spring, when the sun came out and the flowers began to bloom… Iris firmly wrestled her mind back to the present.

'Well, I think it's a wonderful idea,' said Christine Mills.

Iris envied the way Christine always sounded so positive about things. She often wondered how she managed it, what with that big family to look after as well as her full-time job. In Iris's day, women had had to choose between family and career. It had been an easy enough choice for her, never having been blessed with children, and probably easy for Margaret Parker too – she had never married.

'People are always so busy these days they forget what Christmas is really about,' Christine went on.

'What is it about?' Margaret said sharply.

She was hopeless at small talk, the backbone of which, it seemed to her, was platitudes. It was generally thought that her inability to opt for saying the expected instead of speaking her mind may have been the reason Mr Raymond Jr – Managing Director and the only family member of the old firm left – had seen fit to pass her over for promotion, despite her many skills.

'Intimidating' was the word Christine had once used to describe Margaret to her husband, Andy. She always had to remind herself of his response – that she was a strong woman with a supportive family and a lovely home, and she had no reason at all to be intimidated by anyone.

'Weeks of standing in queues followed by two days of enforced joviality,' Margaret went on. 'Then it's back to work with nothing to show for it but an extra half-stone in weight and an overdraft. And now we have to cough up another tenner to buy a present for someone at work.'

I wish someone would explain what's going on,' murmured Emma.

Nothing remained of her flapjack, now, apart from a few crumbs. Just as she did every day, she fervently wished she hadn't eaten it. It was the name that had seduced her in the first place – flapjack. It conjured up a world of home baking, where the delicious smells of treacle, dried fruit and butter combined in an all-too-brief explosion of pleasure.

Of course, the reality was always a let down, a confection of over-processed gloop that turned to glue in the mouth and left a disappointing after taste. A lot like Christmas, in fact, Emma thought. After the age of about seven, when you discovered there was no Father Christmas, it was all downhill.

'It's really quite simple, Emma,' Christine began enthusiastically. She saw herself as a mother figure to all the young girls at work. After all, she had three children – four if you counted Andy – and she knew what they were like. 'Everyone draws a name out of a hat and has to spend £10 on a Christmas present for that person.'

Emma looked appalled. 'Does everyone's name go in? Even Mr Raymond's?'

Christine nodded. 'I wouldn't want to pull his name out, would you?' she asked the table at large. 'What would you buy for the man who has everything?'

'It's a common misunderstanding that material wealth brings satisfaction,' Margaret pointed out.

Christine found herself getting flustered. As if she

didn't know that! She was about to say that surely the idea was to promote goodwill among the staff, when Emma interrupted.

'What's the point?' she asked.

'Exactly,' Margaret agreed. 'How am I supposed to know what to get for a complete stranger? Buying presents for people I know is a big enough headache!'

'I wouldn't have thought you'd have that many to buy for,' said Christine, glad to be able to get her own back. 'After all, it's not as if you've kids and a husband to buy for, is it?'

Margaret was taken aback by Christine's remark. Was she being deliberately cruel? There was no need to throw her lack of a partner and a family of her own in her face, especially not at this time of year. Well, she hoped she wouldn't draw *her* name out of the hat. If she did, she'd buy her a book on manners.

Although she would be 50 next birthday, Margaret still lived at home with her mother and her aunt.

Their lives were for the most part uneventful, revolving round unexciting meals, the weather forecast and television programmes about nature. Margaret's mother and aunt were big fans of David Attenborough.

Margaret was aware that her own life was nothing like the chaotic family whirlwind that Christine was always banging on about it being. That didn't mean it was worth less though, surely? She had her music and her books and her evening class. Well, she would have her evening class when she got round to enrolling on one.

She was so short of time, that was the thing. She may not have a husband and three children, but her mother and aunt made great demands on her. Only when she'd been shopping and done all the chores the two women had long ago relinquished was she free. And by that time, she was usually too tired to do anything more strenuous than curl up with a good book.

* * *

Christine loved Christmas and could never understand why some people dreaded it so. Of course, it was hard work. Andy, to whom she was still devoted after 25 years of being together as a couple, was utterly incapable of planning ahead, and she found it was usually quicker for her to do everything herself rather than watch the children make a mess of things or, worse still, make promises to help that they didn't keep.

Andy was quite happy to give her extra housekeeping to cover the cost, but it never occurred to him that presents and cards didn't get purchased, wrapped and sent all by themselves. Just as it never occurred to him that a self-basting turkey was simply an advertising copywriter's dream and should be treated with the same amount of contempt that he usually reserved for Party Political Broadcasts and the state of the nation's transport system.

But in the end, Christine thought, Christmas was always worth the effort. All those happy smiles around the table made everything worthwhile. Although last year there had been a bit of a to-do with Jamie, her youngest, who had refused to allow any turkey to pass his lips on account of having recently witnessed a disturbing *Blue Peter* report on turkey farming. And her daughter Julie and her fiancé Dave had declared mid-meal that this was positively the last time they were going to do Christmas.

So, things might be very different this year. Julie's Dave – affectionately known as 'Don't-mind-if-I do Dave' by Christine and Andy because he never refused any item of food or drink offered him – had said he and Julie were heartily sick of rampant consumerism and intended in future to take themselves off to a remote corner of the world to avoid it.

It hadn't escaped Christine's notice that their dislike of rampant consumerism hadn't stopped either of them putting away enough bacon-wrapped chipolatas and mince pies to feed a large African village for a year.

Christine had thought it was just Julie going off on one of her crusades, but not even the prospect of mince pies and chipolatas had weakened their resolve. Christine would miss them – not least because they always volunteered to do the washing up so that they could be alone together in the kitchen after lunch. This year she'd probably end up having to do it herself.

But there was another reason she would miss them. Andy's father would be staying with them. He usually spent Christmas with Andy's sister, but they were going away and had made it quite clear they had no intention of taking Grandad with them. He was bound to think he wasn't wanted, so Christine would have to make him feel welcome, and the situation wouldn't be helped when Andy fell asleep on the sofa and the younger two disappeared upstairs to play with their new computer games. Julie and Dave were experts at putting people at their ease, but now it would be up to Christine to entertain Grandad alone.

A week later, everyone knew who they were expected to buy a present for. Emma had been hoping to draw Fay's name from the hat, but it was not to be. It would have been easy to choose for Fay. Fay liked everything Emma liked herself. Shopping for yourself was a doddle.

When she discovered she'd drawn Iris, she could have died. What did you buy for someone who was nearly 60? How much did a walking stick cost, or some of those elasticated stockings? Maybe she should just give her the money and let her put it towards a hearing aid.

Christine felt just as bad when she found she had to buy a gift for Margaret. She rarely disliked anyone, but she disliked Margaret Parker.

'It's not as if I haven't tried to like her,' she remarked to Andy for the umpteenth time one evening.

Andy was beginning to get fed up with listening to his wife on the subject of Margaret Parker and *the present*. The fact was, she'd said everything there was to be said on the subject. All she'd done for the past few days was repeat the same things in a different order.

It went thus: Margaret had once sneered at Christine's taste in literature after she confessed to liking Catherine Cookson. Margaret always looked over the top of Christine's head whenever she mentioned the children. Margaret had absolutely *no* small talk, and she made Christine feel stupid all the time.

'Whatever I buy her won't be good enough,' she complained bitterly.

Andy floundered around and dredged up some ideas, knowing perfectly well that nothing he suggested would be right. The difference between men and women, he had long ago decided, was that whereas men didn't see the point of talking over a problem unless they could be sure of coming up with a solution, for women, simply talking it over was enough. Better than that was talking it over and over and over some more.

He knew he would never be able to suggest the perfect gift because there *was* no perfect gift. There was just Margaret Parker and her unspeakableness. Only when Futura Fashions closed for the festive season would he get any rest from the topic. Until then he resolved to nod sympathetically and say nothing.

* * *

Margaret secretly hoped she might pull Mr Raymond's name from the hat. She had hoped to be able to remind him she existed. She wasn't bitter about not getting the supervisor's job. In fact, she hadn't really wanted it, whatever anyone thought. She knew that her age was against her, as well as the fact she'd only ever worked in one place. Someone young like Jane Markham would bring in fresh ideas. Well, she assumed that was what Mr Raymond had been thinking when he'd made the appointment.

No, the reason Margaret had wanted to draw Mr Raymond's name out of the hat was that she knew he was very shy, and that small talk was just as difficult for him as it was for her. But still he had lingered by her desk once or twice recently. Drawn to a novel or

CD she'd brought to work, planning to return it to the library during her lunch break.

They'd suddenly found themselves deep in discussion about the writer or the composer, or about a particular interpretation of the piece in question. More often than not, they had agreed with each other. But when they'd run out of things to say, one of them, suddenly shy again, would draw the conversation abruptly to a close.

'Well, I'd better be getting on, I suppose,' was a favourite line.

'Goodness me, is that the time?' the other would exclaim.

If she drew Mr Raymond's name, Margaret dared hope that maybe, just maybe, one thing might lead to another. Then who knew what might happen? An invitation to a concert, a dinner date, the start of a loving friendship? Margaret firmly allowed her imagination to go no further.

It was such a disappointment when she drew Emma's name. What did she know about the tastes of young, uninformed girls? The last pop song she'd danced to had been by the Beatles back in her dusty, distant girlhood.

Just five days before present-exchange day, Christine met Iris on her way into the toilet.

'Christine! I am pleased to see you!' Iris said.

Christine wondered why. She always smiled and said hello to Iris whenever their paths crossed, and of course, she'd expressed her condolences on hearing about the death of her husband. But on the subsequent occasions they'd bumped into each other, Christine had never been able to think of anything to say. Their lives were so very different, she imagined. It was impossible to think of anything they might have in common.

'I've been racking my brains about what to buy you since I drew your name from the hat,' Iris said breathlessly, holding the door open. 'I know it's supposed to be the thought that counts, but I would really like to buy you something you'll really appreciate. I always think it's better that way.'

'Iris!' Christine exclaimed. 'You're not supposed to tell anyone whose name you've drawn! Least of all the person you're buying for!'

As soon as she saw Iris's face fall, Christine was mortified by her own insensitivity. She'd made Iris feel stupid, just because she'd felt it necessary to put her right. Wasn't that exactly the way Margaret Parker treated her? After all, where was the harm in spilling the beans? Wouldn't she prefer a nice lipstick in her usual shade rather than something she'd never wear?

'It doesn't matter, Iris,' she said. 'In fact, you've saved me the trouble of having to drop the most enormous hints. Subtlety's never been one of my strong points.'

Iris felt foolish, as she had done more and more often since Edward's death. It was as if he'd stolen her self-confidence when he'd gone. Had she really got this present-giving idea so wrong? Things seemed to slip her mind so easily nowadays.

Was it because she no longer had anyone important to share the events of the day with? She'd stopped taking notice of details in the way she had done when Edward was alive.

Over dinner they had always unpicked their experiences at work, laughed about them and discussed them avidly. All she did now was file things away in the back of her mind, where they withered and died because they were never given a proper airing.

Christine put her hand on Iris's arm. Iris looked so sad, she thought. Like a little girl who has just been told that there's been a mistake and she isn't allowed to play with the dolly after all.

'Come and have a cup of coffee with me at break, Iris,' she said. 'I'll tell you the name of my favourite lipstick.'

Four days to go and Margaret found herself trailing around the shops in search of a present for Emma. The displays of CDs, cosmetics and jewellery aimed at the youth market were bewildering. The cacophony of in-store pop music drowned out the Salvation Army manfully playing carols in the market square. She was getting one of her headaches.

Eighteen. That was how old Emma was. Margaret thought about herself at that age. Had she been as pretty? She'd never thought so, had never been told so by her parents or her aunt. In fact, they'd never missed an opportunity to point out some failing or other on Margaret's part.

But someone had thought her pretty. Pretty enough to ask her out. Not once, not twice, but again and again. She thought he meant it when he said he loved her. He hadn't, of course.

'Boys,' her mother had told her. 'Only after one thing.'

Such a cliché. Margaret had scorned her mother's warning. She was in love, but she was also a fool. When she discovered she was pregnant, she thought he would be delighted. She never saw him again.

Her family managed to keep the pregnancy quiet, although her mother claimed to this day that the shock of it was what killed her father. Margaret had the baby in a lonely maternity ward in a distant town and put her up for adoption. She didn't even bother to give her a name, though there were so many nice girls' names she could have chosen. Emma was a nice name, for instance.

Margaret rarely thought about her daughter these days. She certainly never talked about her. Her aunt had once or twice referred to her as 'that regrettable incident'. Her mother never referred to her at all. How old would her daughter be now? Older than Emma by a good 10 years. Perhaps she even had a daughter of her own.

There was a light touch on her shoulder, and someone spoke softly in her ear, catapulting her into the present.

'Gift buying is meant to be a happy time. You look as though you've just got back from a funeral.'

Margaret blinked and turned her attention to the tall, distinguished looking gentleman at her side. He was standing so close she could smell his aftershave.

'Mr Raymond!' she said, flustered. 'How long have you been standing there?'

He looked so different out of his usual dark suit; relaxed and carefree. He was wearing an open-necked shirt instead of his usual suit and tie, and a pair of casual trousers.

'I'm looking for earrings,' he confided, holding up a particular garish pair. 'I've drawn Mrs O'Shaughnessy from the canteen.' Looking at Margaret's face, he threw back his head and roared with laughter. 'Not in the way you must be thinking, Margaret, I assure you!'

Margaret did her best to summon up a carefree smile, but she was unpractised at flirting. After her one brush with romance, she'd turned her back firmly on affairs of the heart. Her mother was right, she'd decided. She was better off without all that business.

'Good idea of Jane's this, eh, Margaret?' If Mr Raymond was embarrassed by mentioning the new supervisor in front of the woman he'd turned down for the job, he passed it off very well. 'So, who are you buying a present for?'

'One of the young girls, Emma Hope,' Margaret sighed. 'I've been here for ages now and I'm just getting more and more bewildered.'

'I'll help you if you like.'

Margaret felt a girlish fluttering somewhere in the region of her heart. She nodded, but she didn't trust herself to speak. Mr Raymond, on the contrary, kept up a monologue as they rifled through the earring stands. Occasionally, their fingers touched – and each time Margaret pulled her hand away in embarrassment. But when it became obvious that it was impossible to avoid touching in such a cramped space, she decided it was even more embarrassing to keep drawing attention to it, so she left her hands where they were.

'You know, Margaret,' he said, holding up a pair of bright red feather hoops for her inspection and quickly replacing them when she wrinkled her nose in disapproval. 'I've been longing for an opportunity to explain why I didn't offer you the supervisor post.'

'Please, Mr Raymond, you really don't have to,' she said. 'I would never have been as good as Jane Markham, and you know that. I lack… well, I lack the human touch, I suppose.'

His next words came out in a rush. 'But that doesn't mean you're not valued. You do see that, don't you? I value you very much indeed.'

Margaret concentrated hard on her earring search. 'Please,' she said, brushing his words away. 'You're very kind. You mustn't worry about me. Oh, look!'

'Yes, perfect!' With the tip of his forefinger, he tenderly stroked the elegant moonstone drops that Margaret held out in the palm of her hand.

'Do you really think she'll like them?'

It was suddenly very important to Margaret that Emma Hope thought well of her choice.

'Margaret,' Mr Raymond said, and laughed softly. 'Oh, Margaret. You always like to do everything right, don't you? Buy them. Then perhaps you'll come and have a drink with me?'

Margaret thought about it – but not too hard. She'd lived with her mother and aunt for too long, she realised. She was becoming just as suspicious and man-hating as them. Well, she'd had enough of turning her back on enjoyment. If she didn't accept this invitation, she might never be asked out by another man again.

'I'd love to,' she said, warmly.

* * *

Three days to go and Christine still hadn't come up with a present idea for Margaret. She had to pass by her desk on her way to the coffee machine, and she gave her a long look. There was something different about her this morning, Christine thought. Margaret had a habit of hunkering down over her computer, like a clever schoolgirl making sure no one copied her work. But today she was sitting straight, her shoulders down, her arms and wrists relaxed. She touched the keys on her keyboard almost lazily, her head to one side as she gazed dreamily at the screen, and she was smiling. She appeared to be wearing lipstick and her usual severe collar had been replaced by a curved neckline.

Margaret looked up in the way people do when they feel themselves to be under scrutiny. Christine was embarrassed at being caught staring. Margaret beamed at her. Caught unawares, Christine found herself beaming back.

'Bought your present yet?' Margaret asked shyly. 'Not long now.'

Christine had a sudden vision of Margaret with a scarf the colour of fresh watermelon at her throat. She would pop out during her lunch hour and see what she could find.

'It's fun, isn't it? Margaret continued. 'Buying presents for other people, I mean. I never thought it would be.'

Christine nodded, transfixed by the change in her colleague.

'Christmas must be a busy time for you, what with your big family,' Margaret went on. 'How many of you will there be round the table?'

Christine was stunned. For the first time in living

memory, Margaret Parker was showing an interest in her humble self. What was going on?

'Actually,' she said, wondering as she spoke if she was being too free with her words and that Margaret would simply cut her dead. 'I was two down until yesterday.'

'Oh?'

Christine threw caution to the wind. Christmas only came once a year, after all. 'My daughter and fiancé are opting out of this year's festivities. They're off to India to spend two weeks in an ashram.'

'Are they really?' Margaret exclaimed. 'How very exciting!'

There was no getting away from it, Christine decided. Margaret was genuinely interested.

'So, who have you got instead?' Margaret asked.

Christine risked a confidence. 'Iris,' she said. 'My father-in-law will be there too. I just thought… a widow, a widower. You never know.'

'Nothing's impossible if you want it enough,' Margaret agreed, a faint flush spreading along her neck and over her cheeks.

Christine wondered if, on reflection, watermelon might be too strong a colour for Margaret. Ivory would suit her much better.

The final working day before Christmas arrived. There was always a buzz in the air as people began to wind down for the holiday, but this year, the excitement was almost tangible. Two o'clock was the hour that Jane Markham, in consultation with Mr Raymond, had designated as gift-exchanging time. That way, people would be sure to have returned from lunch.

Only Emma Hope was heavy-hearted. She still hadn't bought anything for Iris. After her initial reaction of disappointment when she'd drawn Iris's name, Emma had given the subject very little thought.

She was convinced she had plenty of time and imagined that something would catch her eye on one of the many shopping excursions she undertook with Fay – who was now firmly on the wagon until Christmas, when the next alcoholic onslaught to her system would commence.

The thing was, Emma and Fay frequented Top Shop, New Look and, if there was a sale on, Karen Millen. At the start of every trip, Emma was full of good intentions to slip into House of Fraser or the Scotch Wool Shop, but the unexciting contents of their windows always sent her spirits plummeting so alarmingly that Fay could easily persuade her that right now a Coke was more important, and that there was always next time.

However, as the office clock showed that lunchtime had arrived, it hit Emma that there was no longer a next time. In an hour's time, everybody would be getting a present. Everybody but Iris, that was.

Emma felt awful. She had been catching sight of Iris all morning going about her business like some chirpy Christmas robin, eager for the afternoon events to unroll.

She couldn't get it out of her head that it was almost a year since Iris's husband had died. The poor old lady would be alone at Christmas for the first time in years, and she, Emma Hope, was about to add to her misery by humiliating her in front of the whole company as the only member of the team for whom no one had bought a gift. She felt sick and thoroughly ashamed of her own selfishness and lack of feeling.

Christine Mills came across Emma slumped dejectedly across her computer.

'Oh dear,' she remarked. 'Whatever happened to the Christmas spirit? Not coming down with anything, I hope?'

Perhaps this was her way out, Emma thought. If she went home sick, she could send her mum to pick something up for Iris and give it to her in the new year. But then, full of self-loathing, she realised how cowardly that would be.

So, she blurted it all out, unable to contain how ghastly she felt about the whole business. Christine listened, unjudgmentally. She'd been a girl herself once. She didn't need telling that woollen tea cosies and thermal vests paled into insignificance in comparison with the lure of satin underwear and fancy nail extensions.

'I feel so awful at the thought of Iris spending Christmas all alone, thinking someone at work couldn't even be bothered to get off their backside and make an effort to buy her something nice,' Emma said, close to tears now.

'You don't have to feel bad about Iris spending Christmas on her own because she won't be,' Christine said – and she told Emma about the invitation she'd extended, which had been delightedly accepted.

'But I've still left it too late to get a present,' Emma moaned. 'Look at the time!'

Christine racked her brains and finally came up with an idea.

'Why don't you nip down to the supermarket now and get her a bottle of port? And some nice wrapping paper to wrap it in. I'll cover for you if you're a bit late back.'

Emma already had her coat on. 'Booze! Why on earth didn't I think of that? Everyone drinks at Christmas! Thank you, Christine!'

That afternoon, the present exchange went remarkably smoothly. Iris was thrilled with her port – it gave her the opportunity to announce that it was the perfect gift to take with her when she spent Christmas at her new friend Christine's house.

Christine made a great show of surprise when she received her favourite lipstick beautifully wrapped in rose-petalled paper. 'Fancy someone knowing my exact shade!' she exclaimed, with a wink at Iris.

Margaret loved her ivory scarf and promptly put it on. 'It's absolutely gorgeous,' she said, as she tied it in a fetching bow around her neck.

When she looked up, she caught Mr Raymond Junior – or Richard as she called him these days – watching her. It was obvious he approved. She would wear it later, when he took her out to dinner. They were going to discuss which evening class to enrol on together in the new year.

Emma was enchanted by her moonstone drops. 'You must have spent ages looking for them, Margaret!' she gasped, as she carefully put them in.

'Well, I had a bit of help,' Margaret replied, trying not to blush.

Next, Jane Markham gave a little speech and Mr Raymond handed out the drinks. Someone put the music on, and little bowls of nuts and crisps were passed around. Everyone admired everyone else's gifts and said what a good idea of Jane Markham's it had been. All in all, it was beginning to feel like Christmas.

First published 2000, *Fiction Feast*

A Soft Touch

This job interview was going to be a total waste of time. Craig shuffled forward in the bus queue, getting wetter with every inch he moved. He had no experience of cleaning – his mum would vouch for that. In fact, when he used up his last minutes on his phone telling her he wouldn't be back until later because they were sending him to the hospital, she did exactly that. At great length. Biggest laugh she'd had in a long time, apparently, the thought of him wielding a vacuum cleaner. He told her she needed to get out more.

Besides having zero cleaning experience, he hated hospitals. They were huge, depressing places with long corridors he was bound to get lost in because of his rubbish sense of direction. And sick people made him nervous.

Why couldn't they have found him a job with

animals or trees instead? Those were the two things he'd mentioned when they'd asked him what he was interested in when he'd first signed on. That was after they'd asked him about his qualifications, and he'd said he hadn't got any. Well, he'd got a swimming certificate, but that didn't count, apparently.

But when he'd gone to sign on as usual this morning, they told him a cleaning job had come up at the Hope, and unless he got himself down there for an interview, he'd not only lose his money but be sanctioned too. The woman behind the desk had taken great delight rubbing *that* in.

'Hobson's Choice, really,' she'd said.

He had no idea what she meant so he just took the bit of paper with the name of whoever it was he was supposed to see and said thank you. He couldn't wait to get away from her, frankly. She had long red nails and a face full of makeup, and he could tell she thought she was all that.

Well, she wasn't. If his mum had been with him, she'd have told her to mind her manners. His mum couldn't stand rude people. Manners maketh man, she was always saying whenever she met someone rude, which was often, because people like Red Nails Woman seemed to think they could get away with being rude to people like them. Sometimes all it took was a glance at their address.

He was nearly at the head of the queue now. At least he was finally on the bus and out of the rain.

Plus, he had his bus money there *and* back. Always look on the bright side. Mum said that a lot too. Well, she had to, given her circumstances.

He felt bad then, a bit, for moaning to himself about this job. Maybe, if he got it, Mum would be able to give up one of her jobs. She got so tired these days, working such long hours, first at the supermarket then behind the bar at the Dog and Kettle.

There was one more person in front of him, but there seemed to be some sort of hold up. It was an old bloke. Little and sort of shrunken. He smelled a bit of mothballs too, Craig thought. It worried him that he could smell mothballs even at this distance, because it confirmed what he already knew – that his sense of smell was very acute.

What if he got to the hospital and he smelled something nasty – something in the toilets, for instance, that they said he had to clean up? How would he cope with that? On *CSI*, they dabbed Vic inside their nostrils to block the smell of death. Maybe he should have a look round the pound shop later. See if they sold it there. If he got the job, of course.

He hadn't been listening too closely to the conversation between the driver and the old man in front of him. But he'd already worked out what was going on. The old man couldn't find his bus pass and the driver was telling him that he was holding everybody up, so if he couldn't find it within the next 10 seconds, he was going to have to get off the bus.

Somebody else in charge giving out orders, Craig mused.

Well, he wasn't having it this morning. He'd had enough of rude, bossy people. It was pouring down outside, and this bloke looked so defeated it almost broke his heart. His mum was always telling him he was a soft touch and that he'd never have any money. He told her back that if he was, he got it from her, so it was her fault.

Craig tapped the old man on the shoulder. 'Scuse me,' he said.

The old man looked round. His eyes were little and a bit red, but also watery and sharp, like a little bird's. Craig saw sorrow and anxiety, but also pride.

'Let me get your fare,' he said.

'Oh.' That was all he said at first. But then he added, 'I can't let you.'

'Please,' Craig said. 'It's raining really hard. You can't be walking in this weather. Anyway, it'll be my good turn for the day. I do one every day when I remember, and if I do it first thing, well, I'm done for the day, then, aren't I?'

The old man smiled. It took 10 years off his face. He was going to the hospital, he said. Well, that was a coincidence, Craig thought. He didn't say it, though. Otherwise, he might have felt obliged to sit with him and make small talk for the rest of the journey, which would be a good 20 minutes from what he could remember from two years ago, when he'd gone there to visit his mum when she'd had that bit of trouble that thankfully they'd managed to put right. Craig didn't like small talk. He always ran out after they'd done the weather, which they'd already covered.

He didn't think much about the old man after that. He was too worried about the interview and what they'd ask him, and then he thought he'd lost the bit of paper the woman had given him with the name of the person he was meant to be seeing and all his details. He finally found it in one of his many pockets, but he nearly missed the stop because of searching for it.

The bloke he spoke to about the job was nice, actually. He was called Jeremy, and he had a strong Jamaican accent. He said he thought Craig would be a very welcome addition to the team. When Craig told his mum this later, after he'd got home – he'd had to walk back, of course, plus he'd had no money to buy any Vic for his nose – she told him she was very proud of him. She was even prouder when he told her why it had taken him so long to get home. She gave him a big hug, which was dead embarrassing.

In the end, the job turned out better than he thought. Jeremy continued to be nice to him, and there were lots of other nice people there too. Co-workers, they called each other, which sounded very grand to Craig's ears. They all wore a uniform and had a name badge on a chain too, which made them as professional as the nurses and doctors.

Woe betide them if they lost their badge, Jeremy said, because they wouldn't be allowed on the premises. For the first two weeks, Craig slept with his round his neck because he was terrified he might leave it behind in the morning rush for the bus. Later, when he'd been in the job for a few months and he'd stopped doing that, he told Candice about it over their sandwiches one lunchtime. Candice was a co-worker who was also a friend.

Actually, they'd been for a burger together on their day off, and next Saturday they were going to the cinema together, so technically that sort of made her his girlfriend. It was when he told her about sleeping with his name badge round his neck that her attitude towards him seemed to change.

Her eyes had gone all soft and she'd said how refreshing it was to meet a boy who wasn't always showing off and being macho. When he told his mum what Candice had said, she said she thought she sounded like a lovely girl. She was, Craig said back. She had insight, his Mum said. Craig hadn't known what that meant till Mum explained it.

It meant she could see that Craig was a decent, lovely man. And what most women wanted from a man was for him to be decent and lovely, never mind what it said in that *Fifty Shades of Grey* book. Craig didn't know what made him blush more – the mention of that book, the compliment both his mum and Candice had paid him, or the fact that Mum now seemed to think he was a man and not a boy.

He was in town. It was a half day, and it was near enough to Christmas to definitely start thinking about buying presents. As a rule, he only had his mum to buy for, but this time he thought he would like to buy a present for Candice.

She had long curly hair, did Candice, but she had to keep it tied back for work. She had a different scrunchy for every day, and she said she went through them like nobody's business because she was always putting them down somewhere at the end of the day and then she could never find them again. It was a no brainer really, what to buy her, and Mum had agreed.

'Not from the pound shop, though, Craig,' she'd advised.

So here he was in the big Boots, looking through their selection, which was massive. Somebody tapped him on the shoulder just as he was trying to make his mind up between two colourways. Colourway was a posh name for colour, he decided. Fashion wasn't really his thing.

'Excuse me.'

Craig turned round. He had his answer ready for if it was some store detective asking him if he intended making a purchase. He'd grown a lot more confident since he'd been working, and these days, he liked to think he could stand up for himself a bit more.

But it wasn't a store detective. It was a little old man. Craig had a vague memory of a rainy day and standing in the bus queue and a bit of trouble up ahead.

'I don't suppose you remember me,' the little old man said.

He was carrying a wire basket. It was empty apart from a box of something that had the words 'Denture Fixative' written on it. Craig looked away immediately. It seemed a very personal item.

'You paid my bus fare,' the old man said. 'I was going to go and see my wife in hospital. Do you remember?'

'Of course I do!' Minding his manners, he added, 'How is she?'

The man's face dropped. 'I'm afraid she died,' he said.

Craig didn't know where to put himself. 'I'm so sorry,' he said, stumbling over the words.

'Thank you,' the old man replied. 'She was very ill, and we both knew she was going to die. But I am so glad I saw you. I never thought I would again.'

He put his hand on Craig's arm. 'You see, that day, when you paid for my bus fare, well, it was the last time I saw her alive.'

Craig didn't know quite what to say. He wished his mum was here. She'd have the right words ready. She always did.

'I don't think you understand,' the man said,

obviously noticing just how confused Craig must have appeared. 'If it wasn't for you, I wouldn't have been able to make the journey. We wouldn't have ever got to say our goodbyes. But we did. And so that made losing her so much easier.'

It was funny, but the old man was smiling now. Craig didn't really understand old people. How they could look happy when they'd lost the person closest to them. Well, not happy exactly. But peaceful and contented. Like their story had finished and the only thing left to write was 'the end'.

'So, I've a lot to thank you for,' he said.

It looked like he was getting his wallet out. Craig hoped to goodness he wasn't going to try and give him back the money for his bus ticket. He was starting to wish the ground would swallow him up when he saw his mum coming towards them.

'Craig?' She looked at the little old man for an introduction. 'Do the honours, son,' she said.

He left them to it once he'd introduced them as best he could, given that he didn't actually know the old man's name, which turned out to be Charles Burton. Then he said his goodbyes and scurried off to pay for the scrunchies. Being unable to decide on the perfect colourway, he'd gone for both in the end.

'You made a quick getaway,' Mum said later, when they were having their tea. 'I was talking to Mr Burton for ages after you left. He thinks the world of you.'

Craig carried on eating, trying to ignore Mum's last remark.

'He's a lovely man. So interesting. In fact…' She took a huge bite of her pizza, so it was a while before she spoke next. 'So interesting that I thought, well, him being on his own now and it being Christmas.'

Craig knew what was coming next. 'Yeh, no, course. You got to invite him,' he said. 'He can't be spending it on his own, can he?'

He thought about the denture fixative in the old man's wire basket. With Mum's cooking, this was going to be a bit of a challenge.

'What you thinking?' she said.

'Nothing,' he replied. 'Except how glad I am I inherited being a soft touch from you.'

First published, 2015, *Fiction Feast*

A Bit of a Situation

Irene would be a fool if she didn't sign up to the dating app, Heather, one of her co-workers, said. It was free, easy to use and safe. Above all, it would transform her life. She didn't add that if anyone's life needed a transformation then it was Irene's, but then she didn't really have to.

The last time Irene had had a boyfriend, Gordon Brown had been Prime Minister and Heather had been two years away from doing her GCSEs. Come to think of it, Shane, the man she'd been dating at the time, had reminded her a lot of Gordon Brown. As well as being Scottish, he was thin-skinned, prone to hissy fits and woefully short on charisma.

It had been a relief when he told her he was being transferred back to Edinburgh and that he'd understand perfectly if she felt she couldn't risk her company pension by moving from Glasgow to be with him, when she didn't have another job to go to.

After he'd gone, she spent a couple of days wondering if perhaps he'd been expecting her to make more of an effort to keep him. But her relief at his departure outweighed any mild feelings of guilt about his possible broken heart.

If, over the years that followed, the satisfaction she'd initially felt at no longer having to defer to another person dimmed slightly, she chose to ignore it. She had friends, a nice flat and a good job that paid her tolerably well. You couldn't have everything you wanted in this life, she told herself repeatedly.

Recently, however, something had changed. Perhaps it was her age. Every time she looked in the mirror, she saw yet one more wrinkle and another grey hair. She was a thoroughly modern woman. Was the rest of her life to be a passion-free zone? Where was the harm, she thought, in going along with Heather's suggestion?

She hadn't thought she'd find her Mr Right on a dating app. Nor even her Mr Right Enough. She hadn't even expected anyone to "swipe right", which, she'd quickly learned from Heather, was dating app parlance for moving your finger across an image on your touchscreen phone of a person you might like to meet.

Who was she, after all? A woman nearer 50 than

40, who had never been terribly photogenic even when she'd been at her prettiest. But within a week she'd had three hits, had met each of them for coffee and had a second date arranged with her best match, a history teacher called Geoff. Two years older than her, he was bit on the plump side, but she didn't mind that because she was herself. He had a full head of hair, albeit grey, twinkly eyes and told good jokes. He'd been married, so he told her, towards the end of their first date, but she'd run off with one of her work colleagues. All that had happened five years ago, and it had taken him this long to get his confidence back to try dating again. That night, once she was back home, she found she couldn't stop thinking about him.

'Two-timing the new boyfriend already, are you?'

Irene jumped and snapped her phone shut. She was sitting at her desk, ready to begin her day's work when Heather came swanning by.

'No, no,' she blustered, her face red with embarrassment. "Just checking my messages."

'Any dirty ones?'

Irene didn't know where to put herself. Fortunately, Heather didn't wait for an answer but instead gave a snort of amusement and carried on her way. It was all front, Heather's banter, Irene knew. Deep down, beneath the bluster and the innuendo, she was thoughtful, kind, and a good listener. Irene would have appreciated someone to talk to right now – someone other than Geoff, that was. She couldn't possibly talk this over with Geoff since he was part of the problem. The other part was Pixie.

Geoff didn't know Pixie. After all, they'd only been together for a couple of months. If you could even call it "together". They'd taken things slowly – Geoff didn't much like going out on a school night, which suited Irene fine what with one thing and another. So, what dates they'd had had been spread out over several weekends. Taking into account the week he'd been away on a school trip to Ypres because Year 10 were covering the First World War, they'd only had six dates at the most.

They'd last seen each other at the weekend, when they'd gone for lunch at a lovely village pub that got consistently brilliant reviews on Trip Advisor for its seasonal game pies. It had been a lovely day. Bright sunshine but a nip in the air that made the roaring log fire in The Greyhound all the more welcoming.

Irene had made some comment about the Christmas decorations that were already up, even though it was barely December. She wasn't a fan of decorations till after the 20th, she'd said, but when they were as tasteful as these ones then she could be persuaded. Was it the decorations that had reminded Geoff that Christmas was – if not exactly round the corner – then near enough to start making plans about how to spend it?

She flipped open her phone again to sneak another

furtive glance at the message she'd first read this morning on getting out of bed.

'Is it too soon to suggest spending Christmas together?' it said. 'Just the two of us?'

She must have read it a hundred times already but every time she did, she felt the same response. A sort of sickening thud in the pit of her stomach. And all because of Pixie.

It was ridiculous really, the way she felt responsible for someone who was neither a relative nor a close neighbour. She wouldn't even have called Pixie a friend, really. As a matter of fact, most of the time she didn't even like her very much.

This was hardly surprising, since Pixie Galloway had been the woman who'd broken up her parents' marriage all those years ago. A floozy, so Mother had described her, as well as a string of other colourful collocations that had made the then teenage Irene blush to the roots of her hair.

It hadn't lasted of course, her father's relationship with the floozy. He'd never been one to settle down. But once it was over, he'd made no attempt to return to the family home. Presumably, once he'd rediscovered life as a single man, he had no intention of putting his head back in the marital noose.

Irene and her mother had bumped along together once Dad had gone, until Irene finally plucked up the courage to make a run for it in her mid-twenties, when a job came up in Glasgow. Of course, she'd made visits home over the intervening years. But she'd always had to give herself a stiff talking to before she could bring herself to board the plane back down south. It seemed to her that Mother grew more bitter with every visit, and it was always a relief when it was time to leave.

When Mother died of a fast-growing cancer, Irene had been filled with so many conflicting emotions. Sadness, of course. This was her mother after all, who'd picked her up when she'd fallen over and sung her to sleep when the thought of the monsters under her bed had made her cry out in terror.

But there'd also been relief. No longer would she feel obliged to make any more visits to that dark house with its tiny rooms, low ceilings and décor that hadn't changed in half a century.

Dad didn't turn up to Mother's funeral. Perhaps it had been foolish of Irene to imagine that he would. She'd shrugged off her disappointment just like she'd learned to shrug off all those other times he'd disappointed her. When it was his turn to die, a more spiteful daughter perhaps would have stayed away from his funeral.

But Irene was constitutionally unable to neglect her duty. So of course, she did what she had to do and showed up at the church. Perhaps it was this old-fashioned idea of duty she'd clung to all her life that, over the years, had made it impossible for her to turn her back on Pixie Gallagher too.

Sitting in the front row of the church, her father's coffin directly in her eyeline, Irene had felt vulnerable and so very lonely. She was the last in the line, the only member of the family to attend. There were a handful of other mourners – old drinking chums of her father's – but nobody she recognised. No one with a sympathetic face.

Pixie Gallagher was the only other woman present. Irene couldn't decide if she was to be pitied or loathed. On the one hand, she'd run off with her father when she'd been a vulnerable teenager, not to mention the fact that by doing so she'd ruined her mother's life. On the other hand, look at her now!

She looked, quite frankly, a fright. She was dressed in a riot of pink, and a purple hat was perched on her orange hair like an upturned flowerpot. The hair was a wig, Irene had since found out. Just one of her large collection. Her makeup was a thick mask of orange foundation that stopped at her jawline. Tears had made two jagged tracks down either side of her face and her eye makeup was an even sorrier mess.

When the service finally ended and Pixie left the church, Irene considered following her. Though what she would have said when she caught up with her, she hadn't yet worked out. Excuse me, you don't know me, but I recognise you from some old photos I found in my father's flat the other day, when I was clearing it out. You're the tart with the heart and the cleavage to match, who appears to be hanging off his arm while he raises a glass to the camera.

But that was the kind of no-holds-barred dialogue that was best reserved for Irene's favourite soaps. It was hardly her style. In the end, what kept her in her seat was her usual quiet reserve. What was the point of picking over old scabs, she thought? Tomorrow she'd be going back up to Glasgow. After today their paths would never cross again.

Except they did. Not five months later. It was in the most unlikely of places – the supermarket where Irene did her shopping, just a few streets away from her flat off the West Road. She'd been minding her own business, filling her trolley with two-for-ones even though she knew she'd never be able to consume all of it before the sell-by-date ran out and feeling bad about the inevitable waste.

As she made her way down the aisle, she became aware of a minor confrontation taking place ahead. A fat, red-faced man in a suit, wearing a badge that suggested he was probably the manager, was locked in verbal combat with one of his customers. Other customers looked on. They'd clearly decided this was the best bit of free entertainment they'd had in a long while, since they were making no effort to move away. They stood about, nudging each other, comparing opinions and grinning gleefully at the argument that was unfolding before their rubbernecking faces.

The manager appeared to be accusing a little old

lady of having slipped a packet of biscuits into her own – rather capacious – bag, instead of into the trolley. Irene was about to turn back the other way, embarrassed by the unsympathetic and insensitive way he was dealing with the alleged thief. No one deserved to be made a laughing stock like this, even if she had been shoplifting, she thought. But then she realised who it was.

It was the hair that had initially confused her. The last time she'd set eyes on Pixie Gallagher, it had been orange. Now it was purple. The outfit had changed too. Lime green this time. And scarves. Lots of scarves. The makeup was the same, however. The combination of the pan stick, the mauve eye shadow, the spidery lashes and the bleeding lipstick provided a salutary lesson in how to avoid applying your make up.

Pixie was putting up a strong defence, it had to be said, and all in a very refined Scottish accent. Unless the store manager unhanded her right this minute, she'd call the police and have him for assault, she said, much to the delight of the onlookers. Irene couldn't help admiring the woman's spirit.

There was more, too. Much more. How dare he accuse her of taking something she hadn't paid for? She'd never been so insulted in her life. Did he seriously think she would allow him to examine the contents of her shopping bag? Her own personal, private property?

It was at this point that Irene found herself stepping forward. Could she have a word with the manager in private, she said, drawing him to one side. It took a good five minutes, but in the end, she managed to persuade him to let the old lady go without pressing charges. She even said she could vouch for her. She'd known her for years, she lied. And she'd no more dream of stealing food than she would dream of planting a bomb in the grounds of Holyrood. Stealing husbands, though, that was another matter altogether, she thought but didn't say.

Half an hour later, the two of them were sitting together in a café across the street, drinking tea.

'I got myself into a bit of a situation, didn't I?'

Pixie gazed across the table at Irene, a coy smile playing on her thin ruby-red lips.

A bit of a situation didn't really cover it, as far as Irene could see. She was lucky not to have been hauled off the premises in a police van.

'It was very civil of you to come to my aid the way you did,' Pixie added.

It was nothing, Irene murmured. She'd thought the manager was very rude, she said, which was why she'd stepped in.

'If you'd left it another minute, I'd have lamped him one,' Pixie replied.

The switch from dear little old lady to aggrieved, belligerent warrior almost took Irene's breath away. She didn't know what to think. Who had been right, the store manager or Pixie? *Was* there a packet of biscuits in Pixie's bag? It was an elephant in the room she had no intention of tackling.

And when, halfway through their second cup of tea, Pixie finally introduced herself, Irene realised that here was another elephant. She could have said she knew very well who Pixie was.

But what would have been the point? All that business with her father was a long time ago. If her mother had failed to make a life for herself after he'd left, then that was as much her mother's fault as Pixie's. And as far as she herself was concerned, she'd got over all that upset years ago.

It turned out they lived quite close to each other. A bus ride away in fact. Pixie had lived in the same flat for thirty years, she said. It overlooked the park and held some very happy memories. Was my father one, Irene wondered, briefly forgetting the promise she'd made to herself to let sleeping dogs lie.

Once they'd drunk their tea and finished their scones and Irene had paid the bill, she could have left Pixie at the café door. But instead, she took the bus back to Pixie's flat with her, stopping at the corner shop to pick up the bits and pieces Pixie still needed, because that unfortunate business at the supermarket had got in the way. The thought of going back there was completely off the cards now, Pixie had said in the café, picking at the currants in her scone with her scarlet talons. She had no intention of ever showing her face in that establishment again.

Irene felt it would have been cruel to remind her that actually, she'd been banned. How wonderful it must be to have such self-confidence, she thought, watching Pixie as, on unsuitable high-heeled leopard-skin ankle boots, she teetered to the ladies', head held high.

She did *try* to resist taking a peek inside Pixie's shopping bag to see if there were things in there that hadn't gone through the till back at the supermarket, but the temptation had been too great. She didn't know why she wasn't surprised to see a packet of chocolate biscuits staring up at her.

So, for the last three years, this is how their relationship had progressed. Pixie would get herself in what she called 'a bit of a situation' and Irene would bail her out. There was the time she left the tap running in her bathroom, for example. It had taken Irene the best part of a day to mop up the spillage, as well as all the bother of locating a humidifier to dry the place out and dragging it into the back of her car singlehandedly while Pixie looked on, complaining about her bad back.

Then there was the time she locked herself out of the flat at one in the morning while putting out the rubbish. Irene had been sleeping at the time and had the fright of her life when she opened the door of her own flat to discover Pixie standing there. She was dressed in a voluminous white nightdress with a woollen shawl pulled tight around her shoulders, looking for all the world like Mrs Rochester. 'I seem to have got myself in a bit of a situation,' she'd said.

When Pixie's cat went missing, Irene printed out posters and affixed them to all the nearby trees and lampposts. Not that she was actually lost. Pixie had shut her in the spare room by accident, and it slipped her mind to let Irene know she'd been found. One day, towards the end of September – the day before her first date with Geoff – she'd put out a small fire in the kitchen when she just happened to be in Pixie's neighbourhood and thought she might as well pay her a visit. It was what happened on this visit that prompted Irene to make her offer. The same offer she was now deeply regretting, the closer it got to Christmas.

Pixie had still been in her dressing gown, even though it was fast approaching noon. Irene couldn't help noticing that she seemed out of sorts. Her 'situations' were happening more and more frequently. So frequently, in fact, that Irene was beginning to wonder if she ought to get social services involved.

'Couldn't you smell the burning, Pixie?' she said, as, trying not to panic, she flung a wet tea towel over the frying pan that was fast becoming engulfed in flames.

Pixie didn't move from her chair. If the whole

house had gone up in flames, she wouldn't even have noticed, Irene couldn't help thinking.

'I smelled something,' she said listlessly. 'But I thought it was coming from the flat below.'

There was a newspaper on her lap. Irene noticed it was open at the page marked Obituaries. 'If you don't take more care, I'll be reading *your* obituary sooner than I should be,' she said.

Pixie had a ghoulish sense of humour. This kind of remark would normally have jollied her out of her bad mood. But not today.

'That might be the best thing,' she replied, gloomily.

Irene decided that the situation required a cup of tea. 'Tell me all about it,' she said, once the kettle had boiled and she'd presented Pixie with her usual mug of strong black tea with two sugars.

'Everybody's dying, Irene,' Pixie said, blowing on the steam. 'Two more gone this week. My friends are dropping like flies.'

'So, you thought you should hasten your own end too, is that it?'

She passed the biscuit tin across. Pixie took two, which made Irene think things couldn't be all that bad if she could still eat. But with Pixie's next remark she wondered if her optimism had been a bit premature.

'What have I done with my life, Irene?' she said.

'Now, come on, Pixie. Have your tea, get dressed

and I'll take you out somewhere,' Irene said. 'We can go to the Botanicals. You love it there.'

So far in their relationship, Irene had a done an excellent job of keeping their relationship on a superficial level. They spoke about the weather, films they'd seen on the TV late at night and whatever happened to be in the news that day. Whenever it got personal, Irene steered the conversation back to something more neutral.

'I thought I'd found true love once upon a time,' Pixie said. 'He was the love of my life. My grand passion.'

The conversation was taking a turn Irene wasn't happy with.

'Here, give me that before you spill it,' she said, holding out her hand impatiently for Pixie's mug, which was looking none too steady.

'What's the matter? Is it too much for you to bear, the thought of an old lady like me having had a sex life?' A sly smile crept over Pixie's face. It was as if she were enjoying Irene's embarrassment. 'I didn't have you down as a prude, dear.'

Irene felt the colour rise in her cheeks. Here it was. She was about to get the whole story of Pixie's mad affair. And then, once she'd heard it, she was going to have to confess that she'd known about it all along and that in fact she was Pixie's lover's daughter.

Pixie wouldn't want to know her after that. She

was bound to be suspicious. Why would Irene befriend an old dear like her, a woman who'd ruined her parents' marriage and deprived Irene of a father, unless she was just biding her time with a view to doing her in?

Pixie read a lot of crime novels. This was a scenario that would have been right up her street.

Why on earth hadn't she told Pixie right at the start that she knew who she was? Now it was too late. She was a firm believer that some things should be spoken of immediately or never spoken of again. A bit like that bit in the marriage service where everyone holds their breath when the vicar says, 'or forever hold thy peace'.

She waited for Pixie to begin at the beginning and then proceed to the gory details. But all she got was a couple of sentences.

'This man – he was a little bit older than me. Swept me off my feet, he did. Told me he loved me, wanted to marry me. All the usual guff men come out with.'

She stared into the distance, a smile playing on her face.

'I was a silly girl back then and I believed him,' she said. 'But then I found out he was married. He even had a little girl. Well, I couldn't have that, could I?'

'No.' The single word came out half strangled.

'Dropped him like a hot potato, I did. After he'd

taken the best years of my life. Gave up on all my ambitions. All the dreams I'd had before I met him.'

Irene didn't dare move. She just sat there thinking of ways to change the subject.

'Now look at me,' she said after a while. 'Spending my days reading obituaries. It'll be Christmas soon and this year I'll have no one to spend it with.'

That was when she came out with it. 'Come and spend Christmas with me,' she'd said.

For months now, she'd been able to put her reckless invitation to the back of her mind. But now it was the first week of December and since she'd given it, she'd met a man she suspected she was falling in love with. A man who, only this morning, had sent her a text that said, 'Is it too soon to suggest spending Christmas together? Just you and me?'

In the same way she'd failed to mention she knew about Pixie's relationship with her father, she hadn't so much as uttered Pixie's name to Geoff. What was the matter with her? Why hadn't she mentioned that she'd struck up a sort of friendship with a mad old bat she'd once saved from being prosecuted for shoplifting, who by the way just happened to be her father's ex bit on the side?

It's not as if Geoff had been backward at coming forward about his own family. His parents had been happily married for more than fifty years, he'd told her, round about their third date. But a couple of years ago his mother had died and now his father was on his own. A total pain, apparently, these days. Moody, taciturn and a bit of an embarrassment, especially when it came to political correctness and personal hygiene.

This stuff about his dad – it had been an open invitation to reciprocate. The perfect opportunity. All she'd needed to do was open the door a crack and Pixie would have fallen out.

She could have confided in him just how infuriating Pixie was, always borrowing money and never giving it back; ringing her up at inconvenient times and then getting all huffy when Irene said she couldn't chat about last night's *EastEnders* because she was about to go into a meeting. Asking her if she'd mind doing a little errand for her, it wouldn't take long, but which invariably ended up causing Irene a huge amount of inconvenience. The list went on.

But she didn't utter a single word about the dratted woman. It was like she was stuck in a pattern. No, she had no ties at all, she'd said, when Geoff had asked her about her own family. She conned herself she was telling the truth, since Pixie wasn't actual family, was she? She was just a ball and chain round her ankle she couldn't shake off.

The whole thing was ridiculous. She was going to have to come clean. Tell him that unfortunately she'd made other arrangements and that those other arrangements involved a crazy woman who wore lopsided wigs and makeup that looked like she put it on in the dark and whom she was, quite frankly, embarrassed by.

Except, she didn't do any of that. Instead, after a glance at her work emails, which had mounted up to a frightening number while she'd been sitting at her desk and trying to work out which direction her life was going in, she switched her phone off and put it in her bag.

When she got it out again it was lunchtime. There were six missed calls. Three were from Pixie, who'd left a series of lengthy messages when Irene hadn't picked up. The first said how much she was looking forward to Christmas. The second informed her that her favourite drink was Advocaat if Irene fancied picking up a bottle or two. And the third insisted that Irene wasn't to think about buying her a Christmas present, because she didn't expect one and she hoped Irene didn't expect one either.

The other three were from Geoff. Her heart dipped. It was clear he had no intentions of giving up until she got back to him with her answer. When her phone rang again and his name flashed up on the screen, she had no choice but to answer.

She decided to speak first in case she lost her nerve. She remembered an article she'd read once in a woman's magazine about how to be assertive. Say no first and then give your excuse, but only if you feel you need to.

'Geoff,' she said, her voice a little trembly. 'I can't spend Christmas with you. I have other plans.'

There was a long silence before Geoff replied.

'Oh,' was all he said.

'I'm sorry,' she said, before mentally kicking herself.

Never say sorry, the article had said.

Another pause. Then, 'Is there someone else?'

The very idea that she could possibly have two boyfriends at the same time completely threw Irene. Not to mention the fact that he actually sounded like a man who'd been deeply wounded.

'Someone else? No! Of course there's no one else,' she said.

Except there was, of course. Hovering behind her, she sensed a disappointed figure wearing a badge with the words 'Irene's conscience' printed on it. Before it could speak first and tell her exactly how pathetic she was, she rushed in. 'Yes,' she said. 'There is someone else. But it's not what you think.'

She found herself telling him everything. Suddenly, it was important that she got it all out. She told him about the first time she'd spotted Pixie at her father's funeral and how confused seeing her had made her feel. And how confused about Pixie she'd felt ever since.

'I can't think why on earth I invited her to spend Christmas with me,' she said. 'She's bound to set my house alight or block my sink or fall down the stairs drunk on Advocaat and end up having to stay with me for the next six months till she's mended, like The Man Who Came to Dinner.'

'Which man?' Geoff said. 'Is this an ex you're talking about now?'

'It's a film,' Irene said. 'He was annoying too. They were all glad to see the back of him but then he slipped on the step, and they had to put up with him for even longer.'

Geoff laughed. He actually laughed. Why was this so funny, Irene asked herself.

She'd poured out her heart to him and now he was treating it as a joke.

'Do you know why I was ringing you before?' he said. 'And why I'm ringing you again?'

'To discover my answer, I presume,' she said, aware she sounded like a character from a Victorian novel.

'To cancel,' he said.

'Oh.'

'Before you jump to any wrong conclusions, let me explain.'

There was nothing more he'd wanted than to spend Christmas with Irene, he said, but then he'd had a call from his sister.

'It's meant to be her turn to have Dad this year,' he said. 'But she's just learned her house has subsidence and she and her husband have to move out while it gets underpinned.'

'Oh,' Irene said again.

They'd decided to seize the opportunity to fly to Australia to spend Christmas with their son and his family, which meant that he was going to have to go up to Inverness and bring Dad down to Glasgow for the festive season.

'It wouldn't be fair to expect you to put up with my father for two whole days,' he said.

Irene's heart gave a little flutter. 'Two days?' she said. 'Were you inviting me for two days?'

Two days inevitably suggested the addition of a night.

'Yes. But that was then.'

They'd reached deadlock. There was nothing more to be said. Her Christmas with Geoff – her two days linked by one night – was off.

'Unless...' Geoff said.

'Yes?'

'Well, if I'm going to order a turkey I might as well order one big enough for four.'

'Are you serious?'

'Think about it,' he said. 'It's the perfect solution. Two is always easier to manage than one. They'd cancel each other out.'

'Do you have room enough for all of us?'

She realised she'd never seen the inside of Geoff's house. Apparently, he had four bedrooms. When his ex ran off with her colleague, she felt so guilty she said he could keep the house and all its contents.

'And I'm an excellent cook too,' he added.

'I'll have to think about it,' Irene said.

But she knew she was only stalling. Already she could imagine exactly how Pixie would jump at this change of plan. Not just one man but two to flirt with. Just imagine the fun she'd have with that! It was bound to require a new outfit too. Not to mention a new wig.

'Don't leave it too long,' Geoff said. 'I need to amend my order at the butchers, and he gets tetchy when people change their orders so late, at this time of year.'

She was on it, she said. Like a bonnet, she added. Heaven knew where that silly little phrase had come from. It was probably one of Heather's. Speaking of which, here was Heather at her desk.

'Fancy a spot of lunch?' she said. 'It's been ages since we had a catch up. And I want to know how things are going with you and your Geoff.'

But Irene was already halfway through dialling Pixie's number. 'Just a sec, I need to make a call,' she said, glancing up with a smile. 'I've got a bit of a situation.'

Pinching other people's phrases. There she went again.

First published 2017, *Woman's Weekly* Fiction Special

The Prodigal Father

Claire's Story

Claire braced herself to say the words she had long since resigned herself to never saying. 'A letter, Louise. From your father.'

She had a sudden urge for a cigarette, although she hadn't smoked for years. A bad habit she'd put behind her – along with the other, perhaps more dangerous one. The habit of hoping Tony would come back to her and say he'd made a mistake. That he'd been wrong when he'd decided that at 18, the two of them were too young for marriage, baby or no baby.

Louise was 15 now. Bright, funny, beautiful and confident. The image of her father when he was her age.

When good friends, perhaps late at night after one too many drinks, sheepishly admitted to their own experience of true love – that one mad passion nothing ever had or would surpass – they often said they felt as if they'd known that person all their life.

For Claire, those words were no more than the truth. She'd grown up with Tony Fagan, gone through school with him, played Juliet to his Romeo in the sixth form play, fallen head over heels in love with him and, as their last academic year drew to a close and friends talked of the new starts that lay ahead, found herself pregnant with his child.

'I can't marry you, Claire,' he had said, just before he'd walked out of her life. 'We're both far too young to saddle ourselves with responsibilities. I have a future. So do you. There are things you can do to end pregnancies, you know...'

She hadn't heard everything he'd said, but she'd heard the important things. The word 'responsibilities', as if it were a burden, not an opportunity. The way he'd avoided saying 'abortion'.

She relived that final conversation still. Tony, who she had loved so much, suddenly refusing to meet her eyed as he asked the impossible, adamant that even if she refused, he still intended taking up his place at university.

She'd left it there. Hadn't even tried to persuade him he might be wrong and live to regret such a selfish decision. She'd glimpsed the ambition and the desperation in his eyes. And – because she'd loved him – she'd let him go.

The postman had brought the letter with the Monday morning delivery only half an hour ago. Now it was 8.15, breakfast time, and Claire wondered if she'd been foolish to offer the letter to Louise without first weighing up the pros and cons.

Maybe she should have thrown it in the bin and said nothing. After all, Louise had never received as much as a birthday card from Tony before. Why would she walk into the kitchen two weeks before school broke up for Christmas and ask if the postman had brought anything from her dad?

Or maybe Claire should have broken it to her more gently. But how could the truth ever be that, she wondered, pouring herself another strong coffee.

'Your daddy, after all this time. Married now, I see. To a lovely, clever wife and with a beautiful little girl. Pots of money. Wants to give his first child a holiday – having denied all knowledge of her for the first 15 years of her life.'

No, she could never have said those things. In the years she'd scrimped and struggled to bring up Louise, she had refused to speak one bitter word against Tony. She'd offered only love, and Louise, her pride and joy, had soaked it up and returned it with interest.

She had no intention now of turning her daughter against her in a fit of jealous pique. This invitation, she had to believe, had been offered in the spirit of generosity. It was Christmas after all, or nearly.

Now Louise's azure eyes sparkled as they scanned the letter, and she blinked in sheer delight at the words she read.

'He wants me to go skiing with them at Christmas!' she gasped. 'Can you imagine? A week in a luxury villa in Switzerland. How cool is that!'

Claire marvelled at the sheer breathtaking self-centredness of children. Not that she minded. In truth, she was glad that Louise was able to accept this invitation so unquestioningly. She admired too how easily Louise seemed to have forgotten all about their theatre trip, which she'd taken such pains over.

Claire had managed to get hold of a couple of tickets for the ballet, which Louise loved. She'd seemed over the moon when Claire had said she'd treat her.

One look at her face now, however, showed she'd clearly forgotten all about this outing. Or worse, had already privately ditched the idea in favour of a trip to Switzerland.

'You'd have done the same yourself at her age, Claire,' her best friend Mel told her over coffee at work the next day.

Claire gave a rueful half smile. 'You're right,' she said. 'I knew I could rely on you to stop me skewing everything round. I have to keep reminding myself this is about Louise, not me.'

'That's what friends are for,' Mel said affectionately. 'Just remember, Louise has been out of her father's life for the first 15 years of her existence. The least you can do is milk him for everything you can both get out of him now.'

Claire couldn't resist a wicked grin. 'Well, as it happens,' she chuckled, 'I was just checking out the price of ski wear in that sports shop in town. Don't suppose there'll be much change out of that cheque Tony generously sent!'

Mel laughed. 'Not to mention the après-ski outfits she's going to need.'

For a few days after her chat with Mel, Claire almost convinced herself she was coping well with the prospect of Christmas on her own, and any bitterness she felt towards Tony for taking her daughter away was fully under control.

In front of Louise, she was upbeat and made a good show of being delirious with delight whenever Louise disclosed any more information about her plans.

'Dad says I mustn't worry that I've never skied before.'

Louise had spoken the word 'dad' hesitantly at first, but more confidently over time, so that Claire soon began to wonder if his disappearing act was her imagination.

'He said there's expert tuition available. Abigail skis like a pro, apparently. And Isobel's nearly as good.'

Claire refrained from asking which name belonged

to who – wife or daughter. *Second* daughter, actually, she reminded herself bitterly. The one on whom skiing holidays had been lavished annually for the best part of her young life while his first daughter got zilch.

'That's nice,' was all she said, biting her lip until it hurt. 'It was very generous of your father to send you a new mobile so you could get to know each other before you go off.'

An iPhone. Louise's old pay as you go had died about a month ago and Claire had been thinking about replacing it with something grander as her Christmas present, but now that pleasure had been taken away from her.

'He knows you don't make much money and he doesn't want me making your phone bills any higher,' Louise said.

'Sweet of him,' Claire replied. Fortunately, Louise was too wrapped up in her holiday plans to detect the venom dripping from her mother's tongue.

* * *

'What's his game, Claire?'

It was the last day before the holiday and Claire and Mel were having a Christmas drink in their favourite wine bar before heading home.

Claire had been staring into her glass for some

time. She was exhausted, having slept little since Tony had dropped his bombshell.

'So, it's not just me who thinks he's up to something,' she said, relieved at the opportunity to say what was on her mind. 'I thought I was simply being paranoid.'

'Well, it certainly seems strange that a man should suddenly reappear in his daughter's life after 15 years and invite her on holiday to meet his new family.'

'Appear, Mel. Not reappear,' Claire reminded her. 'To this day, Tony's never set eyes on Louise, remember.'

She pictured him as he'd been all those years ago and wondered if he'd changed. She thought of the wife – Isobel – and daughter. She bet they were both well-groomed and petite, with perfect teeth and manners. She saw them purring contentedly like two pampered cats and decided she hated them already.

'Get me another wine, would you, Mel,' she said. 'I've got to be sociable for when Tony calls later to pick Louise up. Their flight leaves early tomorrow.'

There was a crush at the bar and Claire had plenty of time to plan exactly how she'd behave when Tony turned up. Would she invite him in? She could hardly leave him on the doorstep, the man would freeze to death.

But could she bear to have him in her front room, estimating the value of her property, wondering at the threadbare state of the curtains, detecting the sound of next door's telly through the thin walls and trying to pretend it was lovely?

Or, far worse than that, not even pretending, but sneering at her, feeling sorry for her. She wasn't worried that she still had feelings for him – time had cured her of that. But the pain he'd caused her was still strong. Maybe too strong to make small talk with the man who had so unceremoniously dumped her all those years ago.

She came back to earth as Mel thrust what appeared to be a brimming glass of pink champagne at her.

'I think we've pulled!' Mel giggled. 'Those two at the bar. They bought us these!'

Claire looked over. For a moment, she was puzzled. Then her confusion cleared. She let out a loud laugh.

'Don't you know who it is? Well, one of them, anyway?'

Mel was short-sighted and notoriously too vain to wear glasses outside the office.

'The short dark one is Simon Thingy from Accounts. I don't know the tall blond guy, though.'

'Look out, they're coming over.'

It seemed to Claire that the combination of alcohol and the prospect of a week off work was beginning to have an odd effect on Mel. She was acting for all the world like Louise when she was giggling on the phone to her friends about boys they fancied.

The thought of Louise set off a train of other connections. The prospect of having to make out to Tony that she was totally cool about him taking Louise away, wishing her a lovely trip and waving her off at the door. Then an evening alone followed by a solitary Christmas. And every minute of every day spent wondering how Louise would be getting on with her new family.

The fear Claire had been trying to suppress since the first moment she'd opened Tony's letter bubbled to the surface. What if Louise enjoyed herself so much with Tony, Isobel and Abigail that she decided she preferred their company to Claire's? After all, Louise was so like Tony, and just think of all the things he could give her. He'd already started with a brand-new phone and a skiing holiday.

With icy clarity, she knew what his next step would be. He wanted Louise for himself. He wanted to take her away. She imagined the scene in her head: 'I can give you anything you want. A lovely house, a good school, nice clothes, one day a car of your own…'

'Excuse me, I've got to go,' she cried out. 'My daughter. I've got to get back for my daughter.'

In her urgency, she sent her champagne flute flying. There was a sudden mad flurry of tissues and people shouting: 'Quick, lick it up, don't waste it!'

It seemed everyone was having a wonderful, tipsy time. But there was no way she felt she could stay and join in.

'Mel, ring me,' she said, grabbing her coat and bag.

'Hey, don't I get a Christmas kiss?' said Simon Thingy from Accounts, waving a sprig of mistletoe above her.

'Leave it, Si,' said his friend, noting her glum face.

Claire threw him a grateful smile, thanked him for the drink, then hurried out.

As she turned into her road, the sleek white Jaguar was the first thing she saw. She felt like turning tail and running straight back to the wine bar.

Don't be ridiculous, Claire, she told herself. *You're a grown woman. Go inside and act graciously. It's a holiday for Louise, that's all. Not a kidnapping.*

Louise already had her outdoor coat and boots on, and her face was shining when Claire let herself inside.

'Mum! Where've you been?' she said. 'We have to go in five minutes, Tony said, because of the rush hour traffic. But I couldn't go without saying goodbye.'

Cautiously, Claire inched her way inside, wondering where Tony might be hiding. His voice – all trace of a regional accent erased – assailed her from the living room.

'Isobel doesn't like me driving in these

conditions,' he said. 'She's very highly strung.'

He was standing in front of the gas fire, rubbing his hands in an exaggerated pretence of chumminess. Claire wasn't fooled. She remembered that he'd always been unable to keep still when he was uncomfortable. Shifting from foot to foot like that, several pounds heavier than the last time she'd seen him and with much less hair too, he looked like a man with something to hide.

His pseudo-confident manner inspired in her a boost of genuine confidence. She turned to her daughter and steeled herself to speak with all the enthusiasm she could muster.

'Now, you have a wonderful time, darling, and don't you be coming home with a broken leg!' she joked, pinching Louise's cheek as she hugged her.

Over her shoulder, Claire caught Tony's gaze and held it before his eyes darted away again. But she made sure he read her message. It was a fundamental one.

This is my daughter, Tony Fagan, it said, *and I have raised her all these years. Everything she is she owes to me, and she won't be so easily seduced by your mobile phones and your fancy holidays.*

For the two seconds in which she trapped him in her steely look, she was confident he'd read the message correctly. But then she began to doubt herself and became convinced that all her attempts to warn him off were nothing but bluff.

As she waved them away into the cold, frosty night, her over-bright smile froze on her face, and she felt suddenly drained. She had a sudden vision of a bleak future, with Louise gone from her life because of this new conviction that she belonged with her dad.

It was while she was locking up the house – quiet as a library without Louise's presence – that she remembered Louise had in fact referred to her father as Tony during the brief time they'd all been under the same roof. Or maybe she hadn't. Maybe she'd just imagined what she'd wanted to hear.

For the next two days, Claire did the usual things. She stood in the queue at the supermarket behind families staggering beneath the weight of their trolleys and wondered if they pitied the paltry, unfestive contents of her own.

The next day, Mel rang. As usual, she was off to her elderly parents for a few days, so there was no way the two of them could have got together, which would have been the next best thing to spending the festivities with Louise.

Mel didn't get on with her parents very well and Claire allowed her friend to moan for several uninterrupted minutes about how impossible it was to get out of the visit, because she'd feel so guilty if she did.

'I really envy you being on your own, actually, Claire,' she confessed. 'My mum goes on and on about why haven't I got a husband yet, plus I have to suffer her awful cooking. I'm convinced she puts the sprouts on at the same time as the turkey, but I'd never volunteer to cook myself or I'd have my father complaining about salmonella all through the meal.'

'I can't remember the last time I *didn't* feel obliged to cook,' Claire said. 'This year, I can watch the Queen on the box without Louise making sarky comments. Not to mention her bagging all the caramels and leaving me with the marzipan.'

Small blessings, she told herself. But still, surely her own situation was preferable to Mel's.

'And what about your ballet outing?' Mel wanted to know. 'You'll still go, surely? It would be a pity to waste the ticket.'

Claire had been so preoccupied with Tony taking Louise away that she'd completely forgotten about the ballet.

'You know, Mel,' she said now. 'I've always said you do me good, haven't I?'

'Well, it's mutual, kid.' Mel hated any show of sentimentality and, as usual, deflected the compliment. 'I thought I was doing you some good the other day when those two nice guys came over. Simon's friend seemed pretty disappointed when you bolted like that. He left soon after himself.'

She paused dramatically, and Claire knew she was waiting to be asked for details.

She finally yielded. 'And what about you and Si,

then?' she asked, although she wasn't sure she wanted to know.

Mel paused for a second, sounding unusually shy. 'It was only a drink, Claire, but he asked for my number, and I think this time I may have met The One.'

Great, Claire couldn't help thinking. *First my daughter leaves me, and then my best friend deserts me. Why don't I just jump off a cliff now?*

'Well, you deserve to be happy, Mel,' she said instead.

'And you might be surprised what Father Christmas brings you, too,' Mel said mysteriously, before ringing off with a gleeful laugh, leaving Claire wondering what on earth her friend was going on about.

Claire mooched around the house for a good hour after that, picking up the figs she'd flung into her trolley in an attempt to catch something of the Christmas spirit, fluffing up cushions and marvelling at the house, which had never been so tidy. Then she reread the messages inside the cards on the mantelpiece.

Louise would have had them threaded on golden ribbon by now, she mused, suddenly very close to tears. The tree would have been up in the corner and the two of them would have spent the morning decorating it, with Louise's radio on full blast.

Claire's self-pity soon turned to fury – a fury that

was directed at herself. Why should she allow Tony Fagan to make her miserable this Christmas? Hadn't he given her enough misery in her life already? It was time she stopped this.

Louise would be back in a week's time, and they'd discuss Tony rationally, like two grown women. After all, Louise was old enough to make up her own mind about who she wanted to live with for the rest of her school years.

Besides, Louise was nearly 16, and bright. In two years' time, she would probably be off to university anyway. Once there, her visits home would be bound to tail off. Hadn't Claire raised her for this very thing – her glorious independence? And if Tony wanted to throw some financial assistance her way... well, wasn't that what Claire regarded as his responsibility and Louise's due?

'Don't be pathetic, woman!' she railed at herself. 'You have a ticket to the ballet, which starts in exactly three hours, and a new red dress. Now go upstairs, take a shower and make yourself presentable for the world out there!'

Once showered, dressed and fully made-up, Claire was surprised to find that she felt better. The only thing she had to do now was book a taxi – she was determined to arrive at the theatre in style.

As she reached for the phone, it rang. She picked up immediately.

The male voice on the other end was unfamiliar.

She held her breath, suddenly anxious. What if it was someone delivering bad news – Louise buried beneath an avalanche, or in hospital with a broken leg? Whoever was speaking, Claire was certain it wasn't Tony.

'I hope it's not inconvenient,' the hesitant voice said. 'And I hope you don't think I'm being a bit… well, you know. Only I got your number from your friend. In the bar. I'm David Barlow. From Personnel.'

So that was what Mel had meant by Father Christmas.

Just you wait, Claire vowed.

'Hello? Are you still there?'

'Yes, I am, but not for much longer,' she said breezily. 'I'm off out, actually.' She wanted to sound like a woman with a purpose, even if this David did sound quite nice.

'Oh.' He sounded crestfallen. 'I won't keep you, then. I just wondered if you felt like going for a drink some time. When it's convenient, I mean.'

Claire took a deep breath. *Damn you, Tony Fagan, and your designer wife and daughter*, she thought. *Don't you think for one moment I'll give you the pleasure of feeling sorry for me while you sit round your log fire sipping gluhwein.*

She took a deep breath and said with all the confidence she could muster: 'Do you like ballet, David? Because I happen to have a spare ticket…'

Louise's Story

As the car picked up speed, Louise began to look about her. She knew nothing about cars – for one thing, her mum didn't have one.

'Why would you need to add more congestion to the roads?' her mum often joked. 'Besides, all this walking keeps me fit.'

Some of Mum's friends had cars, but they were all old bangers, littered with sweet wrappers, dog hairs and even once – in the case of Kerrie's mum's car – the remains of her baby brother's breakfast.

The interior of Tony's car seemed oddly sterile by comparison. She wished she could pluck up the courage to ask for the heating to be turned down. Never a good traveller, the combined heat and scent of air freshener was making her queasy.

'So, Lou!'

Louise grinned inanely, waiting for him to continue. Funny, for the past two weeks she'd been building herself up for this moment. At last, she'd be able to address him face to face as 'Dad'.

She'd practised saying it in front of the mirror at first, until she'd started to feel comfortable with it. Only then had she plucked up the courage to pronounce it in front of her mum. She hadn't known what to expect the first time she'd uttered the words 'my dad', but she had expected some kind of reaction.

All she'd got, however, when she'd casually

mentioned she'd been talking to her dad about skiing lessons was a casual, 'That's nice, darling', as if she'd just mentioned she'd got good marks for her homework, when what she was really saying was that she had a father at last – like other girls – and that her mother wasn't the only person who loved her.

'Don't beat yourself up about it,' Kerrie had advised. 'I bet your mum's feeling insecure. I mean, there's never been a dad in your life, has there? Think about it – just hearing you say his name must freak her out. She's refusing to acknowledge it, that's all. Deep down inside she knows it's only a matter of time before he's as important to you as she is.'

Now, as they joined the motorway, Louise pondered her friend's words. She wondered if her biological father could ever play such an important role as her mother did. For one thing, what did he even know about her? What did she know about him, other than that he wasn't how she'd imagined?

'Call me Tony, Lou,' he'd insisted, almost as soon as he'd stepped over the threshold. 'It'd be a bit silly after all these years, don't you reckon, to start thinking we'd got a "dad" sort of relationship.'

It must have been then when she'd started her gormless grinning and blinking. With anyone else she would have said, 'I'm Louise, not Lou,' but something she couldn't quite put into words had stopped her.

So, she told herself it was nothing more than nerves and – fighting off the suspicion that maybe her initial instinct had been correct and that there was something odd about her father turning up in her life after such a long absence – tried to relax.

She must have drifted off, because the next thing she knew Tony was shaking her gently and telling her they were home.

'Straight to bed, I think,' she heard him say. 'We've got an early start in the morning.'

She was thirsty, and hungry, made more so by the rich and flavoursome smell of cooking that greeted her as she heaved herself out of the car and into the house.

A disembodied female voice greeted them as they entered. 'That you, Tone? 'Bout time too. You should have let me know when you set off.'

'I'll just show this young lady to her room – she's all in. Then we can have dinner.' Louise felt Tony's solid weight against her shoulder. She could have woken herself up and made herself sociable for Isobel if she'd tried, but there was something about the irritation in her voice that made her decide that hunger or no hunger, the best place to be right now was bed. Like Tony had said, tomorrow would entail an early start.

Louise was woken by the strange feeling she was being observed from the door of her room. She groped for the unfamiliar lamp switch by her side and reached for her watch. It was 7am.

'Mum said if you want any breakfast, you'd better

get a move on. We leave in an hour.'

Louise blinked herself awake and registered a small, neat child with enviable long hair the colour of straw. She was dressed in casual clothes that sported labels Louise had only ever seen inside the fashion pages of her magazines.

'You must be Abigail,' she said.

'All my friends call me Abi,' the little girl primly replied. 'So, since you're my half-sister, I guess you should be awarded the same privilege.'

Louise grinned. For a little girl, Abi knew some big words!

Breakfast was a rushed affair of cereal and toast, presided over by Abi. The little girl proved a perfect hostess, pouring out fresh orange juice – not the value stuff Louise was used to – and offering up a bewildering variety of jams. At the same time, she kept up a constant stream of chatter about her school friends and her pony, as if Louise was already intimately familiar with them and just needed an update on their exploits.

Tony was nowhere to be seen, but Isobel – a taller version of her daughter, but with darker hair, streaked through with expensive highlights – dashed in and out, clutching a piece of paper and a pencil and checking everything off as she went.

'Well, at least you're packed, Louise,' she said on one of her manic excursions into the kitchen. 'You could teach Abi a thing or two, from the size of your bag. If I let her, that girl would take every item of clothing she possessed.'

She lifted her head from her piece of paper and gave a tinkly laugh. Louise saw how beautifully manicured her nails were and attempted to calculate how much the sparkling jewellery dripping from her wrist and fingers must have cost.

'I haven't got many clothes,' she mumbled. 'I just brought what I had.'

She got down awkwardly from her stool and made to clear the table, but Isobel stopped her.

'Goodness me,' she said. 'We don't have time for any of that. Mrs P will be in later. You go and check that Abi's packed her washbag, and that she hasn't sneaked any more teddies into her hand luggage.'

Dutifully, Louise followed Abi to her room, Isobel's tinkly laugh following them up the stairs. She wondered if the woman found everything amusing. Or was her apparent hilarity just a cover for any antagonism she might be feeling towards Louise's presence in Tony's life?

Isobel had certainly shown little interest in her welfare since she'd arrived – leaving Abi to give her breakfast and not even offering her anything to eat the night before. Admittedly, it had been late when she and Tony had finally arrived, but still. Her own mum would have insisted on visitors joining them, she was sure of that.

At the thought of her mum, she felt a lump form

in her throat and her eyes became watery. What was she doing in this huge house, which seemed to be possessed of every gadget going, yet still managed to give the impression of being empty and soulless?

She wondered if Mum would be up yet, eating her breakfast in the kitchen at home. It was small and cosy and filled with the clutter of living – totally different from the vast white and stainless steel in this house. Everything looked brand new here. It was hard to believe that Isobel ever actually got any of her pots and pans dirty, but presumably she did – hence the necessity for the mysterious Mrs P.

In the kitchen at home, tacky souvenirs and empty wine bottles jostled for space on the narrow ledge behind the sink, because Mum could never bear to part with anything – even when, like the ashtrays she'd bought or been given years ago, they'd outlived their usefulness.

'You girls ready yet?' Tony must have come home.

Louise snapped out of her reverie and called a shy hello down the stairs.

Why be so miserable? she chided herself. *You're going to Switzerland for Christmas – abroad for the first time. And, more important than that, you're going to get to know your dad.*

Yet by the second evening of the holiday, Louise felt that Tony was as much of a stranger to her as he'd ever been. She'd been disappointed when he hadn't sat next to her on the plane. Isobel was a nervous flyer, he'd told her, and needed lots of reassuring. Unless he sat by her side, she would never cope with the take-off and landing.

Louise had been left with no option other than to take her seat behind them next to Abi and endure her half-sister's prattle as politely as she could.

Finding her seat, she'd been forced to disturb a boy of about her own age, who was obviously well settled in his aisle seat. She had muttered her apologies as she'd squeezed past him. He'd nodded in acknowledgement, then clamped his Walkman firmly to his ears and sat back with his eyes closed for the rest of the flight. It would have been nice to talk to someone her own age, Louise had thought, before being distracted by the pilot's talk.

'So, Lou, how are you getting on with your lessons?'

Louise still hadn't got round to telling Tony that no one called her Lou – and now the entire family were doing it, much to her dismay. They were having dinner in the beautiful log restaurant that served the luxury complex of cabins in this thriving tourist resort.

She felt wonderfully relaxed for the first time since her arrival. All she really wanted to do was to savour her mulled wine and be still. If her mum were here, she'd have felt the same too, she was convinced.

Like her, Mum only spoke when she had something to say.

With Tony, on the other hand, it was as if every conversation were an assault course. Every question was prefaced with a 'So, Lou,' as if he felt obliged to fill every second of silence.

Isobel, for her part, had barely spoken to her. She'd ignored Louise's account of her day on the slopes, and simply sat glued to Tony's side, yawning prettily.

Is she making sure I know how much more important she is to Tony than I could ever be? Louise wondered. She certainly gave the impression that she had absolutely no interest in anything Louise said.

At least Abi was chatty – although Louise had realised pretty quickly after meeting her half-sister that you could have too much of a good thing. She'd hoped for a room of her own, but she was sharing with Abi, which meant she was expected to share her bedtime too.

She knew that very soon after this meal ended, she'd be asked to accompany Abi back to the hut, run her a bath and read her a story – just like the previous night. Then she'd been pretty tired after the journey and her first skiing lesson – which, in her opinion, she'd enjoyed but made a complete mess of – so she'd gone along with Isobel's request. It hadn't escaped her notice either how her stepmother had only been able to rouse some enthusiasm towards her when she had a favour to ask.

Tonight, though, Louise wanted to stay here, in the restaurant, maybe drift across to the bar with her father and really start getting to know the man behind the nervous, bluff exterior. Surely Isobel could see how important it was for the two of them to cement their relationship.

From somewhere deep inside, a feeling of bitter mutiny surged through her blood and washed over her like a wave. She fought it, thankful for the candlelight and the flickering flames of the log fire that between them successfully masked her ingratitude. *There was no need for Tony to invite me here,* she reminded herself. *Be grateful.*

So, when Abi began to rub her eyes, Louise didn't wait for Isobel to ask her to take the girl to bed. There was a lifetime ahead. After all, now he'd found her, surely he wasn't going to let her go again so easily.

On the way out, Louise noticed a group of boys and girls about her age sitting round a table sharing a huge plate of sausages and chips. The boy from the plane was there, she noticed, smothering a banger with mustard and laughing at someone's joke.

'Oh, look! That's the boy we saw on the plane, Lou!'

At the sound of Abi's clear, shrill voice, several of them, including the boy himself, stopped talking and looked up from their food, startled.

Louise wished the floor would open up and swallow her. She put her hand roughly round Abi's shoulder to jostle her away, but for someone so tiny and light, Abi became suddenly impossible to move.

'Abi,' Louise urged through gritted teeth. 'For goodness' sake, get a move on.'

She waited for the looks of contempt that would surely emanate from such a sophisticated, world-weary crowd of international jet setters, but all she got were friendly grins and shouts of 'Hi!'

'Why don't you join us,' the boy from the plane said. 'You can help us eat these chips.'

Louise blushed all the more and shook her head. 'Thanks,' she said. 'Only I have to take my sister to bed.'

Someone shouted 'Shame!', and a pale-skinned, red-headed girl giggled, 'Bad luck, Dean!'

The boy looked disappointed and shrugged his shoulders in resignation. Louise smiled shyly and muttered goodbye.

* * *

'I'd say... seventy-five... he fancied... seventy-six... you rotten... seventy-seven.'

Abi, sitting in front of the holly-garlanded mirror in their shared bedroom, spoke between strokes as she applied the brush to her beautiful hair. She was in her pyjamas after her bath, and Louise couldn't help thinking that she almost gleamed with health. She felt her heart squeeze within her. Her logical self could deny all the emotion it wanted, but her heart told a different story.

Who'd have thought it, you nosy little chatterbox, she thought, *but I really like you, little sister.*

Abi chatted on about the coincidence of the boy on the plane again and remarked how wonderful it would be if he asked Louise to go skiing with him.

'Fat chance of that,' Louise muttered. 'You only have to look at him and his cool gang to see they've all been skiing for years. I've just about learnt to stand up, and the way I'm going, that's probably about all I'll master in the time left.'

It would be mean to add that the other encumbrance was the fact that when she wasn't skiing, she was stuck with Abi. Plus, the boy actually had to ask her first.

She didn't have long to wait for this, however. The next day was Christmas Eve and Tony and Isobel had taken Abi off for a visit to Santa's Grotto. All children had to be accompanied by at least one parent, so Louise was off the hook this time, and she couldn't help but offer up a silent prayer of thanks to whoever might be listening.

Abi had gone off happily with her parents, although privately she'd admitted to Louise that she was no longer sure of Father Christmas's existence. 'Let's just say I'm hedging my bets at the moment, in case he leaves me a lump of coal,' she'd said, matter of factly.

That night they would be having a traditional Swiss Christmas dinner together in the restaurant. Louise was already feeling exhausted from being jolly and earnest with Tony. And as for Isobel, well, she'd realised pretty quickly that the only things they had in common were Tony and Abi.

She wondered who Mum would be sharing Christmas dinner with the next day, and she couldn't help wishing it was her.

Outside, the dazzling sunlight soon lifted her spirits. She tramped through the snow to the mini supermarket that looked for all the world like something from a fairy tale, with its twinkly lights and charming window display.

Her plan was to buy a few postcards for Mum, and maybe one more souvenir for the kitchen window ledge – if it would take the weight. Then she would head back to the chalet to grab a shower before Abi got there before her. But on her way over to the cashier, she found herself distracted by the enticing sight and smells of the traditional Swiss bread and cakes on display.

'Hello, again.'

She spun round to find herself face to face with Dean, and her stomach gave a lurch. On the plane she'd barely noticed him, and last night in the bar he'd been just another face in the crowd. But now, one to one, she felt herself drawn to his warm, friendly manner and sparkling blue eyes, made bluer by his tan.

'Tempting, aren't they?' he said.

How on earth can he suspect what's going through my mind? Louise wondered, aghast. It was then she realised he was referring to the cake display. She beamed at him, relieved he hadn't sussed her out.

'You look a bit more cheerful than you did last night,' he remarked.

'You noticed?' she sighed, afraid that because he seemed genuinely concerned, she might give too much of herself away.

'Families, eh?'

She nodded and tried to look cool about it. They chatted for a bit about the skiing conditions, and Louise confessed she was an absolute beginner, and a complete duffer to boot. Then they got talking about where they were from in England.

'But that's about five miles from where I live!' Dean exclaimed when she told him the name of her hometown. 'I go to school there – Randall's.'

Louise gawked at him. Randall's was the exclusive, leafy public school a couple of miles outside the town centre. Sometimes, the boys from there hung round the shopping mall, and Louise and her friends would make derogatory remarks about the way they dressed and talked, just for something to do.

'You don't look like one of that lot!' she said, and

told him the name of her school, a huge, mixed comprehensive.

He grinned. 'You don't look like one of that lot, either,' he countered.

'Touché,' she said.

They continued grinning at each other inanely until Dean mentioned that the next evening – Christmas night – there was to be an under 18s do in the bar.

'Perhaps I'll see you there?' he said.

Louise was desperately trying to work out how to extricate herself from any plans Tony might have made. She was determined to go, but she was also determined to hide how keen she was from Dean.

She shrugged. 'Can't say for sure,' she said.

'Well, how about a definite maybe, then?'

In spite of herself, Louise giggled. 'Fair enough,' she replied.

But the reaction later, when the subject arose, was chilly to say the least.

'You can't possibly go on a date tonight,' Isobel cried. 'You have to babysit while Tony and I step over to the bar.'

It was 7pm on Christmas night and Louise had finally had enough. She'd been roused from her bed at 6am by an excited Abi and forced to spend the rest of the morning playing her stupid games while Tony and Isobel had a lie-in.

Later, over lunch, Isobel had made a big show of

the present she and Tony had bought her – a lovely Swiss watch – over which Louise had been forced to express her delight again and again.

Of course, she loved it, she almost screamed at one point, but how many times was she expected to say so?

She had handed over her gifts too, bought with very little money before she'd even met her new family. Now that she knew Isobel, Louise realised she was probably used to a more exclusive brand of perfume – but did she have to show her distaste so clearly on her face?

Tony had expressed his usual heartiness over the CD she'd bought him, but Louise's relief that at least she'd got that right had soon dwindled when Abi had piped up, 'But you've already got that one, Daddy!'

Thankfully, Abi seemed genuinely thrilled with the hair braids Louise had got her, but it had been these that had precipitated the scene that ensued.

'You'll be able to spend the evening braiding Abi's beautiful hair while we're out, Louise,' Isobel had gushed. 'Won't that be lovely for you?'

After Louise had informed her that she had a date that night and wouldn't be able to oblige, she'd looked on in shocked amazement as Isobel had stamped her foot like a child and said she couldn't go.

She could have shouted back at Isobel, but that wasn't her style. All she said was, 'We'll see about that,' and politely left the room.

'Stupid, spoilt woman,' she fumed as she struggled out of her jeans and into the slinky dress she'd decided to wow Dean with. Yes, she was very grateful for the holiday – she wouldn't have met Dean otherwise. And Abi was a dear little thing. Irritating, naturally. Infuriating, too, especially as she had followed Louise into their bedroom and was now standing watching her. But she would not be bought.

'Who do they think I am, the blimmin' au pair? she snapped at Abi.

'Well, actually, I think they probably do,' Abi said. 'Michelle left just before we came here because she missed her boyfriend in France so much. That's why we had an extra plane ticket, probably.'

Louise felt the blood drain out of her and sat down heavily on the bed. She felt numb. Suddenly, it all became clear. The au pair legs it back to France and leaves Tony and Isobel in the lurch. How very convenient there's a teenage daughter lurking in the wings. She imagined Isobel saying, 'I'm sure if we throw in a free holiday and a Swiss watch, we'll be able to carry on as normal. And just think how handy she'll be in the summer holidays!'

'Are you all right, Louise?' Abi came over to the bed and put her arms around her.

Louise hugged her back. Whatever she felt about her father and his wife was not going to affect the genuine affection she had for Abi. She would not slag either of them off in front of her.

It occurred to her that her mother must have gone through life feeling just the same confusion of emotions as she felt now. Louise couldn't remember her mum ever saying a bad word against Tony. Through all the years he'd remained absent from her life, Claire had only ever said nice things about him. How talented an actor he'd been, how clever, what a brilliant footballer... the list went on and on.

It had been Louise, angry and confused, who had gone through a prolonged phase of demanding to know why her father never wrote or came to visit, and Louise who had cast doubt on her father's integrity.

'He must be a selfish man if he can't see that he has a daughter who needs him,' she'd railed at her mum more than once. Then, in her early teens, she'd simply decided to forget the idea of a father once and for all and get on with her life. After all, she had a mother who loved her enough for two parents.

Loyally, her mother had continued with the same line she'd always spun her. 'We were both young, Louise. And boys of that age are even more immature than girls. I'm sure he didn't mean to stay away so long but think about it. It wouldn't have been easy for him to come back into our lives after so many years. And as time went on, it must have got harder and harder, until finally he must have decided we'd be better off without him.'

He should have stuck to his resolution! Louise wanted to scream. Now she felt doubly betrayed.

There was a knock on the door. Tony, slightly shamefaced, Louise was pleased to note, told Abi that her mother wanted her, and the little girl skipped out of the room.

Tony lingered a moment, then said, 'Mind if I come in, Lou?'

Coldly, Louise finally said what she'd been wanting to say since their first meeting. 'I'm Louise, not Lou. Anybody who knows anything about me knows I hate having my name abbreviated,' she snapped.

Tony apologised, still hovering in the doorway. 'I guess there's a lot of things we still don't know about each other, Louise,' he said. 'I wish you'd let me in. I feel dreadful about what's just happened.'

Louise waved him in, grudgingly. 'I suppose you may as well sit down,' she said.

He perched himself on Abi's bed. It should have pleased her to see him so uncomfortable, but Louise was beginning to feel rather mean. So, when he told her how lovely she looked in her dress, she gave him a gracious smile.

'I'm here to apologise for our assumption that you'd be at our beck and call during this holiday,' he said. 'I guess Abi filled you in about the au pair situation. It was very wrong of us to use you like that.'

Louise had expected all sorts of justifications and explanations. She'd even half-expected Tony to lay the blame at Isobel's feet, and she couldn't help being impressed by his loyalty. He must know Isobel didn't like her and could have used this opportunity to blame her, but instead he'd accepted responsibility himself.

'It's been a difficult holiday, Louise,' he continued. 'Every time I look at you, I feel bad.'

Louise was puzzled. 'How?'

'Guilt, that sort of stuff. I look at Abi and marvel at the way she's growing up, and then I look at you and realise what I've missed.'

Shyly, Louise took his hand and their eyes met. Tony's were misted in tears, and she knew that if she didn't keep a tight rein on herself, she would soon be weeping, too.

'I tried to be so blasé the first night we met,' he went on. 'Insisting you call me Tony and not Dad. I was so sure, you see, that because I'd never treated you like a father, you'd already have decided that you weren't going to use that name, so I decided to get in first.'

'If only you knew how much I dreamt of saying Dad,' Louise breathed.

'Oh, Louise, I'm so sorry. It must have sounded like a rejection. I can see that now. That's one more thing I got wrong. How can you ever forgive me?'

Awkwardly, the two of them embraced.

'It's all right,' Louise said, gently. 'It's not too late to start again, is it?'

'Do you still want to?' Tony said. 'I mean, I know we're all off back to England in a couple of days, but there are half-terms, and so on. Abi's besotted with having you as a big sister. She'd hate it if she never saw you again.'

Thankfully, Tony had left Isobel out of the equation. Rather as if he'd read her mind, he added, 'Just give Isobel time, Louise. She's as jealous as hell of your mum, and it's not surprising she sees you, her daughter, as a threat.'

'But why should she be jealous of Mum?' Louise said. 'Isobel's the one who has got you, after all.'

Tony smiled. 'That's what I keep telling her,' he said. 'But don't let the exterior fool you. Isobel's self-confidence is low. She needs propping up. Something your mum never did.'

Louise was surprised to hear an opinion of her mum she'd never heard before. *Perhaps that's true*, she thought. At any rate, she was certainly more independent than most of her friends' mothers.

'Are you going out, then?' Tony wanted to know.

Louise thought about it. It would have been nice to let her hair down with Dean and his mates. She was dressed up for it, after all. But something was keeping her rooted to the spot.

She wrinkled her nose. 'Nah!' she said. 'It was never a proper date. I think I'd rather stay here. Chat a bit more.'

Tony grinned at her. 'That's the spirit,' he said. 'Treat 'em mean, keep 'em keen.'

'Something like that,' Louise said. 'Actually, would it cost pots of money to ring Mum? I've been dying to talk to her since I've been here.'

Tony clapped his hand over his mouth in dismay. 'My God!' he exclaimed. 'You should have said. Look, go into our bedroom and talk for as long as you like. Don't even think about the cost.'

Claire picked up after the first ring. 'Darling! I thought you'd forgotten all about me! How are you? How's it all going?'

Claire continued with a torrent of questions, all delivered light-heartedly, but the real concern in Claire's voice wasn't lost on Louise.

So much for independence, she mused.

'How are you getting on with your new family?'

Louise wondered how much courage it had taken her mum to ask that one.

'Oh, Mum, I do love you,' she said. 'And you mustn't worry. Abi's a pet but a pain at the same time, and her mother's a bit... neurotic.'

Claire snorted at the other end of the line.

'And your dad? Or is it Tony?'

Louise thought about it. 'Well, it's still sort of Tony,' she said. 'But I think it might soon be Dad.'

There was the tiniest of pauses before Claire said, 'I'm glad, Louise. Genuinely glad.'

Louise decided it was time to lighten the

conversation. 'By the way, did you go to the ballet? On your own?' she asked.

'Well… yes and no,' Claire replied, mysteriously.

'Meaning?'

'Meaning, yes, I went, but no, I didn't go alone. I went with a man.'

'Ooh, you dark horse. Is this what happens when I leave you alone? I suppose you've already moved him in already, have you?' Louise joked.

Claire snorted. 'It was just a date, Louise. Although he's very nice, and I have seen him once or twice since.'

'Good,' Louise said. 'Whoever put the song back in your voice must be nice.'

'You do say some funny things! Anyway, what's the talent like in Switzerland? Do the boys wear those lovely leather pants and braces?'

Louise had a vision of Dean in lederhosen and shrieked with laughter. 'Well, the one I fancy doesn't,' she said. 'And you'll never guess what. He goes to school near me, and he's already asked me out. I stood him up tonight, but I hope he'll forgive me.'

They chatted for a bit longer before Claire said the call must be costing Tony a fortune.

'OK,' Louise agreed. 'Oh, and before I go, there's one more thing I want to tell you.'

'Mmmm?'

'I got you this little pottery figure. A Father Christmas on skis. For your collection.'

'Lovely. Although I'm not sure how many more things we can squeeze onto that windowsill,' Claire said. 'Still, where there's a will…'

Later, as she got ready for bed, Louise thought a bit more about the kitchen windowsill and all the souvenirs that jostled for space along it. In a way, it was like her life. First of all, there had been just Mum. It had been easy enough to find space for her in her heart. She'd had it all. Then, as she'd gone through life, she'd met new people – friends, teachers, boys. Loving more people had never meant for a minute that she had less love for Mum. Now Dad and Abi had entered her heart – she wasn't sure about Isobel, but she was prepared to give it time – and there was room for them, too.

Tomorrow she would search out Dean and apologise for standing him up. Family stuff, she'd say. If he ignored her and slouched away, well, she hadn't lost anything. But if he sympathised, as he had before, then she was sure she'd be able to find room for him, too.

First published 2001, *Fiction Feast*

Being Gerald's Wife

Being Gerald's wife wasn't easy. Things had to be just so, which was a full-time job. Lucky for Sarah, then, that Gerald ran his own company and made enough money so that Sarah could devote her days to making sure that everything in their lovely home was perfect for him.

On this particular afternoon, she was working out a menu for the annual Christmas buffet Gerald liked to throw for the six members of his management team and their partners. The workers had their own party – Gerald would never have tolerated factory employees stomping all over his polished floors.

This would be Sarah's tenth year of organising the event, and that included preparing all the food. Gerald saw to the wine, a subject he was an expert on. Gerald was an expert on a great many things, which was helpful because sadly Sarah, by her own admission, wasn't very bright at all, still less possessed of any expertise.

But she could at least cook, thanks to Gerald's patient criticism of her efforts over the years. Sometimes, in her better moments, she almost felt she was up to providing a buffet worthy of praise, though she never fully relaxed until the last person had left and Gerald had delivered his verdict. Gerald's verdict meant far more to her than anyone else's.

The afternoon had already folded itself away even though it was barely four o'clock. Sarah's heart was heavy as she drew the curtains, automatically flicking away a speck of lint in case Gerald had had a bad day and would use it to upbraid her for her slovenliness. The least she could do when she was at home all day was to keep the place clean and tidy, was one of his constant grumbles.

And of course, he was right. Unfortunately, whatever dirt, dust or untidiness was obvious to Gerald was less so to Sarah. This meant that a great deal of her day was spent looking for any small thing that might be displeasing to her husband's sharp eye, a task so exhausting that it left little time for anything else. Not friends, nor hobbies, nor even children. Children created too much mess, anyway, so they were far better off just as they were, Gerald said.

'How are the preparations coming along?' Gerald demanded that evening, when he arrived home from work.

Sarah couldn't answer him straightaway. She was too busy concentrating on setting the table for dinner. There was a right way to set it and a wrong way, and she couldn't risk getting it wrong. The last time she had... well. They were still short of a water glass. Instinctively, her hand went to her forehead where the shard of glass had lodged. 'It's coming on well,' she said. 'I've done the lists and some preparatory shopping.'

Gerald clicked his fingers. 'Show me,' he said. 'We know what happened last time we had people round to dinner.'

Sarah grew anxious at the memory. It had been an easy mistake to make. And Belinda had been charming about it, insisting that Sarah wasn't to know that gelatine wasn't suitable for vegetarians. She even made a joke about it.

You've done me a favour, she'd said, graciously accepting the plate of fruit that Sarah had hastily assembled for her in place of the pudding. *I could do with losing a few pounds*.

Everyone had laughed, even Gerald. But Sarah had spotted how his fingers alternately flexed and gripped the tablecloth and she knew what it foretold.

Gerald's eyes ran down the page. He was looking for something to find fault with, and he found it soon enough. Sarah braced herself, awaiting his verdict.

'When exactly were you thinking about buying

these avocados you need?' he asked her. 'They're no good unless they're ripe.'

Sarah flinched. And lied. She never used to lie until she met Gerald. 'I've got them already,' she said. 'They'll be perfect on the day.'

He sniffed, almost as if he were disappointed. He shoved the list back at her and she took it. 'Seems like you've got it covered first time for once,' he said.

Next day, Sarah was at the greengrocer's as soon as it opened. She'd barely slept a wink all night, worrying how on earth she was going to make her lie come true. The atmosphere in the shop was festive, with fairy lights and carols, though Christmas was still more than a week away. Only common people put their decorations up before Christmas Eve, Gerald said.

'Looking forward to Christmas, Mrs Grantley?'

Sarah said she was. She smiled at the girl who'd asked the question. Linda was the greengrocer's daughter. She worked at the shop during school vacations and sometimes at the weekend whenever her mother's arthritis played her up. As a family they were very close, even mirroring each other's turn of phrase. They had a stash of them. *Those apples eat well, Mrs G. You can't beat English asparagus. Coriander – it's a Marmite herb if you ask me.*

Today, Linda was wearing a Santa hat and a tinsel necklace, and earrings that were Christmas trees. She fizzed with excitement. How old was she, Sarah wondered? 15? 16? Her memory drew her back to her own happy childhood Christmases and she felt a sudden stab of nostalgia.

How would Linda react, Sarah wondered, if she answered her question honestly and said that no, actually, she wasn't looking forward to Christmas at all. Nor New Year, nor, in fact, anything very much at all.

'Is there anything I can help you with?'

Sarah had found the avocados, which weren't in their usual place. They'd been usurped by dates, brown and shiny, looking like they belonged in some other, ancient epoch. The avocados were rock hard, and Sarah felt like crying.

'How long do you think these will take to ripen?' she asked.

'A few days should do it.' Linda sounded so reassuring that Sarah believed her. Until she got them home.

Immediately, she was on the internet. *How to ripen avocados,* she googled. She soon relaxed. It was doable. You could put them in the airing cupboard. Or in a bowl with a ripe banana or a red tomato. Or in a brown paper bag. Failing the presence of a paper bag, you could wrap them in newspaper.

She had five days. To be on the safe side, she placed them in a paper bag with two bananas and two tomatoes before wrapping the parcel in newspaper and sticking it in the airing cupboard.

Gerald never went there. Airing cupboards were Sarah's domain.

That night, she slept a little better. But during periods of wakefulness, Gerald snoring unthreateningly beside her, she wondered how – almost without her noticing it – it had come about that the life that had once belonged to her now belonged to Gerald. It was as if she'd been dismantled, like one of those components Gerald made, then put back together again as a completely different model.

In the morning, she checked the avocados. No change. She thought about going into town to see if there were any riper avocados there. But she had such a long list of things to do there was no way that she could spare the time.

She checked again three days before the buffet. The tomatoes had exploded, but the avocados were still rock hard. There was nothing for it but to get the car out and sit in the queue for a place to park in the multi-storey behind everyone else intent on doing their last-minute shopping.

It was hell in the supermarket. She found more avocados, but they were just as hard as the ones she was nurturing back home, so she turned her back on them. She needed to take stock.

Recklessly, she decided to treat herself to a cup of coffee and a mince pie. The café in the library would be much quieter than any of the alternatives, and it offered the added bonus of five minutes' browsing time for a nice romance.

What was the least bad thing that could happen if the avocados stubbornly refused to take heed of Linda in the greengrocer's and ripen? she wondered, as she sat with her coffee and mince pie? If it was just a question of being humiliated, she knew she could endure that prospect. She'd learned to hang her head and simply wait until the storm blew itself out. The trick was never to look up and catch Gerald's eye. Her mind blocked out those past scenarios. Sarah was good at blocking things out. It was what got her through the day.

There was a notice board by the lift. As she waited for it to ascend, she allowed her eyes to wander over the notices. There were adverts for Reiki sessions and Pilates classes; piano teachers and French lessons; something about a woman's refuge – a phone number and a website address. Simple numbers anyone could remember and a similarly impossible-to-forget address.

Even as she committed it to memory, she knew this advert was aimed at a different sort of woman. One who lived in a one-bedroomed flat or a council house, not, as she did, a detached house with four bedrooms, a conservatory and a garden an acre long.

When she got home, she checked the avocados. Both banana skins had split, exuding a rich, fecund aroma. But the avocados remained impervious to the ethylene gases produced by their blackening neighbours.

She had one more day remaining. Better not allow her mind to drag her down into those dark corners occupied by the memory of previous incidents. The ones when Gerald had taken his displeasure with her several steps further. Better instead to apply herself to her household tasks for the rest of the day, she reasoned.

That night, when sleep eluded her again, she rose from her bed, made herself a cup of tea and made a decision. She was tired of her life, and she was going to end it.

Next morning, she rose and prepared a perfect buffet. By the time Gerald arrived home from work in the afternoon to uncork the wine to allow it time to breathe before the guests turned up, everything would be set out ready.

But she wouldn't be there. The last thing she did before she let herself out of the house and posted the keys through the letterbox was to remove the avocados from the airing cupboard and slip them into her suitcase.

* * *

The dining room in the women's refuge was a carousel of shiny, clashing colours that would have made Gerald shudder. The clamour of unrestrained excitement as the residents and their children pulled crackers and screamed with delight set her bones alight with the sort of abandoned glee she had never imagined she could feel again. Sarah straightened the paper crown on her head. She had to keep reminding herself that she didn't have to go back to Gerald. He didn't know where she was and he couldn't find her, so Nerissa, who'd answered the phone that night when she'd called, had said.

Nerissa had reminded her too that she was one of the lucky ones. Neither poverty nor children could drag her back. She'd been married to Gerald for ten years, and for nine and a half of those years she'd been abused.

But now she was free of him. She could divorce him. Any court in the land would award her a substantial part of his income and probably the house too. Not that she wanted either. All she wanted was a new start and her true self reassembled.

Later, when the children had all been put to bed, the adults would have their own little party with wine and nibbles. Sarah would make guacamole. She had the ingredients. Red onions, green coriander, limes, chilli and garlic, enough tortilla chips to go round. And three perfect avocados. Ripened at last.

First published 2011, *Fiction Feast*

A Rocking Horse Christmas

December 1998

It was an old-fashioned kind of toyshop. The kind you would expect to find on the high street of any small English town. Julia, his wife, who was from the States, would say it was *quaint*. Pearson's Toyshop, it was called. Greg took no persuading to go inside. It was serendipity, he decided – clearly the shop was waiting for him.

Maybe because last night over a bottle of wine and a good steak they'd made their decision. Now was the time. He was 32. They were never going to be rich, but as long as he remained in the church, they'd always have a roof over their heads. Julia would be 30 in June and like she'd said when she thought he might need persuading – not that he did, of course –

it might take a while to conceive so the sooner they got started the better.

Greg was excited. Delirious even. And the toyshop just happened to catch him while he was in the middle of picturing his soon-to-be conceived son. Or even – after last night and the mood and the wine – his already conceived son. He'd be blonde, like Julia, and sturdy and into everything. A real boy.

Although he wasn't averse to a little girl. A mini-Julia. Smart as a whip and neat as a button. Beautiful went without saying.

Once inside, he nodded to the sales assistant who seemed happy to allow him to wander up and down the aisles picking things up and putting them down again. He put her bright smile and trusting manner down to his dog collar.

For all she knew, he could have coshed a real vicar and stolen the dog collar for the express purpose of coming in here and clearing her out of her entire stock. He imagined the bishop waiting outside in the getaway car. *Where to, buddy? Toytown?* Suppressing a snort, Greg turned his attention to his task.

Up and down one aisle followed by the next he wandered, baffled by the choice. Toys had moved on since he was a boy. Money had always been short at home, so they'd been few and far between too. Fireworks for his birthday because it fell just before Bonfire Night, and at Christmas, sensible things – socks, a book token, once – happy day – a bike. Later, when he got his paper round, he would save up every penny he made to go towards his Meccano collection.

Now, *that* was something you could pass on to a son – if only he'd kept them. Julia being Julia would remind him that a Meccano set was something he could pass on to a daughter too. She was right, of course. He was going to have to remember that if God blessed them with a little girl.

In his day, where he was brought up, toys were divided strictly along gender lines. Although looking around him now, it struck him that any little girl who happened to set foot inside this particular emporium would know immediately which toys were earmarked for her.

A wall of pink boxes and glitter hinted at a future shared between domesticity – (cookers, tea services, vacuum cleaners) – child rearing – (pink prams and dolls of every shape and size) – and man-trapping – (jewellery sets, false eyelashes and hairdressing paraphernalia).

Greg was drawn to the electronic toys that flashed and beeped and zigzagged hither and yon powered by remote control. He wouldn't mind a go with one of those himself, actually.

Julia would tell him he was crazy, spending money on a toy for a baby that didn't yet exist. She was the practical one. She knew more about kids than he did, too. In fact, Julia should be here now.

Someone needed to veto his choice, and who

better than his wife, who taught reception class? He couldn't see her going for the baby doll that drank and peed. Or the drum kit for would-be rock stars. And he already knew her view on toy weapons. No child of hers, etcetera, etcetera.

When he turned the corner into the third and final aisle, he saw exactly what he was looking for. It was an old-fashioned rocking horse, dappled, with a mane and a benign expression on its rocking-horse face. It came equipped with a red saddle and stirrups, and it cost a fortune. Immediately he fell in love with it, and he was sure that Julia would love it too.

It harked back to the past, to simple times. It was non-sexist, non-violent and – now he examined it more closely – non-toxic. The non-affordable bit she didn't need to know about.

Don't wrap it, I'll take it as it is, he told the assistant. Once outside, it was only a matter of moments before he managed to convince himself that the rocking horse wasn't so much a toy as an investment. Heck, no one stopped at one if they'd experienced being an only child like he had. How he'd longed for siblings! Two was the minimum, though he wouldn't baulk at four. Of course, he might want to discuss that with Julia first. There'd probably be grandchildren too. They'd definitely be getting their money's worth.

As he made his way towards the multi-storey, he felt people's eyes on him. A vicar carrying a rocking horse – you didn't see many of those on a day out. He wondered if he was exhibiting the sin of vanity. Why hadn't he asked the shop assistant to wrap Dobbin up? Was it because he wanted to boast that he was about to become a father? Dobbin. Looked like the rocking horse had a name already. Soon they'd be choosing baby names. He was looking forward to that.

December 2000

The millennium. It had to be fortuitous, didn't it? A new century and a new baby. *For a man of the cloth, you sure are superstitious,* Julia had said, smiling at him over her glass of fizzy lemonade. It wasn't champagne but after two long, barren years, she wasn't going to start taking any risks.

It was going to be a June baby. That gave him six months to fix up the nursery. They both agreed they didn't want to know the sex. They only wanted a healthy baby. Everything else was gravy.

Time to get Dobbin down from the loft, said Greg, as he clinked Julia's glass. He'd need a good dusting. If Greg had known it would take them two full years to conceive, he'd have put a dust cloth over him.

December 2001

A new parish for Greg and a new school for Julia. He wouldn't be sad to leave this house. Julia was out tonight. Saying goodbye to friends and colleagues. He had the whole evening to get on with the packing. He was glad he was alone. He didn't want to do anything to remind his wife. She always put on a brave face, but she couldn't hide her sorrow from the person who loved her best.

He'd listened to her about the nursery. *Don't count your chickens before they're hatched,* she'd reminded him. Had she already had an inkling that the pregnancy wouldn't go full term? She wouldn't allow him to buy so much as a pot of paint or a frieze for round the nursery walls.

So, there was no cot to pack away. No highchair to decide what to do with. But Dobbin was still there, up in the loft, beneath his dust cloth. His shroud. Would it be tempting fate to take him with them to their new home? Should he not donate it to the children's hospice instead, so others could get the benefit?

But Julia was still only 33. Okay, maybe he should forget the figure four, but there was plenty of time before her biological clock ceased ticking to push out a couple of healthy babies. Dobbin was coming with them.

December 2004

Julia didn't want to move again. And certainly not at Christmas. She'd recently been promoted and was well loved in her new school by the children, parents and staff alike. It would be a wrench for her to move again, he knew.

But she'd always known what she'd be getting when she married a man of the cloth, she said. Where the good Lord directed, there they must follow. She looked tired these days. Disappointed. And there was a sadness behind her eyes that was never far away.

Two more miscarriages. It wasn't fair. No other woman on earth would make a better mother than Julia, and yet three times now motherhood had been denied her, while 15-year-olds got pregnant at the drop of a hat and feckless families churned out a baby a year without even a thought as to how they could support another child, let alone love it.

Greg knew it wasn't his place to say who should be allowed the gift of life and who should be denied it. But in his darker moments it wasn't possible to refrain from passing judgement on his fellow man and shaking his fist at God, who he believed had made a Big Mistake.

This morning, Julia had walked in on him as he'd been wrestling Dobbin down from the attic. She must have been standing waiting for him to appear, knowing what he'd be bringing down with him.

He looks as good as new, she'd said, while Greg just stood there, mortified, wishing the floor would open and swallow him up.

He'd muttered something, he didn't know what, to hide his embarrassment at being caught with this so solid reminder of his foolish, optimistic younger self. Julia's beautiful face had crumpled, and he'd taken her in his arms and held her till the weeping stopped.

But next morning, when he'd come downstairs, he saw the sticker she must have put on Dobbin's mane for the removal man. He was coming with them. She hadn't given up.

December 2008

Finally, they were settled in a parish of their own. This last move would be their final one for a long time, he'd promised Julia back in the summer, when the news came through that a permanent parish had become available on the death of the present incumbent, who'd been the vicar there for 40 years.

The phone call offering it to Greg arrived a week after Julia's last miscarriage. Her sixth and, so they'd both decided, her final one. They were never going to have children. To go on hoping was just cruel. The conversation had been long, painful and exhausting. But oddly satisfying because it was the last word on the subject.

They both agreed it was time to put parenthood behind them. They had a lot of other things to be grateful for. Enough money to live on, friends, good health and, most of all, their love for each other.

When the time had come round for them to pack

up all their things again, Greg knew exactly what he had to do with Dobbin. He was going to ring the local children's hospice, as he'd thought of doing once before.

But poor Dobbin had spent the last five years at the back of the dodgy shed that had come with the house, where weather and wildlife had left him a mere shadow of his former splendid self. Chipped and cracked and broken, he'd lost his lustre. It was as if he bore the scars on his body of everything Greg and Julia had been through over the years, and it broke his heart.

You've been a long time in the shed, Julia remarked, on his return. *Have you been having a good throw out?*

Later that evening, when the first autumn chill descended, they burned the old rocking horse for firewood.

December 2012

The little town had changed since the last time he'd visited. Money had been spent on it at some time in the recent past – there was a Princess Diana Memorial Garden and a shopping arcade that hadn't been there before. But then, so Greg guessed, the recession must have taken hold, taking some of the new businesses with it.

What brought him to this town today was the same reason as before. On that day, fourteen years ago, he'd been a mere delegate. These days he was the Chairman of the Ethical Investment Committee. The meeting had finished early, and he had some time to kill. There was a toyshop in this town, and he had reason to visit it.

But when he'd arrived at the spot where the old toyshop had been, it was empty, and the shop front boarded up. People seemed to find it easy to take vicars into their confidence, thankfully. Or perhaps it was just little old ladies who did.

If you're looking for Pearson's they've moved to the new arcade, this particular old lady had told him, before proceeding to give him directions. Now here he was, standing in front of the bigger, grander version.

Which one of them had mentioned the *a*-word first? *Adoption*. Really, Greg had no idea. Both of them and neither of them was how he saw it now. It was in the ether, wherever they turned.

Pick up a newspaper and someone had written an article about it. Switch on the TV and there was a programme on the topic. If they found themselves out together socially, sure enough they'd meet a couple who were thinking about it, or on a list, or just about to take delivery. He knew that wasn't the correct phrase, but Greg had never been able to come up with anything that better described it.

Soon they found themselves united. This was the path they both felt they wanted to take. Indeed, it was as if the path had chosen them. It hadn't been easy.

Twice a child had been lined up for them, and twice it had fallen through.

And then yesterday there'd been a call. A little boy. Just two years old. His name was Alfie.

Greg pushed open the door of the shop. It was a cornucopia of delight for any child. Noise and light, children shrieking, anxious parents at the till putting on a brave face when they found out just how much their children's happiness was going to be costing them this year.

Can I help you, sir?

Greg must have looked lost, wandering up and down the aisles. But he wasn't lost at all. In fact, he was a man with a mission. And his mission was in sight. Dobbin, mark two.

'Yes,' he said, beaming broadly at the sales assistant. 'I'm looking for a rocking horse. For my son.'

First published 2012, *Woman's Weekly Fiction Special*

Gemma's Night Out

The atmosphere round the harp-shaped table at the weekly Celestial Case Study Meeting was growing increasingly strained. Even angels have tethers and several of those present were right at the end of theirs.

'I'm sorry, but I think you're all being extremely unangelic. The trouble with you lot is you've spent far too long sitting on clouds polishing your halos. You've forgotten what it's like to have temptation waved under your nose.'

There was a rumble of discord and shouts of 'Not fair' and 'You would say that, wouldn't you?'

Uriel, who was acting as Chair, banged on the table with his gavel and called the meeting to order. Criticism of the Angelic Host was all well and good, but occasionally, Elysia could take it too far.

'Your loyalty is understandable, Elysia,' he said.

'You are the girl's guardian angel, after all.'

'Point of order, but I believe the preferred term nowadays is young woman.'

Uriel was in no mood for this. He'd pussyfooted around Elysia and her points of order for far too long already. Meanwhile, the girl – young woman – was getting herself into bigger scrapes with every day they gave her another chance.

This meeting had been convened to find a solution to the problem that was Gemma Bastion, and find it they would, Uriel stressed.

Elysia sniffed and dabbed her eyes with a stray feather.

'I know you all think I've handled things badly.' She scoured the table with damp eyes, hoping for a chorus of denial, but the only sound was some gentle snoring from Ishmael in the corner. 'But I've done my best.'

'I know you have, dear,' Uriel said, diplomatically.

'But until she actually calls on me for help there's nothing I can do. Clause 39, paragraph 14.' She waved the *Holy Statute* under his nose.

'Well, that's never going to happen, is it?' someone cried.

'She's a lost cause if you ask me,' added another, to cries of 'Hear, hear.'

Once more, Uriel raised his hands for silence. Honestly, it was easier to control the Cherubim – with all their bouncy exuberance – than this lot.

'Ladies and gentleman, the time for discussion is at an end. Now is the time to put the motion to a vote.'

Peering over his spectacles, he read out the form of words it had taken several turns of the celestial egg timer to settle upon.

'Since the human being in question, Gemma Bastion, appears to be oblivious to the damage she is causing herself, her reputation and her relationships with other human beings, this committee decrees that there is only one course of action that remains, to whit a ghostly visitation to take place over three nights, as authorised in Section 39, paragraph three of *The Book of Adjudication*.'

Uriel raised his eyes. All those in favour?

It was unanimous, apart from Elysia, the still sleeping Ishmael and one or two abstentions from the younger members of the committee who were still finding their wings and didn't want to trample over anyone else's.

'Just let me go down and give her a bit of warning in advance,' Elysia pleaded. 'That's all I ask.'

If it would get her off his back, he guessed it was the least he could do.

'You've got 60 seconds with her. No longer,' he said. 'And now I call this meeting to a close.'

Gemma didn't know what all the fuss was about. If you couldn't let your hair down at Christmas, then when could you? The trouble with some people was that they didn't know how to party.

'Gemma, let me help you up.'

When she opened her eyes, all she saw at first were feet and legs. Gradually, she began to make the connection between the legs and their matching faces. A few people were tittering behind their hands; there were raised eyebrows and grimaces of disapproval. Honestly, it was like being at a church social – one where only the teetotal and terminally boring were made welcome.

She finally managed to focus her skewed gaze on Harry, the speaker of those words. He reached out an arm towards her, looking like he wished he were a million miles away. Well, if she was such an embarrassment…

'I can get up myshelf thanksh very mush,' she replied, fishing a strand of tinsel from her mouth.

Fortunately, it was only a small tree, and an artificial one at that. Had it been a towering Norwegian pine, she might very well have knocked herself unconscious when she'd brought it down on top of her during a particularly enthusiastic rendition of the single ladies' dance.

She made several attempts to stand before, defeated, she succumbed to Harry's aid. Why did he think it was his job to stand the tree back up and redecorate it, she wondered. It wasn't even *his* party.

'Don't look so glum, Hal.'

She groped for her shoes and, after several attempts, managed to get her feet into them. It suddenly seemed a good idea to see how far she could kick all those shiny baubles littering the floor.

'For God's sake, Gemma, haven't you done enough damage?' Harry muttered, feebly chasing after them.

'For God's shake, Gemma, haven't you done enough damage?' she mocked.

Someone had put the music back on and the small band of spectators she'd gathered around her began to drift away. She must have closed her eyes for a moment. Harry was back again, this time with his arms full of baubles.

'Where can I get a drink?'

'You can't,' he said. 'Donna wants you to leave.'

'Who's Donna?'

'My cousin. The hostess, remember?'

Harry practically spat out the words. Goodness, she'd never seen him so angry.

'Is you kwoss wiv me, Harry?' Gemma flung her arms around him and began to plant kisses on his face.

'Get off,' he hissed, pushing her away so she staggered back and nearly brought the damn tree down for the second time.

'You're drunk, Gemma. And you're making a show

of yourself. I've rung for a taxi. They won't accept you in the state you're in unless you've got someone with you, so I'm going to have to come too.'

'Oooh, Harry!' she teased.

'For God's sake, Gemma, shut up!'

Gemma felt suddenly deflated. It was too early to feel like that. She needed a drink. A playmate. Something to take the edge off reality.

'What's the matter with you tonight, Harry?' she complained.

'Do I have to spell it out?' He brought his face close to hers. His expression was dark and unforgiving. 'Wait here. Don't move. I'm going upstairs to get your coat. I'll be down in a minute.'

Then he was gone, leaving her alone in a room full of people. 'Wait here,' she muttered. Who did he think he was? He lived in the flat below, was all. They'd bumped into each other a few times – enough to strike up several conversations that could be construed as forming the basis of a friendship. At least, that must have been the impression Harry had formed, since *he* was the one who'd come knocking on *her* door earlier to ask if she fancied going to this party with him, not vice versa. *Wait here indeed.*

No one seemed to notice her leave – they were all trying so hard to ignore her that their tactics worked in the end, and she managed to slip out into the night unseen. Weaving her way down the street, she headed – so she hoped – homeward.

It was a crisp, sparkling, starry night. Her footsteps rang out in the empty streets. Where was everyone? Lamplight glowed from the windows, fires flickered and Christmas trees twinkled. It looked like everyone was home tonight.

God, how could anyone live in the suburbs? It would kill her. Instead of accepting Harry's invitation, she should have headed into town where the lights were brighter. Well, she'd know next time. Not that there would be a next time if his face was anything to go by. Old Sour Face!

In the distance, the clock struck midnight. Her feet were beginning to ache and the cold she'd initially been immune to began to bite at last. How long had she been walking for? She didn't have a clue where she was. Fortunately, up ahead, she spotted a figure leaning up against a lamppost. She'd ask them for directions.

She quickened her pace, keeping the figure in view. From this distance, it was impossible to tell if it was male or female. It was no easier the closer she got. Whoever it was appeared to be wearing a blanket and some sort of goofy headgear. It was a poor attempt at dressing up as an angel, that's all she could say.

It suddenly occurred to her that maybe it wasn't such a good idea to approach a solitary stranger on a deserted street after all, especially one who looked like they'd escaped from police custody. With great presence of mind, considering how much she'd had to drink that night, Gemma made a swift U-turn and retraced her steps.

It was while she was thinking what a fool she'd been to go storming off without her bag – which meant that she wasn't able to ring for a taxi – that she became aware that she wasn't alone. The white blanket had caught up with her.

How had that happened? She hadn't heard a sound. Keeping her head down, she picked up her pace, which only encouraged the white blanket to do the same.

'There's no need to be frightened, Gemma. I'm not here to hurt you.'

If she'd felt uneasy before, now she was plain scared. How did this person know her name? Had they been stalking her? That was it! She had a stalker who'd been spying on her for weeks, months even, lurking in the shadows, watching her every move, finding out all her intimate details. Now, finally, the stalker was ready to pounce.

'Get lost, creep!' she yelled, fuelled by alcohol-induced bravado. 'Go and haunt someone else.'

Gemma turned her stride into a jog that quickly became a run. Infuriatingly, the blanketed stranger bounced along beside her, easily managing to keep up. If Gemma hadn't known better, she'd have thought those feet weren't touching the ground.

'No, no, please. I'm not the haunter. The haunter will be along at one o'clock. I'm your guardian angel,

Elysia. But never mind about that. Oh, dear. Oh, dear. Oh, my goodness. Time's running out already.'

Gemma was briefly reminded of the White Rabbit in *Alice in Wonderland*. She wouldn't have been at all surprised if the stalker had started going on about ears and whiskers and begun to consult a pocket watch – though where you'd keep a pocket in an outfit like this one was a sartorial challenge too many for Gemma at this time of night.

Funny, she didn't feel frightened anymore. Thinking about rabbits wearing suits could do that to you. The best thing, she decided, would be not to even engage with this person. People like this needed no encouragement.

On she ran, her breath coming in increasingly short gasps. With every out breath came an accompanying cloud of white, and each in breath came with a rattle in her chest – she really should give up the fags.

She was concentrating so hard simply putting one foot in front of the other that it was a while before she realised her stalker had disappeared. How very peculiar. Very peculiar, too, that far from being in a strange neighbourhood, she was now standing in front of her apartment block.

Drink, she decided. It was all down to drink. Best thing she could do now was to let herself inside and go straight to sleep.

* * *

She woke from a deep sleep with a dry mouth and a throbbing head. The room was pitch black. A glance at the clock told her it was one o'clock. What on earth could have woken her? She didn't remember anything about getting ready for bed. It explained things when she realised she was still fully clothed – she hadn't actually bothered.

'You're ready for me, then.'

The words echoed round the room.

Ready, ready, ready. Me, me, me.

Gemma almost fell off the bed in shock; someone was standing at the foot of it. If she didn't know any better, she'd have said that whatever it was bore all the hallmarks of a ghost.

Its shape was sort of human, but it was a bit frayed round the edges. It wasn't solid either – she could almost see right through it to her wardrobe. She'd flung open the doors earlier, when she'd been searching for the right outfit, and hadn't bothered to close them. Neither had she bothered to pick up the huge pile of discarded clothes from the floor.

'Ready? What do you mean ready?'

'You were warned,' it said. 'Though why Elysia was allowed to get away with that stunt I have no idea. She always could twist Uriel round her little finger.'

As it spoke, the ghost emitted a sickly green light

from the hole that must be its mouth. It was all very disturbing.

'I have no idea what you're talking about,' said Gemma.

Sleep had dulled her brain. In fact, she decided she must still be asleep. Then she remembered that odd character wrapped in a blanket who'd accompanied her part of the way home before suddenly and unexpectedly disappearing outside her block.

'My name's something-something,' she'd said. Could she have said Elysia, in fact?

'Hey! What's happening?' It was as if a gust of wind from nowhere had suddenly wrapped itself around Gemma, lifted her up off the bed and propelled her towards the door.

'Sorry. I think I've missed something out,' the ghost said.

Gemma was released from the wind's grip and dropped to the floor with a kerplunk.

'Oi!' she yelled, scrambling to her feet. 'What do you think you're doing?'

'Apologies. I forgot. I'm required to say this bit: "I am the Ghost of Christmas Past. And I'm here to take you on a little journey." You'll need your coat.'

* * *

Gemma used to love Fountain Street Primary School. It was small and friendly, and the teachers were kind.

No other school she'd attended afterwards was a patch on this one, her very first school.

Four years she'd stayed there, the longest she'd ever stayed in any one school. She knew the names of everyone in her class and was friends with all of them. It seemed so strange to be standing before it again, 25 years later.

'Recognise the place?'

Gemma jumped. Every time that damn ghost opened its mouth, his words were preceded by the kind of noise that sounded like a dodgy car engine starting up. It was most unnerving. Plus, it would disturb the children, who were all sitting around their tables, deep in their work.

'Oh, don't worry about that,' her companion said, when she complained. 'You can see them, but they have no idea about you. Recognise yourself yet?'

Gemma was starting to get a funny feeling in her tummy. The kind she always got when Something Bad was about to happen. This was Class 4, Miss Turner's class, where she spent her final year before going off to a school called – what was it now? – Park Street Comp, that was it.

She'd left Park Street after a year, to go to another school and then another, because Dad got restless and couldn't keep a job longer than a few months at a time and got drunk and into fights. Or worse, he refused to get out of bed and got the sack, and so they had to move because he couldn't pay the rent.

It must have been summer because all the windows were open, and the children were in summer uniform – shorts for the boys and skirts for the girls; short-sleeved shirts for everyone.

There she was, sitting between Emily and Emma, her two best friends. Emma's hair was long and fair with a natural wave that Gemma, with her short brown bob, always envied. Emily was a fierce redhead whom people called Ginger Nut at their peril.

That afternoon, after school, Gemma was going round to Emily's house to play. So, it must be Thursday. How did she know this? Gemma glanced at the ghost, who was beginning to crank itself up again.

'Yes, Gemma. It's *that* day. The end of your idyllic life. The start of the bad times.'

'I really don't think I need to witness this.' Gemma was growing more and more uneasy.

But it was too late. Even now the classroom door was opening. Here came the principal, Mrs Richter, tall and elegantly dressed as usual, a look of concern on her face. And here was Miss Turner standing up to greet her with a smile, quickly sitting down again when Mrs Richter gestured there was no need. Gemma watched them deep in conversation, their heads almost touching. Every now and then they glanced towards the young Gemma, who was engrossed in her artwork and thankfully unaware that already her childhood had ended.

She was drawing a picture of the caravan, where

she would shortly be spending her summer holiday. Every year they took the caravan somewhere new. She never knew where they were going to fetch up till they got there. 'It'll be a surprise,' Mum said. Surprises were always much better than knowing exactly where you were going to end up.

Gemma's mum wasn't like her friends' mums. For one thing, she was much younger than her dad. And beautiful. Wild. She liked dancing barefoot in the grass and rising early to see the dawn. She had a smile that could light up the dark, and the sound of her laughter would melt even the steeliest heart.

There was never any point asking Mum to help with homework or come to parents' evening. She wasn't comfortable around authority, she maintained. Gemma never minded. She had Dad to help her with her sums and to write her notes to excuse her from games. That was the good thing about having two parents – they shared out the jobs half and half.

Except. Except.

'This is the day, isn't it?' Gemma whispered.

'The last day of term, that's right.'

The ghost rattled and groaned at her shoulder. Why had he brought her here? So she could witness the moment when Miss Turner gently laid a hand on Gemma's shoulder and asked if she'd mind going along to Mrs Richter's office with her?

'The day they found my mother's body at the bottom of the lake.'

'From that day forth, things were never the same for you, **were** they, Gemma?'

Gemma couldn't speak. She was transfixed by the child's bright smile, her trusting face. If only time could stand still, she thought. Right now, the little girl still believed her world was intact. She'd been promised ice cream for tea, and she would get to play with Emily's new kitten.

Later, when she was home again, she and her mother would go through all the clothes they'd take with them on their holiday. 'All our prettiest clothes,' Mum would say. Hours would go by while they tried things on, parading in front of each other like models on the catwalk.

Dad would come upstairs, drawn by the laughter and the loud music, which inevitably accompanied their antics. He'd haggle good-humouredly about their choices, remind them it could get cold and might even rain and that they ought to think about jeans and jumpers and something to keep the rain off. Mum would make faces behind his back, which would send Gemma into fits of giggles, but she always let him have his way in the end.

The grown-up Gemma held up both hands. 'Stop,' she cried, but already it was too late.

Up jumped the young Gemma, keen to find out why Mrs Richter needed to speak to her privately.

She knew she wasn't in trouble – she never was. More likely it would be good news. Perhaps the principal wanted to ask her to represent the school in some way. Perhaps the Queen was coming, and she'd been chosen to present her with flowers! Things like that *did* happen – she'd seen it on the telly. By the time they reached the office, she was already imagining her picture in the newspaper.

In the end it wasn't her picture in the paper but her mother's. Though she was mentioned in the report as *leaves behind a husband and an 11-year-old daughter.*

'OK, I've had enough of this.' Gemma turned on the ghost and stamped her feet angrily. 'Get me out of here,' she yelled. 'Take me home.'

'My pleasure,' the ghost said.

She meant home as in the place he'd dragged her out of in the middle of the night to embark on this cruel journey into her past. But he'd deliberately misunderstood her. Instead, he'd brought her here – to her old home, the one she'd first shared with Mum and Dad, and then just with Dad.

There was Dad, sitting alone in a chair, glass in his hand, bottle by his feet. It was a picture she'd grow familiar with over the years, but from the relative lack of squalor in the room, he was only at the beginning of his downward spiral.

Things quickly got so much worse after the shock of her mother's death. Bills were ignored, food was left to go bad in the fridge, clothes were unwashed.

And when Social Services came knocking on the door, her father decided it was time to leave.

So began a life lived on the run, with Dad taking low paid part-time jobs so he could be there for Gemma when she came back from one of the many schools she attended until, at the age of 16, she could lawfully leave.

'Poor Dad,' she said, wishing she could take him in her arms and tell him that everything would be OK.

'Don't be sentimental,' the ghost piped up. 'He put himself first instead of you.'

'I should have done more,' Gemma said.

'You were the child. He was the adult. I think we both know which one of you should have done more.'

'Nice of you to say so,' Gemma said. 'But I probably wasn't much of a daughter.'

'You had a bad start, I'll give you that,' the ghost said, grudgingly. 'Maybe if your father had paid you more attention you wouldn't have concentrated so much on upsetting your teachers and every other grown-up who happened to cross your path.'

At Fountain Street, she'd been a popular, hard-working child who always wanted to please. With each subsequent move to a new school, she grew more anti-authority. Her insolent manner attracted a certain type of friend, misfits like herself, who she could bunk off with. They would escape down to the precinct, dodging the security guards as they played mayhem charging up and down the escalators the wrong way and terrifying the other shoppers.

At first, their misdemeanours were innocent enough. But it wasn't long before alcohol began to play its part in fuelling their adventures. They took it in turns to steal – from shops and from shoppers who took their eye off their bags for a second too long. Surprisingly, no one ever got caught, which just made things more fun. Until…

'I don't want to be here,' Gemma growled.

It hurt her to see her dad like this, knowing where it would inevitably end. She hadn't seen him in years. Last she'd heard he was living on the street, a drunk, queuing up to get a night in a hostel and the luxury of a bed, a shower and a hot meal, before being turfed out again in the morning.

'Where would you rather be instead?' the ghost asked. 'I could take you to the courtroom where you were given a community sentence for criminal damage.'

'No!'

That wasn't her fault, she protested. It was Justin's. He'd driven her to it. Carrying on with another girl in front of her, deliberately winding her up so that she got drunk and took her fury out on three cars, which she'd keyed as she strode past them home.

'Justin, the one you'd been warned to finish with

by no less than his probation officer, because he was a bad influence on you?'

Gemma hung her head. 'I did finish with him, in the end, didn't I?' she told the ghost.

This was after she'd told him about the baby, and he'd hit her and put her in hospital. After that there was no baby, and for a while, at least, Gemma saw sense enough to finish with Justin, move away and start again.

'That brings you back to the present, don't you agree?' the ghost said. 'Your brand-new start. 'But what do you do with it?'

'I'm trying,' she said.

'Oh, yes, you're that all right,' the ghost replied. 'Ask those people at the party.'

Gemma felt herself beginning to blush. Three months she'd been in this new town where nobody knew her, living in her new flat where she'd made friends with her new neighbours – Harry for one, who started by smiling at her shyly on the stairs or coming out of the lift as she was going in.

Such a sweet face, she'd thought from the start. She'd steadfastly refused to encourage him, still raw from the damage Justin had done to her. And something else too – a certainty that had been with her for most of her life. She wasn't good enough for a boy like him. If she had been, her mother would not have been taken away from her and her father would not have neglected her like he did.

When Harry had knocked on her door earlier tonight, she'd already been three gins into a full bottle. It was Christmas and everyone was out partying except her. One more gin and she'd have headed into town, to a bar or a club. Anywhere where there were people. Where there might be a man who could make her forget, just for a night.

Finding a man for the night had long been her preferred method for stifling the pain she felt whenever she found herself alone with her bad thoughts, ever since she'd learned that sex brought companionship and warmth and understanding, albeit only for a short time.

Since Justin, she'd never dared to hope that she could keep a man for longer than a night. Far better to disappear in the early morning light and leave them with a good opinion of her than to let them see the truth, which was that she was unworthy of anyone's love.

She must have fallen asleep. Because when she next looked around, there was no sign of her heavy breathing companion, and this wasn't her old living room but somewhere else altogether. She appeared to be back at the party.

'What's going on?' she said to no one in particular.

The sound of someone clearing their throat behind her caused her to spin around. She squealed at the sight of the rotund figure before her. He was swathed in a toga, with a crown of vine leaves in his wild, grey locks. When he opened his mouth to speak, her first impression that he was a dead ringer for Christopher Biggins was confirmed.

'Well, they said come dressed for a party,' he said, gesturing to his outfit. 'Ghost of Christmas Present, ducky.'

It was very strange, but the fact was she was oblivious to surprise. After everything else that had happened tonight, if a choir of angels suddenly descended from the sky complete with a harpist section, she doubted whether she'd even raise an eyebrow.

'I'm here to show you what you're missing.'

Gemma scanned the room. She didn't think she was missing much, frankly. Couples snogging, couples dancing – and over by the now upright tree a gaggle of girls obviously in cahoots about something.

'Want to hear what they're saying?'

'Let me guess – they're slagging me off.'

She felt a tug on her arm, and she found herself standing mere inches away from the group, who clearly had no idea that they were being overheard.

'Who *was* she anyway?' a blonde girl wearing a red dress far too tight for her said. 'I've never seen her around till tonight, have you?'

A redhead in green silk shuddered. 'Harry said he felt sorry for her. She spends a lot of time alone.'

'Not surprising is it, really!' a third girl said.

The other two nodded in agreement.

'She's just the type to be found dead in a ditch one morning,' the blonde one said. 'One of life's unfortunates.'

Gemma made a noise in her throat like she was being strangled. *Dead in a ditch!*

'If you ask me, we're the unfortunate ones. She's ruined my party!'

Ah, so the redhead was Donna!

'I've never seen Harry in such a state. He looked all over the house for her. "No use, Harry," I said, "she's fled." Probably on the outside of another bottle of gin by now with some guy just as sleazy as she is.'

The redhead regarded her cronies smugly over her glass. Gemma felt a strong urge to punch her lights out. At the same time, she felt a tiny tug of affection towards Harry, who'd searched high and low for her and had stood up for her even though he knew he'd win no friends through it.

'He's still looking for her, I think,' Donna said. 'He left about half an hour ago and hasn't come back.'

'Good riddance, I say,' the blonde girl said.

The others all muttered their agreement.

'Right. We've heard enough.' The Ghost of Christmas Present clapped his hands together, startling Gemma. 'We're off to find Harry.'

They located him immediately. He was loitering outside the entrance to their block, talking on his mobile.

'Gemma. It's Harry. I've been to your place and you're not there. Well, obviously you know that already. I've left loads of messages. I'm worried about you. You need help. Call me.'

She watched him patrolling backwards and forwards as he delivered his words. He looked like he was about to end the call but then he seemed to have second thoughts. He put the phone to his ear again.

'I just want to say I'm sorry I yelled at you,' he went on. 'I shouldn't have. I hope it wasn't me who made you run away.'

'No, Harry, of course it wasn't!' She went to run towards him but was unceremoniously pulled back.

'No point, Gemma. He can neither hear you nor see you,' the ghost said.

'But look at him! He's distraught!'

Harry held his head in his hands as he leaned against the wall. It was beginning to rain now and he only had a thin jacket to protect himself from it.

The ghost sighed. 'It should be snow at Christmas,' he said, looking up at the sky. 'Global warming! Damn nuisance.'

'Never mind the weather,' Gemma yelled. 'What can I do about Harry?'

'Oh,' he said, a note of dry humour in his voice. 'So, you care about Old Sour Face, do you?'

Gemma shuffled her feet. 'I say things when I'm…'

'Drunk?'

She didn't bother to reply.

'Look, someone should have been here five minutes ago to show you the future. But I've just had a message. They're not coming.'

'Does that mean I haven't got a future?' she said, tears in her voice.

'Oh, dear. Please. Don't upset yourself. I can't bear to see people cry.'

'It's all right for you,' Gemma said, finding her spirit again. 'You can just clear off and leave me down here to muddle through on my own.' She stopped staring at Harry, who was still walking up and down, and transferred her gaze to the ghost. 'Thing is... I don't think I *can* muddle through. I'll just carry on making a mess of it.'

There was silence while the ghost deliberated on her words. Finally, he spoke. 'I could try again with the other angel,' he said. 'Only this rain seems to have blocked the connection.'

She shook her head miserably. 'Don't bother,' she said. 'What do I need with a Ghost of Christmas Future? I know my future. Too much booze. Too many men.'

What was it that girl had said? *She's just the type to be found dead in a ditch.*

The Ghost of Christmas Present hitched up his toga, which had slipped from his shoulder. 'It's a poor show, this is, Gemma. A damn poor show.'

'I know,' Gemma sniffed. 'I'm a waste of space.'

'No, not you! Us! We've let you down. You'd be

within your rights to write to Head Office and make a formal complaint. Imagine you'd ordered a three-piece suite and they forgot to deliver the settee.'

Put like that, he had a point.

'I must say, the longer I kick around in this job, the more faults I find in the organisation,' he said. 'Not turning up when we're called. Leaving the clients dissatisfied. You know, sometimes I think we're just redundant and you human beings would be better off on your own.'

'No!' Gemma protested. 'Didn't I just say? I can't work out my future on my own. All I can do is drift into it. That's not what I want. I want to take control this time.'

The ghost appeared to be fading. Just like the other one, he started to fray around the edges.

'But don't you see? You don't have to work it out on your own, and you don't need celestial advice either. You human beings are lucky. You've got each other.'

He was becoming fainter and fainter. She could barely see him now.

'Where are you going?' she cried. 'Come back. I demand that you come back!'

'Goodbye, Gemma! See you on the flipside, sweetheart!'

Then he was gone. And she was lying on her bed. And her phone was ringing.

It took her a while to answer it. She felt so drowsy. Like she'd been in a very deep sleep.

'Hello?' she croaked.

'Oh, thank God! You're there, Gemma! Are you safe?'

She looked round at her room. It was a tip. But it wasn't on fire. There was no rain dripping through the ceiling.

'I guess so,' she said.

'Can I come up?'

'I'm surprised you want to see me again,' she said. 'I made a total show of myself.'

'You did. But maybe you've got your reasons.'

'I don't know about reasons. I've certainly got baggage.'

A beat, then, 'I'd like to help you,' he said. 'If you'd let me. You can help me too.'

'You? You don't come with baggage. You come with a halo!'

'I hate to say it, Gemma, but I'm a fallible human being. Just like you.'

You've got each other. Where had she just heard that?

'Well, that's fine by me,' she said, with a chuckle. 'Angels are overrated, anyway, in my experience. Come up. I'll buzz you in.'

First published 2012, *Woman's Weekly*

The Love and the Laughter

There's a bit of an atmosphere in the room. Hardly surprising really. Oh, I've had the odd email. A birthday card. Flowers on Mother's Day. But this is the first time she's been to the house for over a year. She's looking well. Blooming, even. I'm not going to ask her if she's still with him. I can't even say his name.

We're in the kitchen having a sort of catch up. Very polite and superficial and awkward. Nothing like we used to be before everything happened. I'd been baking when she arrived. Now the cake is cooling on the rack and I'm washing up. Abi's telling me about some extra teaching she's been given at the college. It's not permanent, apparently. And then she says it. 'I don't mind admitting the extra money will come in handy for Christmas.'

There! The word is out. Christmas. If only it were

simply a word. But it's far more than that, isn't it? Christmas is love, family. It's forgiveness. And it's reconciliation. Am I ready for that? Is she? After what I said and did?

'Goodness,' I say, suddenly flustered. 'It's far too early to start thinking of Christmas.'

'That depends,' she says. 'It's all right for you and Dad. All you need to do is lift up the phone and book that posh hotel like you did last year.'

Desperate for something to do with my hands, I grab a tea towel and start drying the bowl furiously. She'd make a brilliant goatherd. Little by little she inches me into a corner. There's no escape.

'So,' she says. 'Will you be going again this year to the... what was it called again?'

'The Palladian,' I remind her.

A 19th century country house set in rolling grounds complete with four-poster beds and antique fireplaces. My first Christmas ever away from home. Away from my family.

'Why are you doing this, Mum?' Jenna, my youngest, wanted to know when I rang her to say she and Mike were going to have to make alternative arrangements for Christmas this year.

I told her she should ask her sister. I said the same to Hugh when he rang up to ask if it was true I'd abolished Christmas this year. I told him not to be so silly.

'Is it because of this guy she's got involved with?' he wanted to know.

That made me even madder. It looked like everyone but me and her father had known about Abi's new man. It was clear from his tone that Hugh thought I'd gone overboard on the disapproval ratings. I didn't like him making light of my reasons for not opening my house to Abi's new man friend, and I told him so. A married man. Father to teenage children. A good 15 years older than my Abi. She was worth more than that.

'I love him, Mum,' Abi told me on the day she rang me up to say that Darius had finally left his wife and moved in with her.

It was November. A month before Christmas. She'd never even mentioned him before. Not that I hadn't had my suspicions. She'd stopped visiting so often and when she was here, she was always checking her phone. Married men. They never left their wives. An older man too. It was a cliché, and I told her so. Then I slammed down the phone. That same evening, without consulting Graeme, I booked the hotel.

'Don't you think you're being a bit hasty?' he said, when I told him what I'd done.

I said I didn't want to talk about it. Abi had made her bed and she was going to have to lie on it. If she wanted to spend Christmas with her married man, then she was welcome to. But they wouldn't be doing it under my roof.

'If that's what you want, he said. 'But I think you're making a big mistake.'

It wasn't a very happy Christmas, despite the spa treatment, the champagne breakfasts and the carols by candlelight. In fact, we were both thoroughly miserable. But, like Abi, I'd made my bed and had no choice but to toss and turn in it. I don't know what sort of Christmas Hugh and Jenna had. I never asked. This other 'C' word had suddenly become taboo in our family.

It's a word that's easy to forget once the season's gone. But now, once again, it looms large. It fills my kitchen. I can almost smell the cloves and cinnamon, savour the warmth of a roaring fire, feel the love and hear the laughter. We've always been the stubborn ones, Abi and me. The other two – placid and accommodating – take after Graeme. Sooner or later one of us is going to have to say sorry. I'm just not sure I'm brave enough. So, I go for different words.

'I didn't enjoy that hotel one bit because I missed having you all here so much,' I admit, at the exact same time as Abi says, 'I'm pregnant.'

It takes a long time for the words to sink in. When they do, some instinct pushes me forward. The same instinct allows Abi to open her arms and receive my embrace. This is how Graeme finds us when he wanders into the kitchen making murmurs about a cup of tea.

'Goodness! What's all this, then?' He shuffles his feet in that awkward way men do when faced with naked, raw emotion.

Abi and I, still locked together, are both in tears.

'I thought I could do this without you,' she says. 'But my baby needs its grandparents.'

'Grandparents!' squeaks Graeme.

The doorbell rings. There's a change of pressure from Abi's arms. She holds her breath. Me too.

'We love each other, Mum,' she says. 'Don't make me choose.'

I look up, catch Graeme's eye. He's still dazed from Abi's news.

'Do you want me to let him in?' I ask.

'Do you think you can?' asks Abi.

She loosens her hold on me and I make my way to the door.

'Yes,' I say. 'I can.'

Perhaps I already have.

First published 2005, *Woman's Weekly*

She's Leaving Home

December 1999

Dear Father Christmas,

This is my Christmas List. You can't give me what I want most of all, which is, in this order:

1. My dad
2. My mum before she got sad about Dad
3. Si to move out
4. My old bedroom
5. Si to stop picking on Scarlett
6. Scarlett to stop picking on Si back, and to understand that Mum won't stick up for her

anymore now Si's on the scene. (I suppose that's two things.)

Anyway, since you won't give me any of the above, I'll just ask for the following instead:

1. A Nintendo games console
2. Plus games
3. A mobile phone for Scarlett because I don't think she believes in you anymore and so I don't think she's written her own list.
4. *Who Wants To be A Millionaire* – the board game. If we can all sit round the table and play a game, it might stop Si and Scarlett from picking a fight with each other and upsetting Mum and spoiling everything.

Luv from Callum Barnes

January 1 2000

Dear Callum,

When you wake up and see this letter by your bed, I'll be long gone. Now, you mustn't start crying and think horrible things of me, because:

1. I am definitely coming back one day soon, and when I do it will be to collect you and all your stuff and move you into the brand-new pad, which, by that time, I'll have sorted out for us.
2. If it hadn't been that particular row, it would have been another, so you are absolutely NOT to blame for me going. Believe me, if life was like it was when Dad was here, before he got ill, the chances of me ever leaving home would be zero.

But things will never be like they used to be ever again. You're not 11 yet, Cal, and some people will say I'm being cruel saying stuff like this to you. But I tried telling you lies before, remember, when I said Dad would get better and he didn't. It's a wonder you ever trusted me to tell the truth ever again. You did, though. Because you're the trusting type.

Funny, isn't it, that instead of learning from my mistake and refusing to tell you any more lies ever again, what did I do but tell you more fibs?

Like, how Mum would get out of bed soon and start taking you to school again in the mornings, and then pick you up in the afternoon.

Like, how taking those pills and pouring all that alcohol down her neck instead of the tea and coffee she usually drinks was just a temporary measure to help her get over everything, in exactly the same way that putting up with Si was only temporary, too.

Except time has proved me a liar, once again. You still have to take yourself off in the morning and come back on your own in the afternoon. Mum still prefers to drink from a glass instead of a cup, and Si's showing no signs of leaving. Which is why there's just no choice for me but to go.

You don't need me to remind you how much worse it's been getting lately between me and Mum, or how much Si resents me being here. With me gone it'll be better for everyone.

Callum, I can't tell you where I'll be when you find this note because, the truth is, I don't know myself. I'm not a fool, though, so you mustn't worry I'll get into some maniac's car. I might not know where I'm going, little brother, but I sure as anything intend on getting there in one piece! So, you really, really mustn't worry about me.

And like I said, it won't be forever. Once I'm settled, I'll be in touch again to see how you are and to let you know where I am.

Your loving sister, Scarlett.

P.S. Please keep this letter a secret from Mum.

January 2 2000

This is my first entry in my new diary. It was a present from Scarlett. She said I can put all my secret thoughts in it and need never worry they'll be discovered because there's a key that goes with it. That makes me think that when she bought it, she already had the idea in her head that she'd be going away soon, so she got me the diary as a substitute for her. Which it can never be, of course.

It's a five-year diary, so when I get to the end of it, I will be nearly 15 and Scarlett will be 26, which is really old. She might even be married then, with a baby. I hope not because if she finds somebody else to love then what's going to happen to me? There's no way she'll come back and get me if she's got a new family.

I didn't get my Nintendo, by the way. There was a waiting list that you had to put yourself on months ago, and Mum and Si didn't because they were both too busy, they said. Now I wish I'd never asked for it.

Because if I hadn't piped up, in front of Scarlett, that I hadn't got it after all, then she wouldn't have started yelling all that stuff about Mum and Si being too selfish to put themselves out for anybody but each other. And he wouldn't have turned on Mum and demanded to know how much longer she was going to put up with her daughter speaking to him like that. And Mum wouldn't have yelled at Scarlett and repeated all the stuff she always says when she's had too much to drink.

It's always about how Scarlett only ever sees things from her own point of view and doesn't know the half of how she's suffered, what with Dad's illness and the debts mounting up. And other stuff about if it hadn't been for Si there wouldn't have been a Christmas dinner at all, or a tree for that matter, since he'd paid for most of it and cooked it too, and we should all be grateful.

All this just because of me wanting a Nintendo. I wish I'd put down a puppy on my list instead. They might have got me one of them, because you don't have to go on a waiting list for a puppy. There are always puppies no one wants. Just like there are always children. I don't even believe in Father Christmas anyway. I only wrote the list because it was something Dad always used to tell us to do.

January 3 2000

Another day without Scarlett. Mum crying. Si saying over and over he never intended to drive her away, but he was sure she'd come back within a day or two. She's just playing the Drama Queen, he says. I keep thinking I should show them the letter. It might make them worry a lot less. But if she'd wanted them to know anything, she wouldn't have written the PS. And Mum might not be too happy about Scarlett's plan to come back and get me once she's found us a place to live.

January 5 2000

All day, I've been thinking that if only Scarlett had left the argument there instead of going *bla bla bla* in Mum's face when she started crying and saying how hard it had been for her with Dad so ill and how she couldn't have coped without Si.

It might have been all right if she'd just let Mum get it out of her system and cry herself out like she usually does. But she had to go and do that. And when Si went for her, I think we all knew that this time it was different from all the other times.

I just wish she'd spoken to me instead of writing me that note. Just so I could have checked with her that she means what she says about coming back to get me and she's not just saying it to make me feel better like she did the other stuff.

January 19 2000

Dear Callum,

This is a picture of the Millennium Wheel. You may have seen it on the news. Soon people will be able to ride on it, but it's got teething problems so all we can do for now is look at it and buy postcards.

Hope you're being good, and you haven't forgotten me. I am living in a squat with some cool people. It's only temporary so I can't give you the address. But I haven't forgotten my promise and will be back one day LIKE I SAID.

January *21 2000*

Si is angry with the police. They haven't lifted a finger since the first time he went to ask them to look for Scarlett, he says. I didn't even know he'd been to the police in the first place. No one ever tells me anything. Mum just cries and stares at the telly and drinks. It's like she's forgotten I exist.

What makes it worse is that when I take out Scarlett's postcard and read it – which I do every night – I can't help comparing it to the letter she left me. I've noticed that 'soon' has changed to 'one day'.

I don't think she's ever coming back. I don't know what a squat is, and I can't ask Mum because she goes mental every time I bring up Scarlett's name. And I can't ask Si because he'll just tell me to leave it, and that Mum's got enough on her plate. His catchphrase, Scarlett used to say.

I really need to speak to Scarlett and tell her she was wrong to say that with her gone it would be better for everybody. It's 10 times worse.

Feb 1 2000

I'm going to be in charge now for a bit. Si is going away. On business, Mum said, when I asked her. I don't know why but I think she is lying. Scarlett says I'm the trusting type, but I am not as trusting as she thinks.

This morning I asked him if going away 'on business' meant that he was never coming back, and he said why on earth would I think that. I said it was because that was what Dad did, and he said that was different because Dad died.

I went and sat on the back doorstep then, even though it was freezing cold, and thought about Dad being ill all over again. It made me sad and long for Scarlett. And for my Mum too, because it's like, when my dad died, she died too. And she doesn't show any signs of coming back, either.

Later, Si came and sat down on the step next to me and told me not to worry about Mum. She's got stuff going on in her head, he said. What stuff, I asked. He just shook his head then and said something about me being too young to understand.

Grownups always say that, I told him. Just so as they don't have to be bothered explaining. But he said, no, it wasn't like that at all. Maybe 'too young' was the wrong choice of phrase, he said. Because he was 35, but he didn't really understand everything that went on in Mum's head either.

We sat there on the step, neither of us saying anything, until it got too cold, and we had to come inside. By that time, I'd stopped thinking about Dad and started thinking about Si instead. Sometimes, I think Mum makes him as sad as she makes me. Scarlett said he was only with Mum because it was convenient for him. But I don't think there's anything convenient about living with Mum.

When we came inside, he gave me some money and said I wasn't to go to bed without my tea while he was away, and that he'd phone. Then he took me to school in his car. He's done that a lot recently. Just while the weather's so bad, he says.

February 7 2000

Scarlett told me stuff before she went away about Mum and Dad, and where Si fitted in with all of it. She said that Mum was disloyal to Dad, even when he was alive, which was even worse, she said, than being disloyal to him when he was dead.

Sometimes, I worry that if she were here and heard me on the phone, talking to Si about my day, she'd say I was being disloyal too, and that makes me just as bad as Mum.

But I'm not, honestly. If Dad were here, I'd ask him to help me with my maths. But he's not. And if Mum were here – properly here, I mean, not just upstairs in bed or sitting staring at the TV with a glass in her hand, I'd ask her to help me with my science project. But she's not either. So, that's why I ask Si instead.

February 17 2000

Dear Callum,

This is my new address. It's a hostel. All girls. It's a laugh. Better than the squat, which, to be honest, was a bit rubbish. Here the water is always hot, and I have proper bedclothes. But you have to get out at 10 in the morning, and it can be cold walking the streets until they let you back in at night.

How is Mum? I bet she hasn't missed me one jot. And what about Si? Has she kicked him out yet? Don't answer that because I bet I can guess the answer. I bet he's rubbing his hands with glee now I've gone. I miss you, poppet, and I will come and get you one day, but I don't know when that day will be. Flats are very expensive in London.

Love from Scarlett

P.S. You must promise me you won't let Mum know where I am staying.

February 20 2000

When Mum talks to Si on the phone, it's in a quiet voice like she doesn't want me to hear what they're saying. Every now and then she looks round to check I'm not listening, so I have to pretend to be doing stuff. Sometimes, she sends me out of the room to get something for her, but I know it's only to get rid of me because she doesn't want me listening in. What secrets do she and Si have, I wonder? If it's lovey-dovey stuff, then I'm not interested. I'm only waiting for my turn to speak to Si, so I can tell him about my day.

February 20 2000

If Scarlett were here now, I know exactly what she'd say about me telling all my stuff to Si, like he was part of the family. She'd say that he *wasn't*. That he just moved in and took over the moment Dad died. Worse, that all those months Dad was in and out of hospital, Si was doing his best to take Dad's place. Running Mum back and forth, always at the end of the phone when she needed to talk, nothing too much trouble. Just waiting for Dad to die.

Before Scarlett left, she told me something I've tried to push to the back of my mind. Most days, I don't think about it, but some days, when I'm missing her really bad and missing Dad too, and I'm hungry because Mum's forgotten to get any food in again, it comes into my head.

It's about Mum and Si, and it's this, Scarlett told me, that made her hate them both. She cried when she told me, which made me think it wasn't just hatred for them she felt but sadness that our lives had changed so much, and that things could never go back to being like they were.

She told me she'd seen Si coming out of Mum's bedroom on the morning the call came from the hospital to tell us Dad had finally died. I remember that day, of course I do. But only the bit of it that happened to me. Me crying and Scarlett comforting me, and Mum shut up in her room and nowhere to be seen.

It was early and the phone had been ringing for ages, she said, and in the end, she got up to answer it, just as Si was coming out of Mum and Dad's room wearing nothing but a towel.

And that was why Si hated her, she said, and why mum avoided her, because she knew their secret. Their Dirty Little Secret, she called it. She said it was disgusting, and when she explained it to me properly, I thought so too. She's my sister, and Dad was our Dad. So, it has to be right, what she said.

February 22 2000

Last night, I couldn't sleep. It had been trying to snow before I went to bed, and I kept hoping it would snow some more. Thick, fat flakes – so many that they'd bury us all – the street, this house, even school! That way, I could stay at home and make sure Mum was all right. With Si not here, someone needs to make sure she eats something, and to keep an eye on what she drinks.

There were other reasons I couldn't sleep too. I felt bad, really bad, that Scarlett's latest letter lay tucked between the pages of my diary, with her new address on it. I kept thinking I should give it to Mum, because that might be one less thing for her to worry about. At least if Scarlett's safe and tucked up in a warm bed, it might help her to stop imagining the worst.

But Scarlett made me promise. And I don't want to be disloyal. Because, if she finds out I've been disloyal, she might not come back for me. And I'll be stuck here with Mum and Si forever, or until I'm 16 and can go to London on my own to find her. Will she have found a flat for us by that time, I wonder?

The other reason I couldn't sleep was because I was worried about Si. Mum said he should have been back hours ago, and I said to ring him on his new mobile, but she said no, not while he was driving, it might cause an accident.

I kept listening out for his car and getting out of bed to look up and down the street for it, and to check on the progress of the snow (which had decided to turn to rain).

I must have drifted off at last, but not deeply, because the sound of his creaky brakes outside woke me, and I heard him turn his key and stamp his feet on the mat. I left it a bit before I crept downstairs. Mum and Si were talking – or rather Si was talking, Mum just seemed to be asking questions.

Now I know where Si's been all this time. Not on business. He's been looking for Scarlett.

February 23 2000

What should I do? Si hasn't said a word to me about where he's been and what he's been doing, so if I bring the subject of Scarlett up, he'll be suspicious and know I was listening outside the door. Not that I heard much. Just stuff about the Salvation Army and an advert or something and London being a big place and not having much of a clue where to start looking.

But I keep remembering I've got Scarlett's address in my diary. The one she said I mustn't, under any circumstances, give to Mum. And it's like it's burning a hole through the page.

March 10 2000

This morning, Mum was very sick. It was a good job it was Saturday, and I didn't have to go to school. Si had just left – an urgent call to London, so he said, so there was no one to help her but me.

He has a mobile phone, and I could have rung it, but Mum said no, I mustn't. She'd manage, she said. What Si had to do in London was important, and he needed to concentrate. I couldn't help wishing he'd been here, though, because he'd have known what to do. I hate not knowing what to do.

Later, Mum said she felt better. She said we should go for a walk. Just me and her. We went to the park, and it was fun. The sun came out and it felt warm for the first time in ages. We took some stale bread and fed the ducks, just like we used to. One of the ducks was fatter and greedier than the others. It made us laugh. On the way back, she asked me if I would help her to do something.

'I want to start again,' she said. 'So that Scarlett will want to come back and stay this time.'

And then she said she was going to tell me the truth about where Si had gone, even though Si had said she shouldn't because I'd be disappointed if it didn't work out. I felt hot and funny inside then because I think I'd already guessed this trip to London was something to do with Scarlett, and that was why Mum had cheered up.

All the time she was talking to me, I couldn't stop thinking about the promise I'd made to my sister not to tell Mum where she was. If Si did find her, would she blame me and refuse to speak to me ever again? And if he didn't, and then later found out I'd had her address all along, then what? I couldn't even start to think about that!

Someone who was watching out for her – a friend of Si's, Mum said, had seen a girl matching Scarlett's description. She told me I should look happy, not sad. Didn't I want Scarlett to come home?

Of course I do, I said. That's all I said. Because what was the point of saying that Scarlett has no intention of being found and that she hates Si so much she would never consider coming back home?

Seeing Mum smile, well, I just didn't want to do anything to spoil her mood.

It'll all work out, she said, on the way home. Things have been bad between me and Scarlett, and I've not been a proper mother for a long time. But when she comes home, we'll sit down and have a long talk and try again. Sometimes, with Mum, I feel it's me who's the grownup and Mum who's the child.

When we got back home, we cleaned the house from top to bottom. We took all the empty bottles we found to the bottle bank, laughing every time we dropped one through the hole into the big bin and it made a crash.

Then we bought some chips on the way back and ate them out of the bag. Mum had a large fish as well and lots of vinegar. You could smell it all the way home. I hate vinegar, but today I didn't mind it.

P.S. There is no alcohol in our house anymore. Vinegar might smell horrible, but it smells nicer than alcohol.

March 11 2000

No Scarlett. It was a wild goose chase, Si said. Mum cried and said she wished she hadn't thrown the last half bottle of wine away. Si said she had to take one day at a time. He was proud of what she'd done today and proud of me for helping, and on Monday, now she'd decided she was going through with it, he was going to go with her to see the GP. Something about putting her on the programme. Something else too, but I can't think I heard that right. It's not easy hearing things through heavy wooden doors.

March 14 2000

I've not written in my diary for ages. There's nothing to say. No more trips to London. It's like Si and Mum have given up. No more letters from Scarlett, either. I think she's forgotten all about us.

Mum seems better – on the outside. The house is clean. There's always proper food at mealtimes. But all Scarlett's photos have been removed and no one ever talks about her. It's like she's died, too. First Dad, now Scarlett.

March 15 2000

Today, Mum told me a secret. I knew what it was before she told me. I'd heard it through the door that time, but I thought I'd heard wrong. She and Si are having a baby. In December, she said. Round Christmas.

Are you happy for me, she wanted to know. I knew she wanted me to say yes, but I just shrugged. Truthfully, I don't know how I feel. I am going to write a letter to Scarlett. But first I have to work out what, exactly, I want to say.

March 17 2000

Dear Scarlett,

Have you found us a flat yet? Although I'm not sure if I can come to London right now because I have been picked to play football for the school and, like Si says, it's a great honour.

We have some BIG NEWS in this house. Mum is having a baby. It would be lovely if you could come and visit us, when the new baby arrives, which will be around Christmas time. I know that's what Mum wants, but she won't say it. She never mentions you at all anymore.

I used to think it was because she hated you, just like you hate her. But I don't think that's right anymore. I think she loves you and she misses you, and the only way to get through the days is to keep you locked out of her heart, because as soon as she lets you in the tears flood in, too. And tears are not good for the baby.

Si told me this. He also told me that he loves Mum and would do anything for her. It's hard being a woman, he says, because women are mothers too, and sometimes their daughters can't see beyond that part of them. He says that you'll see that one day, too, when you become a mother yourself.

He told me lots of other stuff too. It was like once he started telling me things he couldn't stop. As if he needed to do it. He told me all about how hard it was for Mum when Dad was ill. Because she loved him very much. He was your dad, after all, Si said. And when she found herself falling in love with Si, too, it made her feel guilty, because she didn't know what to do.

I don't know if you understand that, Scarlett, but I think I do. Maybe that's because I feel a bit guilty too – same as she does. I'm torn between my feelings for Mum and Si and my feelings for you. Knowing if I choose one, I lose the other.

Can you see that, even just a tiny bit? Can you stop thinking bad things about Si just for a minute and stop thinking that Mum has been disloyal to Dad and to his memory? Because nothing's black and white, even though I can see how it makes things easier for you to think so.

Everything in my life at the moment comes in so many different shades. Si, for instance, is nowhere near as bad as you told me he was. He's helped Mum to stop drinking. There's no alcohol in our house anymore. You used to say that Si encouraged her, but I wonder if, in fact, the opposite was true. Si only ever drank to keep Mum company – to keep up her story that she was only having a drink to be sociable. He helps me with my homework, too. He comes to watch me at football. He's my friend, Scarlett. I can see you pulling your face at that.

But you're my sister, and I made a promise to you. And now I have all this guilt, too, just like Mum had. I could tell her where you are. It would make her happy to know you're safe. But you won't let me.

Yours, Callum

March 24 2000

Scarlett isn't at the hostel anymore. The letter came back. NO LONGER KNOWN AT THIS ADDRESS. Mum opened it. She couldn't imagine what was in it, she told me later.

I thought she'd be furious with me, but she just put her arms round me and said she understood. Everything happened really quickly after that. Si phoned the hostel, and they said the last they'd seen of Scarlett was a month ago. Si asked if he could go to the hostel and interview some of the girls to see if they knew anything about her whereabouts.

I think the person at the other end said no. She doesn't trust me, I heard Si say later to Mum, when I was supposed to be doing my homework. You can hear it in her voice. Probably thinks I was up to no good, and that was the reason Scarlett left home in the first place.

The house has been very quiet all evening.

March 28 2000

To whom it may concern,

This letter is about my sister, Scarlett Barnes, who stayed at your hostel in February and perhaps for some of March. Si, who is not my dad, but who is a bit like a dad, spoke to you and asked if he could come and talk to some of the girls who might know where Scarlett had gone, but you said no.

Si said you probably did not trust him, so I am writing instead. I can't come to London, but I am putting my phone number on this letter and enclosing a photo of Scarlett, so that if any of the girls in your hostel see her, they can ring me up. Or better still, tell her to come home because we all miss her.

My mum is having a baby and she shouldn't be worried.

Love from Callum Barnes

April 2 2000

I'd forgotten it was April Fool's Day till Si called me down for breakfast. He said he'd made me a boiled egg for a treat and because I had a game, so I needed the protein. I should have spotted Mum trying not to laugh, but I didn't. Just bashed my egg. Course, it was just the shell of his old egg turned upside down, wasn't it! We didn't stop laughing for ages.

Si went to wash up and I went to get my kit ready for the match. I was the only one to hear the knock on the door because Si had his Walkman blaring and Mum was in the shower. I looked out of my window and saw her on the step. Scarlett.

It was like my heart had stopped beating. She looked smaller, not so confident looking. Funny hair in higgledy-piggledy plaits. I pelted over to the bathroom and hammered on the door, yelling Scarlett was here over and over.

That was when Mum came out of the shower, dripping wet, wrapped in a towel, and started having a go at me. But then she heard the knocking on the door too. Then she pushed past me and ran down the stairs and into Scarlett's arms.

December 25 2000

Nobody keeps diaries for long. I was clearing out my room yesterday – Mum said I had to, otherwise Father

Christmas would break his leg trying to climb over all the rubbish (ha ha!) – and that's when I found this, down the back of the bed.

I sat on my bed and read it, and then I thought about everything I could have written in it since. The day Scarlett came back, for instance. Well, I did write a bit about that, but not much because I missed most of it.

Si took me to the match, I remember, and then for a burger afterwards. Mum and Scarlett had a lot to talk about, he said, and it was probably better that we weren't there.

I felt sorry for Si. He'd been so happy that morning, playing that trick on me, with the egg, and making Mum laugh. He loves to make Mum laugh. I tried to cheer him up, but he had that look on his face, just like the team we'd played and thrashed that morning. Kind of defeated.

After we'd had our burger, I could tell he still didn't want to go home, and that it was nothing to do with Mum and Scarlett needing to talk. More like him worrying about what was going to happen between him and Mum now Scarlett had come back.

So, I said we should go bowling, and he agreed. We spent all afternoon there. I lost count of how many games we played. I love bowling. But you can get sick of anything if you do it too long. By the end of the afternoon, I don't think either of us ever wanted to see another bowling ball again.

But Si was still quiet. So, I told him what I'd never told him before. That he was like a dad to me. Not *my* dad, obviously. But somebody I looked up to and liked loads, and that Scarlett would just have to get used to it. Because if she wanted me to choose between her and Si then I couldn't. And what's more, Mum would refuse to do so too.

Si cheered up after that.

I wish I could say it's been a breeze since Scarlett came back. But Scarlett's Scarlett, like Mum says, so it would have been odd if she'd walked back in and said, 'Oh, goody, Si's still here, and what's even more exciting, you're having his baby.'

But things *are* better. She's grown up, she says. Stopped thinking everything in life's so simple. Living in London has taught her that, she said. That's all she's said about London, by the way. I don't think it was anywhere near as great as she said it was in her letter.

She's got a job now. And next year, she's going to college, she says. She's decided she wants a career. And a place of her own. She said I needn't look so worried, she didn't expect me to up sticks and move in with her.

The biggest change has been the arrival of Georgie the Bruiser, which is Scarlett's name for him. She's besotted. Though you wouldn't catch her having one of her own, she says. Not till she's made her first million, anyway. Ambition, she says, is the best contraceptive. She says some weird things, does Scarlett.

Mum said, on the day that Georgie was born, that she was glad she'd had a boy. Scarlett would have hated the competition. I'm glad Georgie's a boy, too.

This is a five-year diary. But I'm not sure if I'm going to have the time next year to fill it in every day. What with Georgie and the extension, which me and Si are going to build together. And then there's football and, in September, secondary school. I'll have a lot on my plate. 2001. A brand new century!

Then there's this other thing Mum and Scarlett can't stop talking about. Mum and Si's wedding in June. Mum wants me to be a page boy. Only if I'm allowed to turn up in my footie kit.

First published 2008, *Fiction Feast*

When Sally Met Holly

Christmas Day and everyone's inside, full of pudding and snoring through the Queen's speech. Except me and the occasional motorist driving past. I can't stop myself hoping that the next one will be Frank, and that he'll pull up, wind the window down and tell me to jump in because we're turning round and going back to his place.

But it never is, and after what I've been and gone and done, I just can't see it happening, frankly. It's Frank's fault as much as mine, though. If he hadn't said what he said while we were putting the tree up, then maybe I wouldn't have felt so threatened by everything that happened afterwards. Oh, dear, I'm getting ahead of myself. I should explain.

Frank has a daughter, you see. He dotes on her. But he's rarely allowed to see her. That's what it's like for fathers, he told me once, blinking the tears away.

Holly is her name. She's 15, soon to be 16. Old enough to make her own mind up about where she wants to spend Christmas, Frank told me, the day he had that row with Yvonne over the phone. Yvonne's his first wife – but you've probably guessed that.

I say first wife as if there's a chance I might become his second. Well, there is not. Not even a remote chance now. Of course, when he invited me to spend Christmas with him, I can't pretend that I wasn't hoping he might use the occasion to pop the question. I may even have hinted as much to colleagues at work. I'm going to look a right berk when I go back after the holidays, aren't I?

And I can't pretend I wasn't disappointed when Frank told me that Yvonne had given in and said that if Holly wanted to come to him at Christmas this year, for a change, then there was nothing she could do to stop her. But I decided to make the best of it. Three days max and she'd be off, was how I saw it, then I'd have Frank all to myself again. Meanwhile, all I had to do was show Frank what a generous nature I had.

The first thing I did was insist on a proper tree, fairy lights and all. For Holly. To show her how special we think she is, I said. A judicious use of the 'we', I remember thinking. Frank's face lit up when I switched the fairy lights on, and for a moment I thought, *This is it, he's going to ask me*. I was all butterflies.

But instead of asking me to share the rest of my

life with him he started on about Holly. About how she ought to be allowed more of a say about which one of her parents she wanted to live with after next month, when she turned 16. I can't tell you how much it threw me, though of course I did my best to hide it, fiddling about with the fairy, trying to get her to stay upright as I replied. 'Honestly, Frank,' I said. 'Can you see her wanting to move away from her friends to be with us?'

'She'll make new friends,' he said.

I could have battered him with the fairy. But instead I decided to try and blind him with a bit of psychobabble. Friendship bonds are important for young women, I said. Removing Holly from her circle would affect her development. She may end up resenting you and blaming her inability to find a new friendship base on you. He went quiet then.

We went to meet her at the station. On the platform, Frank was dancing about like a big soft puppy, and I had to tell him off because people were staring. But he didn't care. I'm not the jealous type, but honestly, I couldn't help thinking, *Would he be dancing a jig if it were me arriving on the train?*

The first thing she complained about was the cold. Frank and I have a little joke about the correct temperature to maintain the house at 20 degrees and a sweater we say. I don't think Holly has a sweater and I've seen less midriff on display on a Turkish belly dancer. Frank was all for turning up the temperature to pacify her, but then I reminded him about the world's energy resources. I lent her one of my woollies in the end. She made a face, but she did wear it.

We'd planned a little treat for Christmas Eve. Pizza at a nice restaurant followed by Midnight Mass. Well, the pizza was a roaring success, but I'm not able to say the same about Midnight Mass.

'You two go and I'll make my own way back,' Holly said, when we told her of the plan to walk there from the pizza place. 'I don't do church.'

There's nothing wrong with my sense of humour, but for the life of me, I couldn't work out what Frank thought there was to chuckle at when she came out with that remark. But he practically fell over laughing and then she joined in, the two of them clutching each other, laughing fit to burst. I looked on, baffled, and I have to say, sorely disappointed in Frank's display of childishness.

So, he chose to go back home with Holly. He couldn't let her walk back on her own or she'd get lost, he said. He was happy enough to let me walk home alone, though. Past that gang of unsavoury yobs outside the Red Lantern Takeaway and the drunken wassailers pouring out of The George and Dragon.

When I got back, it was as if me being abandoned like that had never happened. Frank was his usual cheery self and Holly, exhausted from the long train journey, had gone to bed. The heating was right up, though.

She's got her own way, then, I said. Well, it's only for a few days, Frank replied. I can't pretend I didn't feel resentful as I sat and watched the late film with him, but I had no intention of starting a row, as it was obvious whose side he'd take. But later, in the bedroom, despite the fact the heating was on full blast, things were chillier between Frank and me than they'd ever been, thanks to Holly.

This morning – Christmas morning – I'd planned a special breakfast. Waffles and champagne – well, sparkling wine. I'd intended mixing it with orange juice, but I couldn't seem to find the two cartons I'd put in the fridge just before we'd picked Holly up the day before.

When she finally deigned to get out of bed it was gone eleven o'clock – which was the time I'd put on my Christmas lunch countdown list to start the Festive Roulade – and she let it slip that she'd drunk the orange juice. When she said she thought that was what it was there for, I managed to bite my tongue. But when she added that she never ate breakfast anyway, so she'd be skipping the waffles, something snapped.

Maybe it was a mistake to have that glass of undiluted sparkling wine on an empty stomach. 'Can't you make an effort to join in with some of our traditions at least?' I snapped. She disappeared after that – back to her room to phone her mum and complain what a harridan I was, no doubt. Frank followed in her wake, muttering stuff to her about me not meaning it, which in my humble opinion was not really for him to say.

After a while he came back into the kitchen and said never mind, it was nearly time to start the dinner anyway, and to be honest, he'd never been a great fan of waffles himself, either. I had another drink then.

The Festive Roulade was not turning out well. I blame the fizzy wine I kept refilling my glass with. Frank was bothering me – running in and out of the kitchen asking if there was anything he could do. Placating me. And then Holly crept in to ask when we were going to open our presents. I wasn't sharp with her, but I did say that if it was all right with her, I'd prefer if we waited until we could do it together, and that right now, I was at a rather tricky bit with the chestnut stuffing.

She gave this sigh – an exaggerated, tragic teenage sigh and said whatever. She looked like she was about to flounce off again, but instead she sniffed the air, scoured the kitchen surfaces with her eyes, put on this puzzled look and said, 'Where's the turkey?'

'Didn't your dad tell you?' I said. 'We're vegetarian.'

Well, from her reaction you'd have thought I'd said we eat babies. 'No turkey?' she said. 'No chipolatas, no bacon rolls and no gravy?'

Then she demanded to know if this was another of our bloody traditions, alongside me getting plastered before noon on Christmas Day. Well, that did it. 'How dare you?' I said. 'How dare you accuse me of being drunk?'

Which is when I went straight upstairs, grabbed my bag and coat, struggled into my boots, marched back downstairs and right out of the house. Holly was staring at me, open-mouthed. Frank was in the front room, so he didn't see me leave, which made me even angrier.

There are no buses running on Christmas Day in these parts and I couldn't get into a car, fuelled as I was – still am, maybe – with sparkling wine and boiling resentment. So, this is what I'm doing now – walking. Nearly in a straight line.

My little house is just up ahead. No lights in the window, unlike the other houses. There'll be nobody there to welcome me and it'll be cold inside. My head's beginning to ache and I've just realised I've still not eaten anything today, and it must be gone four o'clock.

As I let myself in, I get to thinking of the last time Frank and I were truly happy together, just a few short days ago – the day we brought in the tree. And I'm starting to wonder if buying that tree, dragging it, laughing, into the house and dressing it together had maybe given Frank the hope that somehow he and Holly could get back the missing years, and that I was worthy to be included in his small circle of very special people.

But all I'd done to repay his love and trust was to make him choose between us. Of course, he'd chosen her – his little girl. I'm supposed to be the grown up. Supposed to know that where there's love enough between two people it will always move over to make room for more. Instead, I'd wanted to keep the love just between us, and stifled it instead. What if I've killed it stone dead forever? Is there a way to breathe new life back into it?

What if I go downstairs, pick up the phone and say I'm sorry? What if I ask to speak to Holly and apologise to her, too, will that soften his heart just a little bit? Will she be able to forgive me? In time, will she even begin to like me? Well, there's only one way to find out.

First published 2010, *Fiction Feast*

My Stupid Lies

Kath felt glum. All her workmates were talking non-stop about Christmas. Was she really the only one who didn't have a family to spend it with?

'There were 14 round the table with us last year,' Dot was saying. 'A bit of a squash, but we managed in the end.'

'You must have been exhausted by the end of it! I know I always am,' Pat laughed.

'Thank goodness I won't be doing it this year. It's my sister's turn.'

Dot sighed with relief and ground out the stub of the cigarette she wasn't strictly allowed to smoke beneath her feet. 'What about you, Marge?'

Marge was teasing her hair into place in front of the restroom mirror. Kath had been at the bottle factory for less than a month, but already she'd picked up the fact that among the women who worked here, Marge had status. She was always deferred to on any matter, and Kath suspected it would be no different now the subject of Christmas had come up.

'Oh, I don't mind how many I cater for.' Marge spoke to her reflection. 'I've got my daughters coming and their partners, and then there'll be the grandchildren. Our Rebecca's third's due any day so that'll make it even more special.'

The women oohed and aahed, their faces wreathed in indulgent smiles. Bonus point to Marge, Kath noted. Babies pipped everything at Christmas.

'What about you, Kath?'

Marge's radar was working well today, Kath couldn't help thinking. Her deep-set eyes narrowed to slits as they honed in on Kath, who was doing everything she could to keep out of her eyeline, waiting for the others so they could clock on together.

It didn't do you any good here to act individually, and to clock on a minute before she needed to would have provoked all sorts of sly comments among 'the girls', as they liked to call themselves – though with an average age of 48, Kath being the youngest at 42, it had been a long time since any of them could have rightfully laid claim to that title.

Suddenly, they were all staring at her, and she didn't think she was imagining the look of pity on their faces. Kath knew they had decided she was a freak. She rode her bike to work instead of taking the bus like all the others. She'd brought her own lunch on the first day because she'd been trying to lose a couple of kilos and, having seen what a diet of pie and chips did for her workmates, she thought it safest to continue doing so.

She didn't have a TV either – weird in itself here, she knew – so she couldn't watch any of the soaps. As a consequence, she hadn't a clue what the girls were talking about when they recapped the previous night's events down the *Street* or in the *Square*.

But the thing that set her furthest apart from all the others was the fact that she was single. No husband, no boyfriend, no kids. Not everyone here was married but most of those that weren't had been, or at the very least they had a son or daughter from some previous relationship that had fizzled out. It didn't matter if the marriages weren't happy or if the teenage kids were a pain or the toddlers were clingy. All those things were simply the intricacies of family life, the glue that held them all together and kept Kath – who'd been brought up in care and had never experienced family life at all – outside the inner circle.

Marge slowly repeated her question. 'So, Kath,' she said, louder this time, to make sure she had everyone's attention, Kath was convinced. 'Where will you be spending your Christmas?'

Kath could just imagine the gleeful look of triumph that would appear on Marge's face if she told her the truth, and the pitying looks her confession would invite from everyone else. The fact was that she'd be spending Christmas alone, because the few friends she had would all be with family for the festivities, assuming – as people always did – that she would be, too.

There and then she decided that there was nothing else for it. She would tell a lie and hang the consequences. Or else those pitying looks would follow her around the factory for the next seven days until they closed for the annual week-long break, when she would be free of the lot of them.

She'd rather be working anywhere but here, but jobs were scarce, and she had her rent to pay. If there was one lesson she'd learned thoroughly in care, it was that beggars couldn't be choosers.

'Christmas? Me?' Kath widened her eyes and looked round at the assembled company. 'Actually, I'm spoiled for choice,' she said. 'There's my kid sister in Wales. They want me to go but I'm not sure.'

Suddenly, it was like someone had turned a tap on, and once one lie popped out, a flood of others came pouring after it.

'Her baby's actually due on Christmas Day, but, well, it's her first and you never can tell, can you?'

She waited for the effect of her announcement to sink in, inwardly revelling in the frown of disapproval that was spreading over Marge's face. She hadn't finished yet, not by any means.

'Then there's my oldest brother. He's got four kids and they're all at that magical age. D'you know what I mean?'

Everyone did and nodded, bar Marge.

'Did I tell you there were triplets between me and my oldest brother?'

This was the icing on the cake, judging by the look of unconcealed loathing on Marge's face and the whoops of amazement from everyone else.

'Every year it's a race to invite me first, just like when we were little, and they used to fight for my attention. I remember one time—'

'Right, girls, let's be having you.' Marge was looking at her watch.

Realising she'd rattled her enough to change the subject, a glow of satisfaction spread through Kath.

But in her newfound enthusiasm for telling porkies, as the week progressed, she found herself losing count of how many members of her non-existent family there were. If she carried on much longer, she was in danger of turning her fictional mother into a modern-day equivalent of the old woman who lived in a shoe.

By the end of the week, the triplets, her older brother and her kid sister had names and ages, as did the spouses and the eight children they had between them. Not to be left out, somewhere along the line she'd even acquired a couple of pets. A budgie called Blue and a Yorkshire terrier called Missy.

She should have felt great. For the first time since she'd started working here, she fitted in. People asked her opinion about the best kind of present for a 14-year-old. They asked whether her family fell out at Christmas like theirs did. They wanted to know if she'd worked out the logistics of getting from one end of the country to the other yet, so that no one in her family should be left out when it came to sharing her out fairly during the holiday period.

But she didn't feel great. She felt miserable. You had to have a good memory to be a good liar, and already she'd almost been caught out by Marge, whose ears were as sharp as her eyes, because she'd stumbled a bit over one of the triplet's names.

The situation had been retrievable – just. But she didn't know for how much longer she could keep it up before she got someone's name totally wrong and blew her cover completely.

One morning, as on every morning for the past week, she was on quality control, and it was as she watched the bottles sail by on the conveyor belt that she'd taken to muttering the names of her recently acquired siblings and their kin beneath her breath.

'Sam and George and Toby,' she intoned. 'Tim, no Tom. Tom, Tina, Tracey. Samantha, Sarah. Oh, my God, what was the name of Sarah's youngest?'

She'd been dimly aware of a white coat moving in and out of her line of vision, but she was so engrossed in her chanting that she'd thought nothing of it. But now, the white coat seemed to be getting rather agitated. It was waving its arms and calling out her name from the other end of the conveyor belt.

Now it came scurrying round to her side. 'Steady on, Kath!'

'What?' Kath blinked, irritated by this interruption, which made her lose her rhythm.

Now she'd have to start all over again. Why on earth hadn't she written those names down?

She looked up from the conveyor belt, which for some reason had come to a standstill, and found herself staring straight into the concerned brown eyes of Alec Maitland, the supervisor.

'You've let at least half a dozen bottles go through there with no labels on,' he said.

He didn't say it angrily, but rather with a hint of a question in his voice, as if he didn't really believe that Kath, of all people, could have been so careless, even though he'd seen it with his own eyes.

Kath mumbled a strangled apology. She couldn't afford to make mistakes like this at work or she'd be losing money. It was this wretched lying that was getting to her, making her take her eye off the ball. A fierce hard lump of misery formed in her throat, which any minute she feared would explode into a flood of tears.

'You all right, Kath? Perhaps you should have a break. You look done in,' Alec said.

Kath liked Alec. He was one of the few people here

who was pleasant to her and who didn't seem to care that she didn't fit in, the way the girls did. In fact, once or twice, she'd caught him smiling at her across the shop floor, when she'd picked up her sandwich box at lunchtime, put on her coat and taken herself off the premises. It was as if he approved of her not shuffling off to the canteen with the rest of the herd, exchanging views about the latest *EastEnders* scandal.

'I expect it's Christmas,' he said. 'It can be a stressful time.'

He smiled his understanding smile at her. At which point, Kath's mouth began to wobble, and two great fat tears slid down her cheeks.

'Sorry,' she gulped. 'I'm really sorry about this.'

Men, she knew, hated women's tears. She'd discovered that at an early age, when she'd been shunted about from one home to another. In the end, she'd learned to control her misery to avoid the exasperation or irritation of those in charge. Nowadays, she prided herself on being an expert in self-control. If only Alec Maitland hadn't mentioned Christmas.

At the same moment as those two rare tears spurted from her eyes, the lunchtime whistle sounded. Now at last she could get away. She would go to the park, where she often went on fine days. At this time of the year, it was less busy. And in the park, there would be no Marge to interrogate her with her ever more probing questions.

Unfortunately, however, Alec was still there, intent on doing a bit of detection work of his own. 'What on earth's the matter, Kath?' he said. 'Is there anything I can do?'

She shook her head miserably. Didn't he have any manners? When you saw that people were miserable you were meant to turn your head and walk off, pretend you hadn't seen it. Everyone knew that.

'There's nothing anyone can do,' she said, refusing to meet his eyes, which were boring a hole into her. 'I'm going for a walk,' she sniffed. 'Scuse me.'

She had to pass him to get out of the door, but he blocked her way. What did he think he was doing? He might be her boss, but he didn't own her free time as well as her working day.

'Let me come with you,' he said, 'You can talk to me in confidence.'

'It's none of your business,' she snapped.

'If you're unhappy because of something that's happening at work, then you're wrong,' he said. 'It's very much my business. I know what these women can be like with—'

'With what? Loners, losers, people who don't fit in?'

He looked shocked at her choice of words.

'Is that how you see yourself?' He paused, then added, 'Get your coat, Kath. We're going for a walk.'

A crowd of girls saw them leave together. The nudging and whispering weren't lost on Kath, who kept her head down as she scurried out, keeping close to Alec, who, by contrast, gave them all a cheery wave and a 'How do, girls!'

It was an unseasonably mild day. The sun still held onto some of its warmth and the wind was light and playful.

'I often come here,' Kath said, after they'd walked a bit in silence. 'It helps clear my head after that place.'

'It suits you out here,' Alec said. 'You look like you belong in the great outdoors.'

It was perceptive of him, Kath had to admit. Outside in the fresh air was where she really felt happy. She could stand up straighter, lift her head up higher, stop feeling like she had to make herself invisible or she'd be a target. If there were any jobs going that involved working outside, she'd snap one up. But instead, she was stuck at the bottle factory, trapped in a web of lies she could see no way out of. She gave a sigh that seemed to steal its way from the very depth of her soul.

'Are you going to tell me all about it, then?' Alec was looking at her intently.

He was the sort of man, Kath felt, who never gave up on anything once he started. She could imagine him as a handyman around the house, restoring things to their former glory so you'd never think there'd been anything wrong with them. The kind of man any wife would cherish, and any child would be proud to have as their dad.

She would lay odds that he was one of those dads who, if his son finally confessed to a broken pane of glass after a long struggle of conscience, would listen patiently and forgive him – because he'd told the truth.

'I've told some stupid, stupid lies,' she said at last, before telling him everything she'd said to the girls and exactly why she'd done it. Looking him straight in the eye while she confessed, she decided, was part of her penance, although she wouldn't have expected him to understand that.

He listened seriously for the most part, although once or twice his expression lightened when she described how she'd lost track of all those names and ages, and when she told him just what it had been about the cliquey nature of the girls that had driven her to tell such whoppers in the first place.

'Not that I'm trying to justify myself,' she said, when she'd got to the end of her story.

She finally allowed herself to look down at her hands, which she hadn't realised until now were getting cold. It may have been warm while they were walking, but they'd been sitting for some time, and it was December after all.

'You must think I'm pathetic,' she said. She lifted her fingers to her lips and blew some warmth back into them.

'I think that what you want more than anything is to fit in,' he said. 'I can't think of any other reason why you'd want to make a friend of Marge and her cronies.'

She hadn't expected him to get straight to the nub of it.

'Is it so very wrong to want to belong?' she asked him.

'Not at all,' he said. 'It's human nature. Only it's important to stay true to yourself.'

He pulled his big overcoat more firmly around him. 'When I first saw you locking your bike outside the factory the day you started, with your hair all natural and your cheeks all rosy, I thought, she's different. She looks like someone with a mind of her own.'

'I'm sorry I've disappointed you, then.'

Kath sprung up. She didn't have a watch, but it felt late. 'We should be getting back,' she said.

She'd made a fool of herself twice it seemed. Had she really thought he'd give her a way out of her lie? Nobody could do that, and she'd been stupid to imagine he could.

They didn't speak again until they arrived back at the factory gates. Kath walked with her hands in her pockets and her eyes resolutely fixed to the ground. At one point, at the park keeper's little hut, Alec had paused, then, after a few seconds, run to catch her up.

'See you, then,' was all she said as their ways parted.

'Yeah,' he replied. 'See you.'

She'd made him feel uncomfortable with the wall she'd thrown up between them. She knew it, but that was her way. He'd had his fun with her and now she had to protect herself. She'd given a lot of herself away just then and she would give him nothing more.

That night, he was waiting for her outside the factory gates.

'Haven't you got a family to go home to?' she asked him.

'Me? I'm like you. Footloose and fancy free,' he said.

The cheerful wife and sensitive though impish son she'd created for him dissolved into the cold, black night air.

'I picked this up for you,' he said – and thrust a scrap of paper into her hand. 'At the park, when we were leaving.'

She squinted but couldn't see anything in the dark.

'It's a job,' he said. 'Park keeper.'

She laughed incredulously. 'What? Me? Parkies are old men,' she said. 'Bad tempered jobsworths who run after kids and spoil their fun,'

'Things have changed since our day,' he chuckled. 'Now you'd be a Parks Officer. Outside all day, your own little office, a few squirrels and robins for company. And definitely no Marge. Give it a go.'

She thought about it. If she got it, she'd be able to leave the bottle factory without a blemish on her character. No one would ever know she'd invented a family bigger than the Waltons simply to be one of the girls. Except Alec. He'd know. And if they never saw each other again, it would be as a liar that he'd think of her.

It was the last day before the Christmas break began. Already Kath had heard back about the job. She'd caught the deadline in the nick of time. But as she was apparently the only applicant, the interview, which would take place in the first week of January, looked like a mere formality. Unless she had a prison record, the man on the other end of the line had joked.

She might have told a few lies, but she couldn't be incarcerated for it, Kath thought wryly, as she put the phone down and began to write out her resignation. Maybe she was tempting providence, but she had a good feeling about this job. And if she didn't get it, she'd find some other job she could do in the open air. She wasn't going back to the bottle factory, whatever happened.

The girls had done Secret Santa, so there was no chance that even she could be left out. Her present was an eye mask from Marge, for when she needed a lie down after being surrounded by her big family.

'I've got two things to say,' Kath said, after she'd thanked Marge for her present. 'One is – I'm leaving.'

There were gasps of surprise. Marge looked pleased.

'But you've hardly been here five minutes,' someone said.

'I've got another job,' she replied. 'One that'll suit me better, I think.'

She was prepared for people to ask, but unsurprised when they didn't. She'd already put herself outside the circle. She simply didn't belong here anymore, if she ever had.

'What's the second thing, then?' Marge demanded. This was the difficult bit. But it had to be done, if ever she was going to get her self-respect back.

'Well…' she began.

Later that evening, she was surprised when her telephone rang. Who would phone her the evening before Christmas Eve? Didn't people have supermarket queues to stand in, trains to catch, presents to wrap? She had a turkey joint, and a few veg she could cook in the microwave. It would do her.

She picked up the receiver. 'Hello?' she said.

'I heard. And I'm really proud of you. You are one courageous lady.'

'Alec?'

'It's strictly against the rules to use my position to get the phone numbers of employees like this, but the girl in personnel wanted to slip off home early, and as it's Christmas, I thought, well, why not?'

'So, you covered for her,' Kath suggested.

'How are you feeling?' Alec asked. 'It couldn't have been easy, owning up that it was all a fib. I don't think I could have done it.'

'You would never have told so many lies in the first place,' Kath said. 'Just to be liked. And you're right. They're not worth it. I feel exhilarated.'

There was a beat, then, 'So, how are you spending Christmas?'

She took a deep breath. 'On my own. Without even a bottle of sherry or a mince pie.'

Another beat. 'Me too, but it doesn't have to be like that. If you like, we could pool our resources…'

Christmas with Alec. It would be fun. It would be more than fun; it would be fantastic. Because already she was very fond of him, and she knew that he was just as fond of her. His instincts about her were right – so much so he'd known the Park Officer's job would suit her even before she did, although she'd walked past that advertisement many times, without even stopping to read it.

But more importantly, just now, was that he'd said he was proud of her. It had lifted her self-esteem so high off the ground, where it had been languishing for so many years, that she knew it would never tumble again.

Or even if it did, right now she dared hope that Alec would be there to lift her up and remind her of the best of herself. Together, there was no problem they couldn't face.

First published 2004, *Fiction Feast*

Bearing Gifts

Tye had never felt so nervous. Not running for his life, cop car in hot pursuit. Or before the judge, waiting to be sentenced. Not even just before they took him down, when he glanced out of the window at so much life going on and realised that for the next three years, it would be going on without him.

They'd got a new front door. Dark green with coloured glass at the top, like you see in a church. Mum must have thought they could risk glass now he was no longer there to put his fist through it. Out of their lives forever, once he'd denied them prison visits. Then, back on the outside, he'd ignored their calls and letters until finally they'd dried up.

He hoiked his rucksack further up his shoulder to ease the spot that ached. He'd carried it for miles, biding his time, inching ever closer to the street where he was born. Christmas seemed like the right time to make his move. Or that's what Holly had been telling him, ever since July.

He wasn't so sure. He'd been standing here for ages, thinking about it. The lights were on, and the telly was booming. So, they had to be in. Unless this was Mum's way of trying to fool a burglar they were home.

The easiest thing would be to leave the presents on the doorstep then leg it. Tell Holly he'd paid his visit, but they hadn't wanted to know so he'd left the stuff anyway and now it was up to them what they did with it. But he knew that even though she wouldn't say so, she'd be disappointed if he did this.

It was five o'clock. Teatime. If Mum was still working her usual shift, she'd have had her sit down and would be in the kitchen cooking. What about the twins? Tommy and Kirsty had been seven when he'd gone inside. How much had they really understood? How must they have felt about having such a loser for a brother? A bolt of shame ran through him.

He'd been away a long time. They'd be 14 now, going on 15. Did you feel shame at seven? Or maybe they'd bigged him up in front of their mates? My brother's harder than yours because he's been inside, that sort of thing. There was nothing about Tye to be proud of, this much he knew.

Except. Holly was always telling him to stop doing himself down. She'd taught him so much. How to like himself, though that was a work in progress. Holly did yoga and meditation too. Her clothes were a bit weird, and she had more tattoos than him. She wasn't his girlfriend. She was far too old for him. But when he'd first got out, she'd given him a room in that big old house she shared with some mates, and he'd been there ever since.

He was accepted there. He'd worked out you learned from watching, not from being told. Nobody there ever told him what to do, not like when he'd been inside, not like Mum had. Although he didn't blame Mum for screaming at him. She'd had the twins to think about and no help. She must have been desperate.

Living at Holly's had taught him that mucking in with the chores and keeping your own space tidy was just what people did. It had taught him to wait his turn before he spoke, too. And – when he finally did open his mouth – to engage his brain first.

And because he'd learned about respect there, he'd got some back. They spoke a lot about respect in the nick. On the street, too. Everyone was owed it, but nobody gave it. Behind this green door was his family. He'd demanded so much of their respect and all he'd given in return was heartache.

It was no use. He'd lost his bottle. The presents would have to speak for him instead. It might be better anyway, since he'd never been any good with words apart from the cutting, hurtful ones. He shrugged his rucksack off his shoulder and – terrified in case he made a sound – placed it gently on the step, unzipped it and carefully removed his gifts.

Three sculptures. A horse for Kirsty because she'd always loved horses; a dog he hoped looked just like Snuff for Tommy, who'd been inconsolable when they'd had to put the real Snuff down because he'd got old and was in a lot of pain. And for Mum, a pint mug she could drink her morning tea from, with the words "To the Best Mum Ever" inscribed within a heart he'd fashioned.

They were all a bit wonky, but they were the best he could do. He'd put so many hours into making them. Picking up the metal he found on those long walks he'd taken, when he'd been trying to make sense of the world and his place in it. An old tap or two, some lead piping, bits of cutlery, tin cans. Genius, Holly said when he'd finally plucked up the courage to show her. Now go and deliver them in person. But this was the hard bit.

Footsteps startled him. He saw the outline of someone's head behind the coloured glass and now the door was opening, and it was too late to make a run for it. Mum. Maybe it was the dark night casting shadows on her face, but he didn't think she'd changed. She caught her breath and he braced himself for curses. But when her face registered who was standing there, it softened and opened like a flower.

'I've brought Christmas presents, Mum,' he said.

'And to say I'm sorry for everything. And I hope we can start again.'

He held his breath. Waited for the door to slam. But instead it opened wider.

'You've come home,' was all she said, but it was enough.

When she stood back to let him in, he knew she still loved him. And that was a start.

First published 2018, *Fiction Feast*

Forbidden Feelings

Miriam could feel Patrick's Christmas card through the pocket of her apron. Robins. Holly. A rosy-cheeked child wrapped up warm in a stripy scarf and mittens and grinning at his snowman. A perfect English Christmas, so Miriam had always imagined, although according to her daughter it rarely snowed at Christmas and when it did it only inconvenienced everyone.

Rachel didn't like to be inconvenienced. She was a busy woman with an important job as a theatre nurse, and anything that got in the way of her work was a justification for a display of ill humour. She'd been just the same as a child back home in South Africa, when anything – be it illness or public disarray, of which there was plenty in those days – meant there was no bus to take her the five-mile round trip to school and back.

While the other children cheered because they'd gained an unexpected day off, Rachel would fume and sulk and declare herself to be a deprived individual living in a backward country. She'd leave it as soon as she could, she'd mutter, stamping her feet in frustration – a promise she kept the day she left for England at the age of 20 to take up a position as a nurse in a very important hospital in London.

England was Rachel's home now. She'd met John, a medical student at the time, but now an important surgeon. They had a son, Larry, who'd inherited his father's sunny, laid-back nature, and a daughter, Tansy, who was as driven as her mother and at present studying to be a lawyer at university.

She would ask John to take her to where she wanted to go, Miriam decided. Or better, Larry, who rarely showed any curiosity about anything his elders got up to, so wouldn't even have to be told to keep their trip a secret. John was bound to say something to Rachel, and then Miriam would have to account for herself.

Not that there was anything about this visit that needed to be kept a secret. It was just that since her move from Johannesburg to live with Rachel and her family, her daughter seemed to want to keep tabs on her movements all the time. It was almost as if Miriam was the daughter and Rachel the mother.

She insisted that her attitude was out of concern for Miriam's safety, which made Miriam laugh out loud. Having lived both in the veldt and in the township, danger had been part of her life for years. What possible harm could befall her in this leafy English suburb, she demanded. She was hardly likely to be trampled by an elephant or shot at by marauders on her way to the high street.

Deep down, she suspected it wasn't so much her safety that concerned Rachel as her daughter's deep embarrassment at having Miriam for a mother. Uneducated, with poor English and a dress sense that left much to be desired, she was well aware that she didn't fit in among the elegant dowagers of the home counties, who passed their afternoons playing bridge or taking their pedigree dogs for a walk.

Miriam used to clean the houses of ladies like these. She used to look after their children, too. Now her own child owned a house just as big, with three cars in the drive and a garden that took Mr Jones, who came every week, the best part of the morning to mow.

She could hold up her head just as high as theirs and look down her nose just as snootily too, if she felt like it, though she'd prefer to be friends if these women could climb down from their high horses for long enough to see past her garish dresses and her strange English and make friends.

It would be nice to have a friend or two in this new country. John and Rachel worked long hours, and Miriam got lonely whiling away the hours till they came home. Larry was friendly and chatty when he was up, but he spent far too much time in bed for her to have the pleasure of his company for long.

Larry was doing what he called a Gap Year. It seemed to consist of coming home in the early hours, staying in bed very late in the morning and doing very little else in between. Surely, he could give up half a day to drive her to Rowan House in Oaksey, where Patrick now lived.

She'd ask him later, before his parents got home from work. He could only say no. Oaksey wasn't far, according to the map. Maybe half an hour or 40 minutes' drive from here. She would tell Larry to wait outside, just in case Patrick didn't mean what he'd written inside the Christmas card. People often said things they didn't mean. Especially bosses. Not that Patrick was her boss anymore, of course.

Miriam removed the card from her pocket. It was badly creased now from the number of times she'd held it in her hand and read the words. Although she didn't really need to read it – she knew what it said off by heart. She just wanted to remind herself of Patrick's handwriting. It was shakier than it used to be but still recognisably his.

Dear Miriam, she read. *This will be my first Christmas in my new home. Rowan House is a sumptuous place with marvellous views of rolling green hills. Seasons greetings to you and yours, your old friend, Patrick.*

How many years had they been exchanging

Christmas cards, the two of them? Miriam had lost count. Never as children. That would have been frowned on, of course. When she was growing up, Patrick's father, Mr McKinley, ran the farm before Patrick took it over.

Her parents both worked there – her mother in the house and her father on the land. Miriam and Patrick had played together as children, along with the other kids from the compound where the workers who supplied their labour to the farm were all housed. Up until they were about eight years old, the village children and the white children who lived on the farm intermingled with no reference at all to their different class or colour.

Then Patrick left the farm and went to school. After that he only came back in the holidays. Miriam missed him but dreaded his return even more. She knew what happened to the white children when they came back from school after 15 weeks away. They changed – addressing the children they used to play with as 'boy' or 'girl', or even ignoring them altogether, particularly when in the company of their white school friends who'd come to visit.

The first time Patrick returned for the long holidays, she refused to go up to the house to say hello. She needed to save herself from the humiliation of being ignored. She kept away a whole week, convinced that her old pal had forgotten all about her, but at least with her pride intact.

On the eighth day, Patrick came to seek her out. Where had she been? Why was she snubbing him, he demanded. He'd been waiting for her to come up to the house so he could give her a present for the birthday that he'd missed while he'd been away.

Touched, Miriam accepted the beaten copper bracelet that a proud Patrick said he'd made himself at school especially for her, and she allowed him to put it on her arm. In that moment, something changed between them. It lasted no longer than the length of time it took to breathe in and out, but Miriam felt it as palpably as she felt the warm touch of copper on her skin.

But she knew her place. Immediately fearful, she stepped back, refusing to meet Patrick's eyes. Then she mumbled some excuse and hurried away before Patrick could say anything to stop her.

For a week afterwards, she lay in bed at night and wondered if Patrick had felt the same charge. Maybe that copper bracelet was only ever just that – an innocent birthday present – and not the love token that Miriam had grown to wish it was.

Inevitably, they drifted apart. Patrick's visits home became fewer and fewer. He was a popular, sporty boy. If he wasn't spending summer with friends, he was touring with the school cricket team. When he did come home, he was taller and more broad-shouldered with every visit.

By now Miriam had taken up with Dominick,

whom everyone expected her to marry and so she did. Patrick stopped seeking her out on his visits home and, as she was a young woman promised to another, naturally Miriam kept well away from him too. They lived their lives in parallel, as black and white people in her country had done for a long time.

Life went on, and if not happy – a career as a maidservant had never been high on her list of priorities, but it was all that was open to her – then Miriam considered herself content enough.

But when the rumour went round that Patrick was engaged, she decided she had to go and find out from the man himself if it were true. By now she was a married woman, with a young baby she strapped to her body every morning before she went to do the job she'd inherited from her mother as maid-of-all-work at Patrick's father's farm.

She found Patrick alone on the veranda, sipping a beer and looking contemplative as he gazed out over the hills that stretched for miles before finally merging into the blue haze of the sky.

Miriam watched him for a long time, admiring how tall and strong he'd grown, telling herself that the way her heart suddenly lifted and hovered in her chest was to do with nerves at speaking to her new boss – Patrick had recently taken over the farm from his father, whose health wasn't as good as it used to be – and nothing at all to do with her forbidden feelings for him.

Why was he looking so sad, she wondered, when everyone else was so happy to hear his news. Everyone except for her, that was.

He must have sensed her presence and spun round. He was clearly surprised to see her and oddly nervous, too. It was easy to read Patrick's emotions. With his fair hair and freckles, he flushed bright red immediately. But perhaps *his* was not the only face that was easy to read.

'You've come,' he said, and then they both knew.

The message they read in each other's eyes was a shock to them both. It spelled so much danger that Miriam almost lost her balance through fear. Stumbling, she turned to go, without saying a word. But Patrick caught her by the hand she'd stretched out to save herself from falling. And that was the beginning.

'So, Grandma. Where is it you're taking me?'

Larry leaned across to fix her into her car seat. She should have realised how easy it would be to persuade him to drive her in the end. He was John's son more than Rachel's.

'Not a word to your mother, mind,' Miriam had warned him. 'This is our little secret.'

Larry had been intrigued, which was not what she'd expected. When he'd teased her about going to see her fancy man, however, she was sharp with him. Patrick was her old boss, she told him.

She'd worked for him and his wife for 20 years or more, and for his father before that. Since it appeared he'd made his new home in a village just 40 miles from where she now lived, it was only good manners that Miriam should go and visit, didn't he agree?

Innocently enough, Larry said he did. But there was a hint of disbelief behind his eyes, as if he suspected there was more to his old Gran's story than met the eye. And now here they were at last, bowling along on a fine sunny morning with the cherry blossom just beginning to appear on the trees and Larry on his best behaviour, driving beautifully and asking no questions. He deserved a little more explanation, just for that, Miriam decided.

'When they sold up the farm, Patrick and his wife moved here to England. He made me promise to send him a Christmas card every year.'

'He, not they?'

'I meant they, of course,' she said, stumbling over her lie and already regretting softening towards him.

Larry kept his eyes on the road ahead. Miriam opened her handbag and began rummaging for a tissue, a sweet, anything to save her face giving everything away. How could she possibly tell this boy, her grandson, the real story of her brief affair with Patrick? What would he think of her, a married woman, carrying on with the Boss Man?

She could never open up to Larry about things like that. Nor could she tell him about how when it ended – abruptly and by mutual agreement – she had tried to end her life. And she would have succeeded, too, had not Dominick found her just in time.

She'd brought so much shame on him, but Dominick had forgiven her. For the remaining years of his life, neither of them had ever mentioned Patrick again. They'd moved away from the farm and the village to the township, where life had been harder for them both. But a hard life was what she deserved, Miriam would tell herself, as she stood in line with the other women waiting her turn for water from the pump.

Life went on, as it must. Dominick got ill and she nursed him dutifully. Having to care for him gradually made her realise just how much she loved him, and how deeply he'd always loved her.

And more – how sad it must have made him, as it made her too – that because of what had happened back in the village where they'd both grown up and where they'd met and married, they couldn't ever revisit their shared memories of that time, because the farm and Patrick had played such a great part in them.

Patrick stopped writing at Christmas, though the cards continued to arrive each year. These days, they were signed by his wife, who appeared to have taken over the tradition, though Miriam had never understood why.

Dutifully, Miriam returned them. But for the last two years of Dominick's life, she broke with the tradition. It seemed a betrayal of Dominick somehow. Then, after his death, it was just too difficult to pick up a pen and write the sad words.

After a few more silent years had passed, a card arrived from Patrick, announcing his wife's death. She wrote back, offering her condolences but giving away little of her own life other than that Dominick had died, too. It was best to keep Patrick at arms' length, she decided, as a mark of respect to her dead husband and Patrick's deceased wife. With practice, keeping Patrick at arms' length with a yearly brief message scribbled on the inside of a Christmas card became easier.

She'd thought long and hard about paying this visit to Patrick's big new house. After all, he hadn't invited her. But then, since she gave so little of herself away, he couldn't know that at the grand age of 81, she had upped sticks and moved to the UK.

'Maybe I should have telephoned first,' she said, when she saw the first road sign that pointed to Oaksey.

'Not getting cold feet, are you, Gran?' Larry said. 'We can turn back if you'd rather not go any further.'

'No,' she said. 'We've come this far.'

Her mouth was beginning to feel dry, something

that always happened when she found herself getting nervous.

'Do you have the number? We could ring and ask them to pass on a message.'

Larry was such a cheeky boy. She'd told him about the huge farm that Patrick had inherited from his parents, with its acres of land and outbuildings beside the main house, and how it had seemed like a palace to the young Miriam, who lived her own life in a two-room shack.

There'd been so many servants running around after the family back in those days. But this was England in 2012. Maybe Patrick would have a housekeeper. Or possibly a butler – isn't that what English gentlemen had? But she doubted he would have both, as Larry's *they* seemed to suggest.

'Next turning on the right,' she said, pointedly ignoring his question. 'Oh, look! It's signposted!'

'Well, obviously, your Patrick is a very important man, Gran,' Larry teased.

'He's not *my* Patrick,' she said, in her most withering voice.

The look she gave Larry was a stern one, but she couldn't be angry with him for long. There wasn't a single malicious bone in that boy's body. And by the time the large manor house came into view, peeking out from behind massive wrought iron gates that stood wide open, as if waiting for them to drive right in, she'd forgotten all about his teasing words.

'This is it, then, Gran. Do you want me to come in with you? It looks like it might be difficult to spot him in among all the others.'

The sign at the gate said drive slowly. There were other signs too. This way to the bursar's residence. That way to the main house. Car parking in another direction. It was all very confusing.

'What's going on here?' Miriam said, puzzled. 'Why has Patrick put up all these signs?'

She glanced over at Larry for some sort of reassurance. He was driving very slowly now, looking around him all the time. He seemed awkward, Miriam thought, as if suddenly afraid of breaking some very bad news to her.

'Gran. Don't you know what kind of place this is?' he asked her.

'Of course I do. It's Patrick's new house,' she said, suddenly cross with him. What was it about young people that they felt compelled to speak to you as if you were an idiot, she wondered.

The lawns on either side of the long drive were manicured to within an inch of their lives. There were wooden benches like the ones she'd seen dotted along the seafront when Rachel, on a rare day off, had driven her to the seaside. And on these benches people sat and chatted.

They were mostly old people like herself, though over by that beautiful weeping willow she spotted three generations of a whole family: children, parents and an old lady sitting in a bath chair with a plaid blanket over her lap.

'Gran.' Larry was speaking more urgently now. 'You saw the sign back there, remember? You commented on it. Rowan House Retirement Complex.'

Miriam struggled to grasp the meaning of her grandson's words.

'I... no... I saw only Rowan House. I stopped looking after that,' she said.

Truth was that as soon as she'd glimpsed the word Rowan, she'd shut her eyes, suddenly giddy with the thought that any minute now she'd finally be standing face to face with Patrick after all these years. She wondered how he would react to seeing her. She would know immediately if he was telling the truth when he stretched out his hand, as he was bound to do as a gentleman, and say how good it was to see her.

'I'm sorry, Gran,' Larry said. 'I thought... Oh, God. This must come as such a shock for you.'

Miriam held herself stiff as the car snaked up the drive. Now they were in front of the house.

'It's nothing,' she said, as the truth sank in. 'I came to visit my friend Patrick, not to have a tour of his house.'

But the Patrick of her imagination was the boy she'd played with, the youth who'd captured her heart and the young man whose body she'd worshipped.

Tall and strong and virile. What was Patrick doing in a home for the elderly?

'Come on, Gran,' Larry said, unbuckling her seatbelt and leaning across to open her door. 'We'll go and find him for you, shall we?'

'No,' she said. 'Please. You go and park the car and wait for me. I need to do this on my own.'

Larry was about to protest, but he saw her determined expression and thought better of it.

'Of course,' he said. 'The entrance is just over there.'

'I'm not blind, Larry,' she snapped.

'I'm sorry. I didn't mean…'

At the sight of his crestfallen face, Miriam immediately regretted her sharp tone.

'No,' she said, taking his hand between hers and gently squeezing it. 'It's me who should be apologising. I'm sorry, Larry. Thank you for driving me all this way. I appreciate it very much.'

And then she turned and walked away from him. Holding her head high, she made her way inside. She was struck immediately by the pictures on the walls and the scent from the huge bouquets of tastefully arranged flowers that decorated the reception desk. People were coming and going, exchanging greetings, stopping to chat. Soft music played. Why, this was more like a hotel lobby than an old people's home, she decided.

'Can I help you?'

A pleasant-faced woman in a dark suit had spotted her and was coming to her aid. The badge on the lapel of her jacket gave her name as Janet Figes and her position as Assistant Manager.

'You look lost,' she added. 'Perhaps I can help you. I'm guessing you're here to visit a friend?'

Such kindness in her eyes. How she wished this lady was one of her neighbours, instead of the woman who glared at her through her window each time she walked down the street to the shopping precinct, where she found herself heading more and more these days, in a bid to find refuge among the crowds and to kill the lonely hours until Rachel and John returned from work.

'Patrick,' she stammered. 'I'm looking for Patrick.'

'Now, which Patrick would that be, I wonder?' Miss Janet Figes furrowed her brow. 'Irish Patrick, Scottish Patrick or South African Patrick?'

Miriam dared to smile. 'South African Patrick,' she said. 'Mr McKinley.'

'In that case, he'll be outside. That's where you'll find him at this time of the day, taking his exercise come rain or shine.'

'But I've just come from outside.' Miriam was growing anxious again. 'I didn't see him there.'

Or perhaps she had, and he was just one more old, bent figure in a bath chair. Her Patrick? No, how could that be?

The lady with the name badge rested her hand

very lightly on Miriam's arm. Immediately she felt calmer.

'I expect he's taking a turn around the lake,' she said. 'I'll take you over there if you like.'

Miriam nodded. 'A lake?' she said. 'You have a lake here? And the people who live here are allowed to walk around it?'

Janet Figes chuckled. 'Of course,' she said. 'This isn't a prison!'

'No, I'm sorry,' Miriam mumbled. 'I can see that.'

Again, the touch on the arm that said *Be calm. I'm your friend. There's no need to be frightened here.* It gave Miriam courage. And as they walked outside, through another door this time, she used her newfound courage to ask Janet Figes an audacious question.

'Tell me,' she said. 'Is Patrick happy here?'

Janet slowed her step while she thought about her answer. 'I'd like to think so,' she said. 'But I think he could be happier. He seems quite reserved. A friend from home is probably just the tonic he needs.'

'Yes,' said Miriam. 'I know that feeling too.'

She could see the lake now, twinkling in the dappled sunlight, although to her eyes it was little more than a pond. But then everything in England came in miniature – the heatwaves, the hills, the patterns on the dresses of the women. Why not the lakes too?

She recognised the solitary figure up ahead immediately and caught her breath. She stumbled and almost lost her footing, but the lady with the badge put out her arm and steadied her. It was as if she understood exactly the significance of this moment, Miriam thought.

'He hasn't changed at all,' she murmured. A little older, a little greyer, but still tall and straight, just as she remembered him.

'He's a very handsome man,' her new friend said.

A flock of birds shrieked as they flew overhead in the pale sky. Patrick, who'd been deep in thought, jumped and raised his eyes, following their flight till they were completely out of sight.

He'd been striding round the lake for the past half hour now, and he was getting bored. Soon it would be time to go indoors and have a cup of tea. No doubt he'd be chivvied over towards a table full of widows, as usual, who would simper at his approach and spend the next 45 minutes quizzing him about life in South Africa, each vying for his attention.

Inevitably, the questions would be the same. Had he ever killed a wild animal? What was it like living through apartheid? Did he miss South Africa? Why had he left and come to live in England?

He had his answers off pat – yes; bleak; yes; and, finally, mind your own business. Not that he would ever say that, of course. My wife had family over here and she felt we had better prospects in the UK, was the reply he'd got into the habit of trotting out.

Both these things were true. Yet there were other,

more personal reasons for leaving South Africa that he couldn't possibly divulge to a table full of inquisitive strangers.

The fact that his wife had found out about his affair with Miriam, for one. How disgusted she'd been. A black woman. A servant. What was he thinking of, dragging their good name into the mud?

Mix that with Miriam's attempted suicide and the rumours that spread like wildfire among the other workers following it. Top it with the day he came face to face with Dominick alone out in one of the fields. Witnessing the hatred in the man's face, he immediately understood how much he and Miriam had hurt Dominick.

There was very little love left between Patrick and his wife by then. But for the sake of his marriage, he had no choice but to do her bidding, sell the farm and move right away.

Sensing that he was being observed, he transferred his gaze from the sky inland. Two figures stood at a distance, moving towards him, the sun behind them. He raised a hand to his eyes to cut out the glare. Damn! Once upon a time he'd had 20-20 vision. They were almost upon him now, and still he couldn't make them out properly.

And then he heard a voice that was instantly familiar, speaking his name, bringing with it so many memories, each rushing in all at once. He smelled the sweetness of the night stock on the air; he heard the rustling of the savannah grasses and the warning hoot of the owl that reminded him it was time for them to part. And there she was before him. Miriam.

* * *

Larry had grown tired of sitting in the car waiting for Gran to come and find him. But he didn't want her blowing her top at him like before. He knew why she'd done it, of course. He was just the same when Mum tried to tell him what was best for him.

Gran was independent and she had all her marbles. Truth was, she was also bored and lonely, though you'd never catch her admitting it. Right now, she probably thought she should be grateful. His house – his parents' house – must seem magnificent compared to the shack she'd grown up in. He'd noticed the amazement in her eyes that first day she'd arrived, when she'd gone round the house taking stock of all their mod cons.

But the downside of all these labour-saving devices for a woman like Gran was that she had nothing to do. She would walk around the kitchen ineffectually wiping the top of the cooker, or she'd plump up a cushion or two in the lounge. She went out when the cleaner came, because she said she couldn't bear to stay home and witness some poor woman cleaning up her mess.

No use him explaining that this poor woman got

good money for what she did, and that pushing a vacuum cleaner around was hardly slave labour. Gran simply wasn't comfortable with being waited on.

By this time, Larry had made his way inside the main building and found the dining room, which was, according to the young, pretty girl in an overall he'd just stopped to ask, where most of the residents were at the minute. If he wanted a cup of tea, she'd bring him one herself, she added. Her smile was warm and flirtatious. Larry detested tea. But right now, a cup of tea was what he wanted more than anything.

It wasn't hard to spot Gran from the entrance of the dining room. She was the darkest woman in the room for one thing, and then there was that dress that you could have spotted a mile off. She was sitting at a table with an old man, and they were rapt in conversation.

The expression on Gran's face was one of sheer joy. The man looked delighted too. Whatever they were talking about was making them both happy, Larry decided. Old people talked about the past a lot, he knew that. Well, they had to, didn't they, as they had very little future left.

Though perhaps he was being just a tiny bit judgmental. He looked around at all the other tables. Over in one corner four women sat huddled together. They'd obviously got dressed up to have their tea and biscuits – the jewellery they were wearing between them must have weighed a ton. It was obvious from the sly looks they were giving Gran and her friend Patrick that they were gossiping about them. Jealous, maybe?

A glance round at the other tables revealed people laughing, joking, or in quiet conversation. One frail old gentleman was smiling at a small girl, who was doing a bit of a dance for him. His great-great-granddaughter, possibly? Her movements drew other eyes towards her and soon she had quite an audience, who clapped her loudly when she finished and demanded an encore.

There was life here in this room. And maybe if people didn't have a long future ahead of them, they had something even more special and important. They had the present. The here and now. Glancing back towards his Gran and Patrick, whose fingers now reached tentatively out towards each other, he decided that, actually, that was probably enough.

'Your cup of tea, sir.' The girl in the overall, who'd crept up behind him, held out the cup and saucer. Her smile was beautiful, and her eyes reeled him in like a fish on a hook.

'Call me Larry,' he said.

'OK, Larry, here's your tea,' she agreed.

'And you are?'

She pointed to her name badge. It took him a long time to read it – Ilona Mancovic.

'Ilona. That's a pretty name,' he said. 'Tell me, Ilona. What time do you get off duty?'

Over on the other side of the room, Miriam caught a glimpse of her grandson talking to a pretty young woman.

'Oh,' she said. 'Here's Larry. He must be wondering where I am.'

'Your grandson, right?' Patrick followed her gaze. 'He's a very handsome boy.'

'He's a very lazy boy,' Miriam said. 'But I don't want to talk about my family anymore. I've told you everything you need to know.'

Patrick nodded. 'You're very lucky to have family so close,' he said. 'I'm here because I don't have anyone.'

'I'm sorry there were no children for you and your wife,' she said. She looked down at her lap. 'I wonder. Was it me? Did she guess?'

'Yes, she knew. She did her best to convince me she was upset about it, but she had her own affairs.'

Patrick took her hand and squeezed it between his two. He wouldn't tell Miriam that it was not the fact he had a mistress that worried Anne, his wife, but the fact that the woman he had chosen and who had chosen him was a black servant woman. Some things were best left unsaid.

'Miriam,' he said. 'All that was a long time ago. Let's not waste time dwelling on the past and what might have been. You're here now, right?'

She nodded. He was right. No point going over and over everything. The pain she felt when he'd told her that their relationship had to end. Did he ever find out about her suicide attempt, she wondered? Well, she wasn't going to tell him about that now. Some things were best left unsaid.

'Are you really glad I've come to see you?' she asked him with her biggest smile. 'Shall I come again?'

'Read my face,' he said. 'You always could.'

His eyes softened and Miriam relaxed. It was OK. He was telling her the truth. That he loved her and welcomed her and wanted her back in his life. And that was a good thing. Because it was exactly where she wanted to be.

First published 2012, *Fiction Feast*

Just How Far

The last day of November brings my first Christmas card written in Aunty Linda's frail, spidery handwriting. *Best Wishes To You And Yours*, it quaintly says, as it says every year. I stare glumly at the nativity scene: Mummy, Daddy, Baby Jesus and various assorted animals. The perfect nuclear family. Tears prick my eyes and I remember that Aunty Linda is one more person I've forgotten to inform.

More cards drop through the letterbox as December arrives – a constant reminder that here are more people to whom I'm going to have to write the words, *Luke and I are getting a divorce*.

'There's only one way to tackle it,' my friend Judy tells me over steaming hot mugs of hot chocolate after our therapeutic early morning swim. 'A round robin.'

'Oh, I don't think so,' I mutter into my drink. 'Not my style at all.'

I've been at the receiving end of a few of these myself, I tell her.

'So why don't you like them?' Judy wants to know.

'Where do I start?' I reply.

I tell her it's the impersonality, for one thing. I don't want the same news as everyone else. I want to think I'm special, even though, of course, I know I'm just one more name on a list to be ticked off with a sigh of relief, once my card has been despatched.

Then there's that mean-spirited little twinge of jealousy I find very hard to ignore, when I read how perfect other people's lives are compared to mine. With their combined promotions and multi-talented children, is it any wonder with my recent track record that I want to stop my ears to such blatant displays of achievement?

'Don't believe a word of what you read,' Judy tells me. 'Round robins are works of fiction, each and every one of them. Face-saving exercises in the gentle British art of keeping a stiff upper lip and putting on a united front to the world.'

I may not agree with what she says, but at least her words kick-start a few brain cells and make me feel less like the corpse I've been since that morning in early January, when Luke finally revealed what had been making him so morose over Christmas.

'Give it a go,' she says, as we hug and part. 'It's

got to be easier than saying the same thing two dozen times. Just remember how far you've come.'

Judy's my rock. Solid, dependable, always there. She knows about divorce, having been through a messy one herself and lived to tell the tale. Perhaps I should take her advice.

Later, I sit in front of the computer. I have one hour to compose my words.

Ross and Cat continue to delight and entertain. Teenagers certainly keep one on one's toes!

The phrase pops into my head from nowhere. I type it out with a flourish, deciding that I can always cut and paste it later or simply erase it completely. I haven't promised Judy that I'll do this. I've only said I'll see. Then I write this:

Luke and I have decided to separate for a while.

I think back to Twelfth Night. Always the worst night of the year for me. The day I swear I'll never get a real Christmas tree again, as I struggle to unblock the vacuum cleaner. Or that next Christmas I won't go anywhere near the mince pies or the pud. All that lies ahead is a diet, cold days and chilly nights and the hefty thump of store-card bills as they hit the mat.

And I think my problems can't get any worse.

It's a mutual decision and a completely amicable one.

'But what do you mean you don't love me anymore? You can't leave. What about the children?'

My voice is high-pitched, shrill. My heart flails against my ribs. His words have winded me, and the lack of oxygen to my brain makes me truly fear I may pass out.

And then I start to yell. Who is she? How long has it been going on? I find my strength again as my accusations grow.

'It's no one,' he says. 'There is no one.'

He tells me that he's just stopped loving me. We have nothing in common apart from the children. They're 15, 16, he reminds me, as if I need reminding. Soon they'll be gone. And what then?

'The rest of my life stretches ahead of me like a wasteland,' he says. 'I've stopped having dreams, stopped making plans. And I can't continue this way.'

'But it's what people do,' I scream at him. 'It's life!'

In that case, he tells me, it's no life at all. Better for both of us to start afresh, while we still can. Before time runs out completely.

Of course, any break-up is a cause for sadness, but I think I can safely say we've both managed to be adult about the whole thing.

The morning after Twelfth Night, I fill bin liner after bin liner with Luke's personal possessions. He wants time to find a place of his own, time to work out exactly what he wants to say to the children. I remind him, with bitter relish, that time is the one thing neither of us has, if I've understood him right. I throw his words right back at him. And then I begin to throw other things.

Something is happening to me. Frantically, I tear open drawers, fling open cupboard doors, sweep the entire contents of a bookshelf into a black plastic bag. I have lost control of my senses. I am like one of those demented, bereaved women I've watched on the TV screen, bewailing her loss unrestrainedly, not caring who hears or sees. I am going mad.

Luke is a dark, huddled figure, shivering in his jacket, ducking the objects that come flying out of the windows. If my neighbours see or hear, they don't respond. In my corner of suburban England, grief and madness are private, shameful things.

Luke and I both feel it is important to remain friends for the sake of the children.

At the weekend, Luke comes to pick up Ross and take him to his football match. I make him wait outside in his car. I will never let him set foot inside this house again, I decide, the day he leaves. And I have kept my word.

Weeks pass. I huddle in my dressing gown. I spend most weekends dressed like this now. During the week I am obliged to get up, to shower, to put on fresh clothes and makeup. But weekends are different. Like a skein of wool unravelling, I watch as the structure of my weekday life rolls away from me.

I don't shop. What's to shop for when I've stopped cooking? We live on takeaways or snacks. I don't visit friends. I can't imagine who would want my company nowadays.

Ross and Cat have been really supportive. I couldn't have come through it without them.

When Ross comes home with tales of Jenny, Luke's new friend, I stop my ears.

'Don't tell me anything about your father,' I snap. 'I do not want to know.'

'Well, you'll have to face it! Dad's got a new girlfriend. She's ten years younger than you, and she's slim and pretty and she doesn't drag herself round the house all day pigging out on junk food.'

With one angry movement, Ross sweeps my empty jumbo bag of crisps onto the floor. For a moment, I am taken aback by the force of his anger. He's not my little boy anymore. He has the same reactions as any adult, wounded alpha male, casting a pre-emptive strike.

'Oh,' he adds, as he barges out of the room, 'and she laughs a lot too.'

Later, in my bed – the bed I used to share with Luke and where I still cannot bring myself to move away from my half – I mull over Ross's words.

Cat's music thumps remorselessly from behind her door. She's meant to be revising for her exams. But I know what she's really doing. Avoiding me.

Thankfully, both Luke and I have managed to move on.

Luke's new friend is now his lover. Official. Ross reports sightings of her toothbrush nestling cosily next to Luke's. Her drying smalls casually thrown over the bathroom radiator.

Luke wants to see me about the children. He thinks we should be more amicable in our dealings. I don't think so.

One day, I catch my reflection in the mirror, and I'm horrified by how much weight I've put on. Grief is meant to make you thin. It's happiness that makes you fat. Yet Luke, according to his son, who has taken to spending most weekends with his father and new squeeze, has shed ten pounds, and with it the same number of years.

Of course, I only have the son's word for that, since I will not allow the father through the front door. And Cat can't back her brother up, since she refuses point blank to go anywhere near her dad's place. She prefers her room and her music. And she must work for these exams. It's not going too well, according to her last report. Of course, I know who I blame.

Cat did really well in her GCSEs, considering the events of this year. In the end, she decided to do her 'A' levels at the local further education college where she can also combine a couple of resits.

When she opens the letter that contains her results, I can see right away how disappointed she is. I long to put my arms around her and tell her it doesn't matter a jot. I know how much she's been longing to go to sixth-form college with the rest of the gang. And now, with these results, they won't have her.

I wait for her to say something – anything. But she doesn't say a word. She simply folds the piece of paper into a small square and replaces it in the envelope.

'If your father hadn't left,' I long to shout. 'He's to blame for all this mess.'

I don't say it, of course. But it's there on my face in bold print for Cat to read.

September brought the start of a new term for Ross, the beginning of a new adventure at college for Cat and a new hobby, and with it new friendships, for me.

I decide to pass on summer. Not much sun, little fun, let's leave it at that. It's at the swimming pool, at the beginning of September, that I meet Judy. Pounding the lanes, side by side with grim determination, we finally acknowledge each other after a week or two has passed. We find ourselves drinking our hot chocolate together, engage in small talk and discover we have things in common – children, errant husbands. We gradually open up, mutually displaying hearts in varying stages of disrepair.

She tells me about her divorce, her determination to get through it. To me, she looks as if she has already. I tell her how much I admire her attitude, that it's taken all this time for me to get my act together, to try and lose some weight by coming swimming every day, and to get out of my dressing gown at weekends at last.

'You'll get there,' she tells me. 'I just know you will.'

My hour is up. One of the children is back. I scroll back to my initial sentence.

Ross and Cat continue to delight and entertain. Teenagers certainly keep one on one's toes!

The front door slams. It's Cat. Speedily, I save my document and log out.

'Aye, aye,' she jokes, as she breezes into the room and immediately spots my guilty expression. 'Caught you hitting on some strange guy on the internet, have I?'

I haven't seen her so light-hearted in a long while. She looks positively radiant in her skinny top and tight jeans, her hair a cloud of gold caressing her slim shoulders. There's someone hovering behind her. Male, tall, and shy-looking.

'This is Ben,' she says. 'He's on my course.'

'Hi, Ben,' I say.

He returns a muttered, strangled greeting. He has more hair than she does, I notice.

'Come on,' she says proprietorially. 'Hungry? Mum does a mean cake.'

He looks at her adoringly. Follows her into the kitchen. Sneakily, I re-open my document.

Cat's decision to swap to her present course is definitely the right one. She's making friends and growing into a lovely, self-confident young woman with a great sense of humour.

This time, I realise that I'm not lying. Not even close to embroidering the truth.

The front door opens again. The sound of shoes being kicked off, a heavy backpack being dropped on the floor, a coat slithering to the ground. Ross's usual routine on returning from school.

But then he breaks it, his usual scowl morphing into an expression of surprise.

'You're smiling!' he says, observing me from the doorway.

For a second it feels like we've connected. But the moment is short-lived. He slumps into a chair, without returning my smile.

'Good day?' I ask.

I never expect an answer to this one and it comes as no surprise to get nothing more than a shrugged reply. Perhaps I should get back to my round robin. But there's a heaviness in his posture, a weariness around his eyes. He's going to ask me something and expects me to say no.

'What is it, Ross?'

Not trouble, please.

'Have you forgotten about tonight?' he asks me.

Oh God! Of course. I turn back to my screen. Type something.

'I've got appointments with all my teachers,' he says.

And Ross makes us so proud. Tonight is parents' evening,

so perhaps I should wait till after the event to write those words. Luke and I will both be there to support him, of course.

I brace myself. Smile.

'I wish you'd come,' Ross says.

I can see from his face just how heartfelt his words are.

'Will she be there?' I ask him. 'Jenny?'

It's the first time I have acknowledged that she has a name. It tastes like a bitter pill in my mouth.

'Of course not,' Ross says. 'What has my education got to do with her? You're my mum. And Dad's my dad. And I want you both to be there.'

This is surely the longest speech Ross has made all year. He's bright, articulate and shows a maturity beyond his years. Now, there's a stunning sentence for a round robin.

'You're smiling again,' he says. 'Does that mean you're coming?'

'It does,' I say.

'Think how far you've come.' I recall Judy's words.

'And maybe the three of us can get a curry or something afterwards. There might be stuff we need to say.'

Cat is in the room. Funny how she always is when food is mentioned. The boyfriend isn't far behind.

'What's this?' she wants to know.

I tell her. Her face lights up.

'Can we come?' she asks.

'Depends who's paying,' I joke.

'I'll ring Dad,' Ross says and jumps up from his chair.

I take one last look at my round robin before deleting it. Tomorrow, I'll go out and buy a pack of Christmas cards. I don't care who knows about Luke and me. That was last year's news. I've come a long way since then.

First published 2005, *Woman's Weekly*

Gabriel's Story

The women huddled round the baby's cot like a Greek chorus. This was a huge one all right. Nine pounds! Why, my twins combined weight at birth didn't add up to that, someone said. And wasn't his cry loud? It drowned out the kitten cries they'd grown used to, being on a ward with babies so much tinier.

'We should give him a name,' one said. 'It's not nice for a baby just to have a label on his wrist that says Baby Smith.'

'What about Gabriel? Like the angel.'

'Well, I suppose it *is* Christmassy.'

'I like it. It's classy.'

'Me too. He deserves a classy name. He's not got much else on his side, has he?'

'Poor little mite.'

'What kind of a mother would refuse to visit her own newborn baby? Just because of a cleft palate.'

'A heartless one, I'd say.'

Everyone agreed.

'Is that the lunch trolley? I'm starving,' someone said.

Heads turned and eyes lit up. Breast feeding stimulated the appetite, it was a well-known fact, and there was nothing else to do on the ward between now and visiting time.

The Greek chorus melted away, leaving baby Gabriel alone in his cot, kicking up his sturdy legs defiantly. Apart from the mewling of the other, much tinier babies, the nursery was quiet at last. There was nothing for it but to go to sleep.

Betty Prior was late for work. Christmas meant the buses ran at odd times. It also meant that taxis were thin on the ground. Tonight, Christmas Eve, everyone was set to party and had booked their cabs weeks in advance.

'You really shouldn't have left it this late, love,' she'd been told by every smug taxi operator she'd rung.

Betty was far too polite to let her irritation show. She'd always hated drawing attention to herself and would never have dreamt of screeching down the phone.

'Well, thanks anyway,' she ended up saying lamely,

every time. 'I did mean to, I just forgot. I can't think why.'

Which made her even later, of course. In the end, she had no choice but to walk. It was a cold night, but a dry one, thank God. And the exercise would do her good. She wrapped up well, blessing the fact she'd been clever enough to send for that old-fashioned snood she'd spotted advertised in the copy of the *The People's Friend* she'd found lying on a chair in the patients' TV lounge.

It might not be to everyone's taste, but Betty had never been a fashion victim. The snood kept her ears and neck warm, and if she felt like it, she could draw it right up over her nose. Ideal for this weather!

Before she'd gone far, she decided she needed chocolate – fuel for the long hike ahead, although she doubted there'd be a shop open. Not if her luck with taxis was anything to go by.

But then, up ahead, she spied a lit-up shop window.

'And lo, up above she saw a star!'

Betty spoke the words aloud. Well, there was no one about. Besides, she was only getting into the Christmas spirit.

The other midwives thought she was crazy volunteering to work a double shift over Christmas Eve and into Christmas Day. But maybe they had families of their own. Stockings to fill, turkeys to baste and all those Christmas presents to wrap.

It was different for her. Oh, she'd had the odd invitation. But she'd never felt comfortable intruding in what, after all, was really a family occasion.

Besides, she loved working at The General. With her air of quiet respect, she was a favourite with the doctors. The other nurses liked her and, for the most part, so did the patients. You'd get the odd one or two unpleasant ones, but that was the world we lived in, Betty had long decided. She'd soon learned the best way to deal with ignorance was to be extra polite.

Cheered by the sudden unexpected change in her fortune, Betty approached the shop and pushed open the glass door, reluctantly pulling down the snood so her face was exposed. Well, she didn't want to look like she was going in to rob the place and give the owner a heart attack! The rich aroma of Indian spices hit her nostrils and the sudden warmth, in contrast to the cold outside, made her face flush.

Behind the counter sat a young, pretty Asian girl in western dress, her long black hair hanging down over her shoulders. When the bell pinged to herald Betty's arrival, the girl looked up from her magazine.

Betty was on the point of saying something. The sort of thing you said on a night like this. Parky out, isn't it? I bet you're glad you're behind that counter. But one look at the girl's face told her not to push it.

She decided to pick up a box of chocolates for the other midwives to dip into as well as getting a bar for her journey. In her opinion, it was always nice to bring the festivities into the ward.

It took her a while to make her selection and she became so absorbed in her task that it was a while before she realised she was being watched.

'Could it be?'

A man – Asian, like the girl behind the counter – dressed in a white coat over casual clothes, and with his jet-black hair greying slightly at the temples, was on his knees stacking a low shelf with bottles. Pausing in his task, he beamed up at her. 'I'm right, aren't I?' he said. 'It *is* you!'

'Er. I'm sorry. Do I know you?' she said.

The man struggled to his feet, dusted his hands on his trousers and reached out his hand towards her.

'Amrit Rajania. This is my shop. And the little girl sitting behind the counter over there is my daughter, Jasleen.'

He cocked his head at an angle and called out to the daughter in question: 'Jasleen! Come and say hello to this very special lady!'

The girl slid off her stool with a great deal of attitude but, obediently enough, sloped across to say hello. Betty glanced around the shop. Special lady? There was only one customer in the shop, and she was it.

'You still haven't got a clue, have you?' Mr Rajania was still beaming.

'I confess…'

Time was getting on and if she wasn't out of this shop within the next two minutes she was going to be seriously late. She grabbed the nearest box of chocolates. Too bad they were the most expensive in the shop.

'You delivered her!'

Betty racked her brains. She'd long ago lost count of all the babies she'd delivered over the years. Her eyes flickered over the face of the girl as, tentatively – trying not to look absolutely disgusted by the ordeal she was being forced to undergo – she put out her slim brown hand and muttered, 'Pleased to meet you.'

'May 11th 1986. Remember?'

Of course! A triple celebration. Her own birthday, her first single-handed delivery, and a perfect baby at the end of a relatively simple labour.

'Goodness me! Where does the time go?'

She knew she'd fallen back on a cliché, but she sincerely hoped this response would suffice – the clock on the wall said she had 15 minutes to get to work if she wanted to arrive on time.

Unfortunately, the cliché wasn't remotely sufficient for Mr Rajania, who launched into a protracted reminiscence of the day in question, dwelling in detail on the finer points of his wife's labour. His daughter, looking so bored that Betty could only surmise she knew the story off by heart, stood idly by, looking anywhere but at Betty.

'And it was only after Kiran had been safely

delivered of a healthy seven pounder that you let us in on your little secret – you'd never delivered a baby on your own before,' he finished by saying.

Despite her concerns over the time, Betty allowed herself a little nostalgic wallow. It had, indeed, been a memorable occasion.

Here were two people, man and wife, prepared to put all their trust in her – plain Betty Prior – and calmly and efficiently she'd done her job like she'd been doing it all her life. Perhaps if it had been a different couple – one less meek and mild and more demanding – she'd have faltered and made mistakes. As it was, their confidence in her had proved her inspiration. She probably had just as much to thank them for as they had to thank her.

'Fancy you remembering me!' she said.

'Oh, I never forget a face,' the shopkeeper replied.

Betty felt her cheeks burn. She glanced at her feet, wondering how soon she could make a polite exit.

'Dad!' the girl hissed.

'Forgive me. You are right to reprimand,' he said. 'I'm too familiar.' With a hangdog face, he added, 'She's always telling me off for it, you know.'

'Please, don't worry about it,' Betty said.

She'd rather taken to this man. She felt instinctively that he was kind and honest and an excellent provider for his family. His shop was clean, and his shelves were well-stocked and tidy. She decided that he probably knew all his customers by name. But even so, she had a job to go to.

'So,' she said, in one final, determined burst to draw the conversation to a close. 'You will give my respects to your wife, won't you? I'd stay to say hello, only I'm very late for work!'

Mr Rajania suddenly looked crestfallen. 'In fact,' he said, 'my wife didn't live to see Jasleen reach her tenth birthday. She died of a long illness, unfortunately.'

Betty was covered in embarrassment. Embarrassment tinged with sadness at the thought of Jasleen growing up without a mother and of a life cut short so tragically young. The world was a cruel place indeed.

'I'm really so very sorry,' she said.

The image of a young, frightened girl rose in her mind. Big, dark eyes, a soft voice. It seemed like yesterday. And now the girl was gone, almost before she'd grown to be a woman.

The grocer waved her apology away. 'No, no. It's quite all right. You couldn't possibly have known,' he said. 'But listen, if you're late, why don't you let me take you to work in my car.'

Betty was sorely tempted. Sitting in a warm car instead of freezing to death was infinitely preferable to walking.

'I couldn't presume,' she said, half hoping he'd insist.

Jasleen chose that moment to show her perfect pearly teeth. 'Don't think it's a favour,' she grinned. 'If I know my dad, he'll charge you!'

'Jasleen!' Amrit Rajania cast his daughter a murderous look. 'As if I would ever dream of charging the woman who brought you into this world.'

Then he seemed to think again. 'Or maybe I should charge her treble for being responsible for bringing such a witch as you into my life!'

He wagged his finger at her. His words were harsh, but it was clear from his twinkling eyes that he was devoted to her.

Jasleen grinned. 'My father's starting a new business,' she explained. 'He's taken up taxi driving. You'll be his first customer. And no doubt he'll give you a fistful of cards to pin up round the hospital.'

'Well, if I can be of any help,' Betty said.

'Indeed, you can,' Amrit replied. 'You can do me the honour of being the first in the passenger seat. You are bound to bring my new venture good luck. Jasleen, my coat. We have to hurry!'

So it was that Betty got to work not just on time but with minutes to spare. In the rest room the other midwives were discussing Gabriel.

'He's going to be hard work,' complained one. 'All that spoonfeeding. By the time he's got to the end of one feed it'll be time to start another.'

The others commiserated glumly.

'What's up?' Betty asked, as she removed her snood.

She didn't think she was imagining the shift in atmosphere. Whatever was up, no one seemed to want to let her in on it. It was up to Jane, a small, pretty blonde girl who hadn't been qualified for long, to finally and haltingly relate the story of Gabriel's abandonment to Betty.

'Maybe I should go and introduce myself,' she said.

'Doesn't it make you angry?' Jane said. 'His mum abandoning him like that? I know it does me.'

Betty smiled. 'People want perfect babies,' she said. 'More, they think they're entitled to it these days. Put yourself in the mother's place. All those months spent imagining exactly what he'll look like and then the shock of reality. I'm sure the mother will come round eventually.'

'You're always so fair to people, Betty,' someone else said.

'I'm here to support new mothers,' Betty replied. 'Not to judge them. There's plenty of people out there blaming them for all society's ills without me adding to it.'

There were nods of agreement. 'Right enough,' muttered someone. 'That's true, Betty,' said someone else.

Betty dived into her bag, bringing out the chocolates she'd left the shop with.

There were shrieks of appreciation as everyone fell over each other in their race for their favourite, and with that, all discussion of Gabriel was over.

'What a humungous box! Must've cost you a fortune, Betty,' someone said.

'Actually, they were a present.'

'From an admirer?'

Betty's face grew warm again. First in the shop and now here in the middle of the hospital staffroom. She wished she could grow out of being so self-conscious. But at her age, if it hadn't happened yet then there was little chance it ever would. She sensed everyone was expecting her answer. Oh, well, she had nothing to hide, whatever they might prefer to think.

'Nothing like that,' she said, trying to sound casual. 'Just an ex-patient – or rather the husband of an ex-patient, that's all. Apparently, I delivered his daughter. He simply wouldn't allow me to pay for these, however many times I offered.'

Nonchalantly, she rifled through the box and popped a Caramel Cluster into her mouth. 'Come on now, girls. Help yourselves before the doctors find them!' she added. 'You know what gannets that lot are.'

The rest of Betty's shift was hectic. She loved working on Diana Ward. To her, it was much more satisfying than the conveyor belt atmosphere of the other wards. This is where the problem babies stayed. Some were slightly premature and unable to feed independently; others were jaundiced and needed treatment. At the moment, there were two sets of twins and one of triplets. There was a mother whose infant was over in the special care baby unit, born at 26 weeks and in an incubator. And then there was Gabriel.

Mums and babies stayed longer here, some for as long as a fortnight or more, so often strong relationships were forged. But of course, she was always happy when the sickly babies grew strong enough to be taken home. There was nothing more satisfying, when the time came, than carrying an infant, whose chances of survival had been low, right off the hospital premises and all the way to a waiting car to be whisked home at last.

She didn't have a minute to go down to the nursery until it was almost midnight. One of the orderlies was grudgingly feeding Baby Gabriel with a tiny spoon, and most of the formula was ending up *on* rather than *in* him.

Dismissing the orderly – who she decided would do less damage changing the nappy of a wailing baby nearby – Betty took over.

'So, you're Gabriel,' she said, holding him close as she began to feed him.

Warily, he stared up at her with his huge blue eyes, frowning slightly as he accustomed himself to a change of carer.

'What a handsome young man you are,' she said.

'I hope you don't mind me giving you your supper. Only your mummy's not here just yet. She will be soon, though, just give her a chance.'

All babies, however sick, however young, revelled in being talked to. If Betty had learned one thing over her years as a midwife, then this was the most important one. It amazed her that people still maintained that babies only smiled after six weeks, or that they could barely focus when they were newly born.

Over the years, she'd observed differently. She'd found herself relating her theory to Amrit, as he'd driven her to the hospital through the icy streets.

'When you first look into a newborn's eyes,' she said, 'it's like they know all the secrets of the world. And with every ounce or two they gain in weight it's as if they shed another ounce or two of wisdom. When they're ready to go home they look at you in quite another way.'

'Like they've forgotten everything, you mean?' Amrit said. 'As if they've finally grown into being simple babies?'

'That's exactly right!'

'Then they spend the rest of their lives trying to remember what it was they knew when they first got here,' he added, with a chuckle. 'And they never do. Not even when they get to be as old as we are.'

'You don't think I'm mad, then?'

His opinion was suddenly very important.

'No,' he said. 'I don't think that at all. In fact, I'd go so far as to say that I think you are a very spiritual person.'

They'd reached the lights, which were at red, and for the first time Amrit allowed himself to take his eyes off the road.

'That's a very good thing to be, though not so well appreciated in these material times,' he added, resting his dark brown eyes on her face.

Then the lights changed and once more they were on the move, isolated from the dark, impersonal night speeding past their window. In the velvety warmth of the car, the two of them connected by a thread of unspoken thoughts.

A cough and a splutter from Gabriel jolted Betty out of her reverie. How long had she been sitting here, thinking about her conversation with Amrit, lulled into a trance by the warm proximity of Gabriel's little body in her arms?

She'd have liked to stay here all night, in lieu of his mother ever putting in an appearance, but there were other babies making other equally urgent demands on her time.

The rest of the night followed with periods of calm interspersed with sudden eruptions of activity. In the morning, one of the paediatricians did his turn as Santa, to the admiration of all the young nurses – not to mention quite a few of the older ones, too – who secretly harboured a crush on him. A skeleton choir made up of anyone who could be persuaded to take part, either going off or coming on shift, sang under the tree as usual, and Secret Santa gifts were exchanged among the staff to varying degrees of delight and disappointment.

Now it was time for Betty to go home. She was exhausted, but first she felt compelled to go and say goodbye to Gabriel. Maybe it was sentimental of her to think that he'd grown as fond of her as she had of him, but more than one of the mums had remarked how he seemed to respond to her feeding him much more than he did the other nurses.

She'd said it was just practice. After all, she'd been in the job a long time. But inwardly she'd wondered if perhaps Gabriel sensed how much her heart went out to him – a helpless baby, neglected just because of a disfigurement.

It was quiet in the nursery. A woman was bending over Gabriel's cot. At first, Betty assumed it was one of the orderlies checking up on him, but it was apparent from the woman's dress – sweatpants and a baggy t-shirt – that the figure rocking the cradle could only have been Gabriel's mother.

For a while, Betty remained with her hand on the door, observing the mother, as, awkwardly, she scooped Gabriel up in her arms. Then, almost as if she sensed she was being observed, the woman turned round, spotted Betty and let out a startled cry.

'I didn't mean to frighten you,' Betty said,

approaching warily. 'I'm going off shift in a little while and I wanted to say goodbye to... to your son.'

The woman's eyes remained transfixed on Betty's face. Suddenly embarrassed, Betty put her hand to her mouth, to cover it.

'I'm sorry,' the woman said. 'You must think I'm really rude. I didn't mean to stare.'

Then she glanced away from Betty and down at the face of her own son. Tears began to trickle down her face.

'He's going to be all right, you know,' Betty said, gently.

She felt that if she took one step towards this poor, dispirited young woman, she might collapse completely.

'I can imagine how hard it must be for you to think that your son's not perfect,' she said. 'But, believe me, they can do wonders nowadays.'

Awkwardly, she touched her own mouth again. 'An awful lot better than the job they made on me,' she said.

'I just want him to have a normal life, like any other child. I can't bear the thought of people looking at him like he's a freak,' the woman said, staring down at her son.

Betty shrank back. The woman didn't mean it, she was sure. She was so wrapped up in her own concerns that it was easy for Betty to forgive her choice of word. She'd been called a freak before, anyway, and got over it.

Through a mist of tears, the woman took her eyes off her baby and addressed Betty angrily. 'Tell me, how do you cope?' she said. Her eyes were the same fierce blue as Gabriel's, Betty suddenly saw.

She shrugged. 'You just do,' she said. 'You take some knocks, but then who doesn't? I bet even Kate Moss has her fat days.'

The woman blinked back her tears and smiled a wobbly smile. 'He's got such beautiful eyes, hasn't he?' she said.

Betty nodded.

'After a bit, you know, you almost don't see it,' she added.

Betty nodded again.

'And after the operation you won't,' she reassured her.

'They all think the world of you in here, those other mums I've spoken to. The nurses do, too,' the woman said.

'Nonsense.' Betty brushed the words away. 'I do my job, that's all. Just like everyone else in this place.'

'You're like me,' the woman said. 'You can't bear compliments.'

Betty didn't say that she'd had so few in her life that she hadn't had much practice in accepting them gracefully. 'Thank you for taking care of him for me.

You look tired. Please. You don't need to stay. We'll be all right now.'

'I'm sure you will be,' Betty said.

Dropping a kiss on Gabriel's head, she wished him goodbye and Happy Christmas. Then, with a wave to the other babies in the nursery, she turned on her heels and left the room.

Home, she decided. A hot bath, a cup of tea and bed. She dug into her coat pockets for her gloves. Then her fingers made contact with something else. A card. Of course, Amrit's business card. Maybe she should ring him. Put a bit of business his way.

But she didn't need to. Because, as she stepped outside to meet the chilly Christmas morning, there was his cab, with Amrit at the wheel.

First published 2005, *Fiction Feast*

After Christmas

Since his father's heart attack, Nazir had been running the shop more or less single-handedly, apart from some help from his mum and his sister Laila at busy times. But it was still his father's name above the shop door, as he never failed to point out whenever he thought Nazir was overreaching himself with his suggestions of how to improve the business.

'What's the point opening up at the usual time on Christmas Day?' he'd grumbled to his mother last night, just before he'd sloped off to bed.

His mother had been on Dad's side, of course. No matter that Nazir was a grown man of 22. As far as she was concerned, he was still a kid in short pants.

'You heard your dad,' she said. 'Because people expect it. What happens when they pop in for a paper on their way to work an early shift one day and they find out we're not open? Next day they make a detour and go somewhere else.'

'But that's my point!' Sometimes Nazir felt he was banging his head against a brick wall. 'There *are* no papers tomorrow. And people don't work on Christmas Day. Most people, anyway.'

'Just do it, son, OK? We can't have your father upset.'

There were dark shadows under her eyes, and her face, like the hand she laid on his arm as she spoke, had grown thinner these last few months. Dad was home from hospital now and he was on the mend. But it had been touch and go for a long time and the worry of it had left its physical mark on her.

Nazir propped the newsstand by the shop door, then loitered for a minute on the pavement, hugging himself against the cold as he scanned the street for life. Wasn't it supposed to snow on Christmas Day? He looked up at the sky expectantly. Only on films and in books did the weather reflect nature's mood. He knew all about that from when he'd done his English Literature 'A' level at college. Pathetic fallacy, it was called.

By rights there should have been a howling storm the day his dad collapsed and was rushed to hospital in a wailing ambulance. But it was a beautiful day at the end of summer; the sun shone from a blazing blue sky and every park and garden he drove past en route to the hospital – sick to his stomach with the fear that when he finally made it through the mad traffic he'd be too late – was ablaze with colour.

Much good it did him now, knowing all those literary terms. Three 'A' levels and what was he doing? Serving in his dad's shop. He'd more or less given up his place at uni because of Dad's heart attack. They'd told him they'd defer it for a term if he wanted. Stupidly he'd said no, convinced Dad wasn't going to make it and he'd have to stick around to look after his mum and sister.

'Don't commit to your decision just yet,' the lady he'd spoken to on the phone had said. 'Ring again after Christmas. Hopefully, you'll be able to think a bit straighter then.'

After Christmas. It was like this woman thought the phrase had special powers attached to it. Christmas was just a few days – 12 at most. When it was over, he'd still be stuck behind that counter, waving an envious goodbye to his friends as they left for the spring term.

'You open yet, Naz?' Someone's gruff voice roused him from his meditation.

It was Tom, one of his mates from school. In his first year at Leicester. Lucky beggar. He was looking the worse for wear, it had to be said.

'You on the way out or on the way back?' Naz said.

'Back, man,' Tom said, adding that his hangover was starting to kick in and he was in need of painkillers.

'In that case step this way.' Naz bent low and made a sweeping gesture with his hand as he opened the door for his first customer. 'We've got more choice than the chemist's. Plus, we're open and they're not.'

'Cheers, mate.' Tom strode through the open door. 'Any chance of a bag of crisps for being your first customer of the day?'

'What do you think it is? Christmas?' Naz said. He grinned as he playfully pushed his friend inside.

Julie wasn't asleep. She could only ever sleep fitfully when Tom was out late. Funny, she had no idea what he got up to or what time he got in these days, now he was away at university, and most of the time she didn't give it a moment's thought. But as soon as he was home, she reverted to her old habit of staying awake till he got back.

Next to her, Brian snored contentedly. Nothing would ever disturb his sleep. How she envied him. She worried too much about Tom, he was always telling her that. 'You've got to cut the apron strings, Julie,' he was always saying.

He was right, of course. If only it were so easy. She didn't choose to be such a worrier. But it had been impossible not to notice the change in Tom since the last time she'd seen him at the beginning of autumn.

For a start he was pasty faced, a bit spotty, if truth be told. Too many pizzas and take away curries, Brian had concluded in that no-nonsense way he had of dismissing her maternal worries. A couple of weeks of home cooking and plenty of fresh vegetables and he'd look as fresh-faced as he had when he'd left in the summer.

But what if Brian was wrong? Tom had been so restless since coming back for Christmas. Always dashing off here, there and everywhere. Unwilling to sit and watch TV with them of an evening or have a natter over lunch. It was like he was avoiding staying in one place deliberately, in case she started quizzing him.

The sound of footsteps trudging up the path alerted her that Tom was home at last. Five-thirty in the morning. Where on earth could he have been till then? No point asking. She knew what answer she'd get. Just chillin', Mum.

If he *was* avoiding them, she wondered, then why? She was going to have to have it out with him sooner or later, even if it meant positioning herself in front of the door and refusing point blank to let him leave the room until he'd told her what the reason was. But not till after Christmas. She didn't want to risk ruining the celebrations.

Yasmin heard voices coming from the shop downstairs. She smiled to herself. Abbas would be pleased to be able to tell Nazir that he'd been right to insist they opened at their usual time today. Nazir wouldn't be too thrilled to hear it, though. *Rubbing my nose in it*, he'd say, and he wouldn't be far wrong.

Since his heart attack, it was as if Abbas had to remind everyone that he was still the man of the house. She tried to be supportive. But he'd never been an easy man at the best of times. Just the slightest suggestion that perhaps it was time to think about retiring sent him into one of his tirades.

He'd be back to full health in no time, he insisted. Meanwhile, Nazir was perfectly capable of holding the reins. Should she have made more of a stand? Disabuse him of his conviction that Nazir was more than happy to give up his place at university to serve in the shop?

Abbas was so old-fashioned. Family came first. Never mind a person's individual hopes and dreams. He was proud too. Happy to let Nazir do the donkeywork but adamant that it was *his* name that remained over the shop door.

'Perhaps if Daddy made Naz manager, then he wouldn't mind so much giving up his place at uni,' Laila had said, only last week.

She noticed things, that girl, even though she was still barely 13. She'd seen how serious her brother was these days, witnessed his sense of fun withering away. Yasmin hadn't replied, just smiled.

It would have been lovely, had it been true. But Nazir wasn't interested in becoming a businessman. His vocation lay elsewhere. Sooner or later, she was going to have to confront Abbas. Tell him a few home truths. But not today. Today was Christmas Day. Those things she was determined to say would still be there in a few days. She'd do it after Christmas.

Why had he drunk so much? Tom's head was still spinning as he pulled the duvet over his head. In about five hours' time he'd be expected to get up and wish Mum and Dad a Merry Christmas and do his share before everyone turned up for the spectacular lunch his parents always concocted between them. How was he going to keep up the relentless jollity that was bound to be expected of him, back from his first term at university and with a hundred and one tales to tell?

Except he didn't. He only had one. And it was that he never should have gone. He hated it there. The block of student flats he was in with its thin walls and its thin curtains that made it impossible to sleep; the other students who all seemed far more confident than he was.

As for the lectures – they were impenetrable – so

much so that he'd stopped going. Hadn't been for four weeks now. Hence the letter from the Dean that he'd stuffed inside one of the many pockets of his big suitcase.

He'd had other letters – at least two from his tutor. But this was the Big One. They were going to kick him out. He was sure of it, however they dressed things up in fancy words. He should have felt deliriously happy. After all, it was what he wanted, wasn't it?

Yes, if it meant he didn't have to look at those physics textbooks again. Every time he did, he got panic attacks. He'd only scraped a halfway decent 'A' level grade in the subject because Dad had coughed up to pay a tutor to go through the practice papers with him and knock the wretched subject into his head.

He'd just about got away with it, as long as Mrs Banks was at the end of an email address to explain the hard stuff when he felt himself going under again. But there was no Mrs Banks at uni. Just a bunch of lecturers who spouted stuff at you that you didn't get, then sent you away with a pile of experiments to do.

Whenever she came across him pouring over one of his textbooks, his mum always used to say that physics was like a foreign language to her. It wasn't like a foreign language to him. French and German he used to *get*. But he'd had to give them up after GCSE.

'It's science and maths you need these days if

you're going to get a decent, well-paid job,' Dad had insisted.

And so, he'd gone along with it. Why hadn't he put up more of a fight? Just said no, he wanted to carry on with his languages and his drama. He knew why, of course. Because Dad was bankrolling him, and he wouldn't have had a leg to stand on.

Well, look at him now. He'd still failed. And his dad had failed too, because he wasn't going to be able to brag to all his mates at work about his clever son who was doing a science degree.

The clock radio by his bed said 6.45 in luminous green digits. Why couldn't he go to sleep? He didn't think he'd slept for weeks. He was going to have to tell them, sooner or later. What about round the dining room table, just as Dad was about to carve the turkey, his face tinged pink with the first of many glasses of wine?

He could see it now, the gasps, the groans, the tears, the embarrassed hush of the relatives as they put on their coats and slid silently away, leaving Tom to suffer the worst of the fallout alone.

No. Not today. He couldn't bring himself to ruin the dinner his mum always put so much love and effort into. He'd tell them after Christmas. He'd be ready then.

Julie pushed open the door of the corner shop. They weren't Christian, the Dars, but they still put the decorations up. It was Twelfth Night today and she could hear Nazir's mum humming as she set about her task of taking down the tinsel for another year. She seemed very cheerful, hopping on and off her little stool to reach for another paperchain. Perhaps her husband was finally getting properly better.

Naz was nowhere to be seen, she noticed. They'd always been good friends at school, Naz and Tom. Had Tom confided in Naz first, before he'd come clean to them? Surely, he couldn't have kept his terrible secret to himself all this time!

'Oh, I'm sorry. I didn't see you there!'

Naz's mum – what was her name, Julie felt bad for not remembering – stepped off her stool. She couldn't remember the names of *any* of Tom's friends' parents, if truth were told. It had always been Jack's mum, Harry's dad, Rob's step-mum.

'Just getting rid of the remains of Christmas,' she said, beaming at Julie. 'I tell you, I won't be sorry to say goodbye to the old year.'

'I'm sure,' Julie replied. 'How *is* your husband now?'

'He's well,' Naz's mum replied.

Julie couldn't tell if she was speaking the truth. Stuff went on in families that everyone covered up. Heavens, she should know all about that! The rows they'd had, backwards and forwards. Tom in tears, her too. On and on it went. Till finally Brian's fury had burnt itself out and the point had been reached at last where they could all start talking to each other as civilised human beings who loved each other.

'I'm glad,' Julie said. 'And Naz? He's not in the shop.'

Naz's mum smiled. 'No, you're right,' she said. 'Actually, he's upstairs, sorting out his future.'

'Oh?'

'From now on it will be me running the shop,' she said. 'Abbas will help, as and when he's able. But Naz is off to university next term. They've said they'll take him late, though he'll have a lot of work to catch up with.'

'I'm sure he'll manage,' Julie said. 'He's a very clever boy. I'm so glad it's worked out for him in the end.'

Yasmin smiled her serene smile. It *had* worked out in the end, yes. But it had taken an awful lot of persuasion and scraping away at that thick, tall wall of stubbornness and pride that Abbas had surrounded himself with.

In the end it was love that had won. Abbas had always loved his family. He just didn't always notice things, he'd said, when she'd explained just how unhappy their son was. And how *she* would love to run the shop. It was from her that Naz got his ability with figures after all, she'd teased, even though they didn't make him happy like they did her.

'Give me the chance to share the running of the business,' she'd pleaded, 'while you concentrate on getting 100 percent well.'

The best thing he could do for her, she'd said, tenderly, was to live. Because if he carried on the way he had, with the weight of the business on his shoulders alone, then he would have another heart attack. And she would never forgive him if he died. Shock tactics were the only thing ever to work with Abbas.

'And what about your son,' Yasmin asked. 'How is Tom enjoying university?'

Julie had never been very good at pretending. She suspected it was from her that Tom had inherited his own inability to hide his anxiety.

'Actually, Tom won't be going back next term,' she said.

There, she'd managed to get it out for the first time. It would be easier next time, and every time after that.

'Oh? I'm sorry.'

To her credit, Naz's mum looked like she meant it. What she dreaded was the fake concern she suspected some would show, while inwardly rubbing their hands in glee that her family wasn't as perfect as the picture she'd always tried to paint.

'It's for the best,' Julie said. 'To be honest, he should never have applied to do the subject he did.'

Naz's mum nodded sagely. 'You can't push a round peg into a square hole,' she said.

Julie smiled, felt better. 'He should have done languages,' she said. 'And he thinks he will. Just not this year. He's going to apply again. Meanwhile, he's decided to spend the rest of this year on a crammer, getting them back up to speed.'

'Well, that sounds wonderful!' Naz's mother clapped her hands.

'Yes,' said Julie. 'It is, actually, isn't it.'

And for the first time she really believed it was.

'It takes some people a while to discover where their true talents lie,' said Naz's mother. 'Good heavens, it's taken my husband half a lifetime and a heart attack to realise that I'm probably as good a businessman as he is! Or businesswoman, I should say.'

The two women laughed.

'You know,' Julie said, 'it's funny, but all these years our boys have been friends and I still don't know your name.'

'I'm Yasmin.' She held out her hand.

'And I'm Julie.'

The two women shook hands solemnly.

'A new friendship for a new year,' Yasmin said. 'That's a good omen.'

Julie felt her recent gloom fall away from her. A good omen. Yes, she felt it too. Things would work out. For Tom. For Naz. And hopefully, Naz's father would make a full recovery too. But who knew, maybe he'd discover he enjoyed retirement and take up golf, gardening, friends. And Yasmin – well, anyone could see she would run the shop as well, if not better, than it had ever been run before.

But what about her and Brian? They'd been lucky so far – no health scares or money worries. One little blip, that was all. Heavens, it hardly figured compared to the troubles some people had. They'd get over it. Already they were looking forward and putting the past behind them. They'd rub along. They always did. This time next year things would be different again.

First published 2014, *Woman's Weekly*

Nicole's New Year

Nicole let herself into the flat. Reaching down to pick up her mail, she stabbed the front door shut with her behind. Definitely less wobbly today, she thought. Even with Christmas butting in to interrupt the good work, those early morning gym visits combined with the diet were finally paying off.

Lobbing her jacket on the sofa, she gave the mail a cursory glance then dropped it into her bag for another day. It would only be bills and junk mail anyway. No one wrote letters anymore. It had been another long, frantic day at the office and what she needed right now was a mug of one-cal soup to ward off the starvation pangs till she could muster up enough energy to grill her cod fillet and steam any remaining broccoli spears that might be lurking at the bottom of the fridge. But as soon as she spotted the parcel leaning up against the wall her exhaustion evaporated. Perfect! White Van Man had delivered the ruby red pashmina she'd ordered online – and just in the nick of time too!

Tomorrow she was off to spend New Year at Villiers Hall. A proper stately home, to which she'd been invited by two of the most prestigious clients of the publishing house she worked in – Lord Giles Villiers and his toothsome wife Lady Ursula.

She'd been schmoozing them since the moment they'd stepped into her office at the beginning of the year, with their idea for a biography of one of Lord Villier's ancestors, Lord Baliol Villiers. Ten months on, her invitation was in the bag.

The New Year festivities at Villiers Hall were a large and welcoming affair, Lady V had declaimed, and one more body – particularly one as young, witty and attractive as their publisher's assistant – would be more than welcome.

For the weeks leading up to the visit, Nicole had been on a mission to look as good as possible. She'd seen the guest list and googled every single person on it. There were at least two Baronets and any number of Honourables. She didn't know the difference, but she wasn't remotely fussy which of the two titles she bagged – as long as she bagged a 'somebody' prepared to keep her in the manner to which she longed and – in her opinion – deserved to become accustomed to.

After all, she'd worked hard to escape her impoverished past, largely made up of flitting from various squats, communes and caravan sites with the occasional settled spell in a proper house depending on her mother's success at bagging a temporary father for her.

These men never lasted long. Given a choice between the steady, homebody type and the adventurer with a roving eye, there was never any doubt which of the two her mother would go for. Diana craved excitement and change. The downside to that was that she often found herself dumped and homeless.

Nicole, whose disillusion with her mother had set in at an early age, had parted company with her at the first opportunity, tired of always coming second in her affections, and longing to better herself.

University had never been an option, as she was never in one place long enough to complete a full school term. But she was bright and hardworking and ambitious, which is how she'd managed to wheedle her way into the position of Publishing Assistant at Trentworthy Publishing.

She'd kept her nose to the grindstone, her ear to the ground and her eye on the main chance. And, just as she'd known it would, less than one year on, her perseverance had finally paid off with this invitation to spend New Year singing *Auld Lang Syne* with the aristocracy.

The pashmina was exquisite. What if it did cost almost as much as a week's rent? If she wanted to make connections, then slipping an old cardigan round her shoulders at breakfast was hardly going to bring the suitors running, was it? A pashmina suggested casual elegance and that the wearer wasn't a slave to fashion. And, with her dark hair and pale skin, ruby red was a good colour for her.

'Such a pleasure to make your acquaintance, Lord Hetherington! Nicole Brown, Trentworthy Publishing.'

May I say you're looking particularly ravishing tonight, Miss Brown!

'Please call me Nicole, Lord Hetherington.'

In that case, I insist you call me Chaz, like all my friends.

'Oh, are we friends then, Chaz?'

Nicole batted her eyelashes at her reflection, swishing the pashmina from side to side depending on which role she was playing, and altering her voice accordingly.

I'd like to think so, Nicole, wouldn't you?

'Well, then, Chaz it is. Why, thank you! Another glass of champagne would be simply mah-vellous.'

Nicole removed the pashmina and rolled it into a neat enough boulder to fit into her weekend case. Capsule dressing was the trick, so she'd read in *Vogue*, which, now she was about to join the ranks of landed gentry, was her fashion magazine of choice. Now, sod the champagne. Where was that soup?

Next morning, Nicole set her mirror at a jaunty angle and strapped herself into her seat belt. A taxi had just pulled up in front of her, its engine thrumming noisily above the sound of the Amy Winehouse CD she was playing. Nicole watched the driver get out, stroll round to the boot in the disgruntled manner of someone not usually prone to helping passengers with luggage, and remove a large, battered suitcase. Then, after a prolonged struggle with the door, his female passenger finally emerged.

She was small, delicately built, heavily made up and dressed in a cheap coat and flimsy shoes that Nicole doubted offered much protection against the late December early morning damp. The woman glanced at her case then simpered at the taxi driver who, after some moments of internal debate, picked it up and trotted after her to the house she was presumably visiting.

Nicole sat transfixed behind the wheel, as the full realisation of the woman's identity sank in. In one perpetual loop her thoughts rolled round and round her brain until she thought it would explode.

Villiers Hall. Champagne. New Year celebrations. Dukes. Baronets. Honourables. Marriage prospects. Castles. Riches. Security.

Spanner. In. The. Works.

Her Mother!

What on earth did she think she was doing? Turning up without a moment's notice like this? Then Nicole had a sudden flashback from last night, as she'd reached down for her mail. Her handbag, open on the seat next to her, revealed the lilac envelope poking out. Furiously, she snatched it up, tore it open and glanced at the light blue scrawl on the page.

My darling Nicole!

Nicole swore mutinously at the salutation. The only time her mother addressed her as darling was when she wanted something. Well, it was clear from the suitcase that what she wanted this time was free board and lodgings for the rest of the festive season.

I absolutely wouldn't ask you if I had even one single alternative, but the truth is you are my last resort!

Nicole let out a long shudder of dismay.

Due to circumstances beyond my control, I find myself without a roof over my head, and since all my friends are off to stay with relatives...

'I bet they are,' Nicole muttered, darkly.

...I am throwing myself on a daughter's mercy.

Guilt-tripping me, more like, Nicole decided, screwing up the page and tossing it into her glove compartment. Crossing her arms she fumed silently, occasionally peering through the window at her mother, who was trilling Nicole's name through the letterbox. After her fourth futile attempt to summon her daughter, Diana turned her face to the taxi driver in that little-girl-lost way Nicole remembered of old.

He looked like he'd had more than enough of this particular passenger, Nicole decided. Probably wondering when, if ever, he was going to be getting his fare. You've got a lot to learn, mate, Nicole was tempted to roll down her window and cry out. Diana, in common with the Queen, never carried money. She had none, for a kick off, plus it had doubtless been her intention to get Nicole to foot the bill as soon as she'd dialled the number of the taxi firm.

She could just drive off, she supposed. Her mother would never know. Nicole's car, at least 10 years old and punctuated with the odd dent here and there, wouldn't even have registered on Diana's radar. Sooner or later, surely, her mother would just have to give up, turn round and sling her hook.

Maybe it was Diana's complete failure to charm the taxi driver that softened Nicole in the end. At one time, her mother would only have to squeeze out a tear and any male bystander would have been putty in her hands. But even at this distance, Nicole could see that time had been cruel. The driver, clearly, was only interested in his fare.

Diana kept up the performance of scrabbling about in her bag, searching for non-existent notes for so long that Nicole was unable to bear it any longer. She leapt out of the car and ran up the drive to her house, pulling notes from her purse as she did so and then pressing the 20 pounds demanded of her into the taxi driver's hands.

'And a Happy New Year to you too, mate,' she sang out in a voice ringing with sarcasm, when he asked her where his tip was for lugging that great heavy suitcase up the path.

'Odious little man.' Her mother presented her cheek to be kissed. 'Now, please, open this door before I freeze to death.'

Any pity Nicole had been feeling for her mother dissolved instantly. Not a word of thanks for bailing her out with the fare and no apology for turning up with less than a day's notice. What was the idea, she demanded? Couldn't she have guessed that Nicole had made plans for New Year?

'Plans? What plans, dear?'

Nothing ever changed, Nicole thought, grimly, as, half an hour later, toilet visit and phone call to Villiers Hall made and warm invitation extended to include her 'unexpected visitor', she set out on her journey for the second time that morning, but this time with more baggage than she'd bargained for.

'So, are you going to tell me why you have no roof over your head – again?'

They'd been driving half an hour, during which time Diana had kept up a constant stream of inane chatter that included her thoughts on taxi drivers, motorways, the Government and the inadequacy of the heating system in Nicole's car.

At Nicole's question, Diana trilled a little laugh. Nicole recognised avoidance tactics when she came up against them. She wouldn't get the truth from her mother – she never had – so she didn't even know why she was asking.

'Oh, you know, man trouble,' she said. 'Or perhaps

you don't. I don't believe I've ever met any of your boyfriends in all the years I've known you. Apart from that – what was his name? – Jonathan.'

Nicole gripped the wheel. 'Jonah,' she said, through gritted teeth.

Her mother smiled, amicably. 'Whatever,' she said, with an absent-minded wave of her hand. 'Now, when can we stop?'

Nicole fumed inwardly. How could her mother act so normally at the mention of Jonah's name? He'd been Nicole's first love, and Diana had practically thrown herself at him the one time he'd come to stay. By the end of the weekend, he was besotted with her, completely ignoring Nicole. Was it any wonder she'd refused to introduce any other men to Diana since?

Well, at least she'd have a clear run at the Villiers. Whatever glamour her mother had once possessed had completely faded. No amount of slap could hide the deep ridges in her face, thanks to her smoking habit, or the puffiness around her eyes, which Nicole put down to her years of excessive martini consumption.

'There's no stopping till we get to Villiers Hall,' Nicole said, firmly. 'And you can think again if you think I'm going to let you smoke in my car.'

A crestfallen Diana returned the packet of cigarettes she'd just removed to her bag with a martyred sigh. 'You haven't changed, then,' she said.

'Still never happier than when you're making me miserable.'

Nicole reminded her mother that less than an hour ago, she'd managed to wangle her an invitation to one of the biggest stately homes in the county and rescued her from spending the night on the street. What was that if not generous?

'Oh, darling! Honestly, it was just a joke. Where's your sense of humour?'

Nicole longed to reply that it had deserted her as soon as Diana's taxi had pulled up in front of her house, but the road ahead was tricky now that they'd turned off the motorway and she needed all her concentration to get them to Villiers Hall unscathed.

The prospect of the next 24 hours in her mother's company loomed over the event she'd been looking forward to for so long. She was suddenly 14 again, at her birthday party, sulking because her mother had walked into the room uninvited, just as she was daring to hope she'd been accepted by the girls from the sixth school she'd attended in as many years.

It had been humiliating, the way she'd turned up the music and taken centre stage, dancing around in that ridiculous mini dress of hers like she was trying to be 14, too. The room had emptied before you could say *mutton dressed as lamb,* and that had been the end of any further attempts by Nicole to edge her way into the popular girls' circle.

And now her mother was about to repeat herself,

of that Nicole was certain. She'd have one too many martinis and start talking louder than anyone else, and before you knew it, everyone present would tacitly agree that she and Diana were just *not their sort*. There'd be no more visits to Villiers Hall for Nicole and gone would be her chances of latching onto an Honourable for all time.

But a couple of hours into their stay, Diana had so far managed not to disgrace herself. Nicole could only put it down to her mother's awe at the plush surroundings she'd suddenly and so unexpectedly found herself in that was keeping the lid on her natural over-exuberance.

The house – if you could call anything a house that consisted of four wings, each of which her own modest abode would fit into twice – was frighteningly grand. Maybe not quite as magnificent as those country manors she'd seen on the telly, where murders took place with alarming regularity, and Hercule Poirot was only brought in after the tally of corpses had reached ridiculous proportions. For a start, some of the carpets were a bit worn in places, and the furniture had seen better days, well, the bed she was sleeping in certainly had. But even so, Villiers Hall was by far the grandest location she'd ever visited.

This evening there was to be an informal buffet, though what was informal about the flunkeys in penguin suits she'd spotted carrying in silver tureens of soup and platters of cold meats, Nicole couldn't imagine.

From the corner of her eye, she glimpsed Diana, who was wandering ill at ease among the throng. She's obviously out of her depth and looking for me to hold her hand, Nicole decided. Well, she'd had that! Nicole was here to eye up the male guests, not to play nursemaid to her mother.

She too had been circulating round the drawing room, keeping as great a distance between herself and Diana as possible and sipping her mulled wine, which, as far as she was concerned, tasted like warm cough medicine. Where was the champagne she'd re-enacted herself necking last night, in front of her mirror at home? And, frankly, she was disappointed at the lack of talent.

There were plenty of old men with hearing aids, and almost as many middle-aged ones with paunches and red faces, all reeking of cigars. Occasionally, the odd male, not all *that* much older than herself and vaguely passable – though she'd need several more glasses of mulled wine to be entirely convinced – would flit in and out of her line of vision, but by 10pm, she was getting desperate.

At this rate, she'd never grab a title, she mused. And to make things worse, even from this distance, she could see that Diana was getting decidedly twitchy. She was clearly scouring the room for Nicole and wondering how soon she could latch onto her for the rest of the evening. Throwing her pashmina over her shoulders, Nicole decided to escape onto the terrace. Her mother hated fresh air and would die before braving the cold to look for her outside.

The terrace was festive and inviting, with twinkling fairy lights stretched between an avenue of trees. It was nice out here – like *real* countryside. Or at least as near as she'd ever got to it in her lifetime! The braying voices of the guests were barely audible outside. Funny how, in her quest for a toff, the one thing she'd left out of her equation was that he might come as a package, wrapped up in layers of an ancestry that barked loudly at the servants, shot pheasants and hunted foxes. Frankly, Nicole had no desire to follow any of these pursuits.

It was all very well planning to grab her own piece of landed gentry action, but just how deeply had she thought about the Hooray Henry lifestyle she'd have to put up with once she'd landed him?

'Well, hello there!'

Nicole stiffened at the sound of the voice of the Leslie Phillips soundalike as it wafted towards her on the cold night air. Spinning round in the dark, with only the fairy lights for guidance – the moon and stars both sulking behind the clouds tonight – her eyes finally came to rest on the dark figure of a man who emerged from the shadows clutching a bottle of champagne in one hand and a cigarette in the other.

Finally, Nicole thought, proper booze. And though

he might have sounded like Leslie Phillips, he was, thankfully, several decades younger. And passable in his dinner jacket, too, though she wasn't sure about that haircut, and his jawline wasn't quite as firm as the one she'd had in mind either.

Still, beggars couldn't be choosers and time was running out. If she could snare a partner to link arms with at midnight, then everything else would follow. They'd be engaged before spring, tra-la, and this time next year, maybe she'd be hosting her own New Year's party.

'Charles Hetherington. Most people call me Chaz. Except the servants, who call me sir, of course! You must be the lovely Nicole. I heard all about you from my aunt.'

Nicole's heart skipped a beat. It was just like she'd imagined! Her very own Lord, whom she'd googled as soon as she knew she'd be coming here. He was the only son of Lord Harry Hetherington (widowed), who was in possession of a huge estate somewhere in the wilds of Scotland. And he was making a beeline for her! He was holding out the bottle and telling her he'd brought his own stash this year because he'd learned the hard way after being forced to drink mulled wine when he was last here five Christmases ago. Already they had so much in common, Nicole thought, as he added how lucky he was to have found someone so pretty to share his champers with at last. Wowsers!

They were getting on like a house on fire, though to be honest, that might have been more to do with Nicole's over-exaggerated appreciation of Chaz's repertoire of feeble jokes than them tumbling upon common ground. Chaz seemed remarkably uninterested in Nicole, she thought, and seemed to see her as more of a sounding board for his semi-drunken monologue than as a prospective companion and helpmeet.

But Nicole gritted her teeth and persevered. It would be worth it in the long run, she decided, foxes and pheasants notwithstanding. And Scotland was no distance from London these days. And it couldn't be any drearier, living up there in the Highlands, than living in her poky little flat always worrying about her rent and having to choose between food and a manicure.

'I say, you're awfully pretty, you know.'

Chaz had broken off his patter to get a closer squint at Nicole, who simpered up at him, wondering when he was going to pass her that bottle again. So far, she'd only managed a couple of mouthfuls. She didn't like to think in stereotypes, but what they said about the Scots being a wee bit parsimonious carried more than a little truth.

'Nicole!'

Chaz was at the point of going in for the kill when the sound of Diana screeching her name jolted him out of it. Nicole, furious, jerked her head away from his and spun round.

'I need to talk to you. Now. Upstairs. My room.'

Nicole was ready to embark on just the kind of indignant reaction she'd employed as a teenage girl, whenever her mother had gone too far, as she clearly had now. But it was important to show Chaz her gentle side. The sight of her screeching like a fishwife might make him reconsider making any further advances, which would be a pity just when they were getting on so well.

So, meekly lowering her eyes, she bade a fond farewell to a clearly disappointed Chaz and timidly followed her mother inside and up the stairs to her room, whereupon she promptly and enthusiastically let rip. Diana, to her credit, remained speechless, simply waiting till the storm that was Nicole had blown itself out. And then she told her daughter exactly why it was she'd decided to break things up between Earl Charles Hetherington, son and heir of Lord Harry Hetherington of Tweesdale Glen, just at the point when he was about to kiss her.

Nicole hadn't a clue where she was heading. She just knew she had to get away from Villiers Hall, Lord and Lady Villiers, Earl Charles Hetherington, her mother, and the whole shebang as fast as she could. And she could never go back. Not after what her mother had told her, as she paced up and down the bedroom, with its mullioned windows and miniscule double bed that, judging from the width, must have been installed somewhere around the mid 1600s, when people never grew much bigger than 10-year-old children.

'What do you mean Charles Hetherington could be my brother?'

'Please, Nicole, don't screech!'

Her mother clapped her hands over her ears. As if *she* was the one who deserved to feel affronted!

'I can't be 100 percent sure, but surely you can understand it's better to be safe than sorry.'

Nicole groaned. She remembered Hetherington's wobbly chin dipping down towards her own, his cigarette breath and the soppy expression on his face. She'd practically snogged her own brother! Fortunately, when she staggered backwards, the bed was there to catch her.

'I've been catching glimpses of him on and off all night. His father, I mean. Harry. Of course, he's changed. Much older. Bit of a paunch, no hair.'

Diana could have been describing 99 percent of the men present.

'But his voice is unmistakeable. Like treacle. Deep, rich, velvety…'

Diana's own voice had shrunk to a whisper. It was like she was back in her past. In a time when she'd been young, and hopeful that maybe, just maybe, this time she'd met *the one*.

It was disgusting! Nicole had been humiliated. Staggering to her feet, not really having the faintest idea of her intentions but certain she had to leave right now, she'd run next door to her room, snatched up her case – which she hadn't bothered to unpack on arrival, being far too eager to head downstairs to embark on her quest for a prospective husband – and pelted down the back staircase and outside, where, after wandering around in the dark for quite a while, she miraculously stumbled upon her car.

Fortunately, by this time, everyone had gathered in the Grand Hall for the buffet, so apart from one or two looks of restrained curiosity on the faces of the flunkeys guarding the back door, her departure went unnoticed.

After speeding away from Villiers Hall, she travelled down country lanes, through hamlets and villages, and down yet more country lanes, all the while narrowly avoiding all manner of wildlife that dodged her headlights (apart from one or two unfortunate rabbits, who failed to get out of her way quick enough). Eventually, she found herself approaching the outskirts of a small town.

It was grim and dreary, with boarded-up shops. A couple of revellers, arm-in-arm and in the throes of celebrating the New Year even before it had arrived, were staggering down the main street between two pubs. Nicole spotted an Indian takeaway and a chippy, but definitely no four-star hotels. The place didn't even boast a B&B.

Her heart sank. For the first time, she realised that unless she turned back and retraced her journey, she would have no roof over her head tonight. A quick glance at the petrol gauge showed her she was low on fuel.

She could sleep in the car, of course. But her mother's long, protracted complaint about the heating, or rather lack of it, had been well and truly justified, if irritating. All she had to keep her warm was her pashmina.

She *couldn't* go back to Villiers Hall. The thought of seeing Charles Hetherington again made her feel queasy. She should have known something was up with her mother from the restraint she'd shown almost as soon as they'd crossed the threshold.

Nicole had put it down to nerves. But it was obvious now she'd had time to think about it that Diana must have spotted her ex-lover across a crowded room, made a connection between him and the only half-decent looking man of marriageable age, spotted Nicole eyeing him up and predicted which way the wind would blow if she left her daughter to it.

Quick thinking on Diana's part, Nicole had to admit. How on earth had she put two and two together so speedily? Nicole, grown suddenly anxious at the approach of a figure emerging from a nearby building and apparently heading her way, wound her pashmina even more tightly round her shoulders. Well, her mother's thought processes were hardly rocket science.

Diana knew which way Nicole's mind would be working because it was the way her own mind worked. All her life she'd been on the hunt for someone to provide her with a more comfortable existence than the one she could provide herself. Was it any wonder that Nicole, who'd only ever had Diana as a role model, had imitated her mother's behaviour so skilfully – though denying it even as she did so?

Why else would she have submitted to the pawing of a man who, on any Saturday night in any bar in any town, wouldn't have merited so much as a glance from her? Because she was desperate to escape her life of scrimping and saving, that's why. She'd seen a way out by going after a man with a title, and she'd allowed Charles Hetherington – her own brother – to come onto her. The whole thing was just too gross to contemplate.

Diane had some morals, at least. She could have let things run their course. Turned a blind eye – something she was expert at. Maybe Nicole should be grateful for that at least and not be so hard on her.

'What the...?'

She put up her hands to shield her eyes from the torchlight shining on her face. Whoever was flashing the light at her must have realised he was blinding her and switched it off once they'd registered her startled reaction.

Nicole made out a face at her roadside window. Male. Concerned looking. If he'd been at Villiers Hall, he'd have been the star turn. But right now, she wasn't interested in eyeing up men as husband material. All she wanted was to be able to feel her feet and the tips of her nose and fingers.

Star Turn mimed winding down the window. Resolutely, she shook her head. He must think she was soft. She'd seen enough episodes of *Crimewatch* to work out that just because someone looks trustworthy doesn't make it so.

She wound down her window.

'You look lost,' he said, with a country burr that made her feel she was being bathed in warm chocolate. 'Have you come for the party?'

With the back of her hand, she wiped away the condensation from her kerbside window. The cheerfully lit entrance of the building she was parked in front of – some kind of social club, she gathered – looked warm and inviting. It wouldn't hurt to pop inside, surely, and have a drink or two?

Though, if they were all country yokels like Star Turn seemed to be, she'd never find anybody here who could afford to buy her Gucci shoes and Prada bags. Briefly, her mind flitted back to Villiers Hall, Diana and her newfound family.

She was related to a Lord. On the wrong side of the blanket, maybe, but all the same. Funny, just yesterday that news would have had her singing and dancing in the street. But now she couldn't care less if her second cousin turned out to be Prince William.

Star Turn was peering at her hopefully through her window. Nice eyes, she thought.

'I don't know,' she said. 'I don't know anyone.'

'You know me,' he said. 'Dave Parks. And you'll soon get to know everyone else. We're a real friendly crowd.'

Nicole wavered. A couple of girls in flimsy dresses were standing at the door sharing a cigarette, oblivious to the cold. They waved at Dave, who waved back.

'The one on the right's my sister,' he said. 'And the other one's my cousin. Everyone's related to everyone else round here.'

'Tell me about it,' Nicole said.

'Bit like that where you're from, is it?'

Nicole grinned. 'You could say that,' she replied.

Maybe she'd tell him, later. Once she'd thawed out and had a glass of something warming, which she hoped with all her heart wouldn't be mulled wine. Of course, she could always tell him no, she didn't want to come inside and join the party because she had a date with an empty flat, an empty fridge and *Hootenanny* on the telly.

'There's only 15 minutes of the old year left,' Dave

said. 'It'd be a pity to spend them out here in the cold when you could be socialising inside.'

Nicole had made her mind up. New Year's Resolution Number One – if a nice guy comes along don't ask him his pedigree. Dave seemed like a nice guy. Better, he seemed to think she was a nice girl. New Year's Resolution Number Two – *be* a nice girl. Stop sizing people up and wondering what they can do for you. First thing tomorrow, text Mum and wish her a Happy New Year. Ask after your half-brother. Show her there's really no hard feelings.

New Year's Resolution Number Three – make sure that when midnight strikes, you're standing next to Dave. Tonight's Star Turn.

First published 2009, *Woman's Weekly* Fiction Special

Acknowledgments

Charles Dickens may not have invented Christmas, but he certainly left his legacy when he wrote *A Christmas Carol*. I can't be the only author to be influenced by his tale of ghostly visitations leading to a drastic change in behaviour. Thank you, Mr Dickens, for *Gemma's Night Out*.

About the Author

Geraldine Ryan is a proud Northerner who has spent most of her life in Cambridge – the one with the punts. She holds a degree in Scandinavian Studies, but these days only puts it to use when identifying which language is being spoken among the characters of whatever Scandi drama is currently showing on TV. For many years, she worked as a teacher of English and of English as a second or foreign language, in combination with rearing her four children, all of whom are now grown-up, responsible citizens. Her first published story appeared in *My Weekly* in 1993. Since then, her stories have appeared in *Take a Break, Fiction Feast* and *Woman's Weekly,* as well as in women's magazines abroad. She has also written two young adult novels – *Model Behaviour* (published by Scholastic) and *The Lies and Loves of Finn* (Channel 4 Books.) *The No-Hopers Christmas Club* is her second short story collection. Her first, *Riding Pillion With George Clooney*, was also published in 2022.

Keep up to date with Geraldine's news, be the first to hear about her new releases and read exclusive content by signing up to her monthly newsletter *Turning the Page*. By adding your details, you'll also receive a free short story. Use this link to subscribe: https://bit.ly/Turningthepage

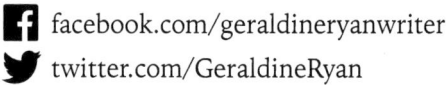

facebook.com/geraldineryanwriter
twitter.com/GeraldineRyan

Printed in Great Britain
by Amazon